BENEATH THE MISTS

OF ASTRAL AND UMBRAL BOOK ONE

BONNIE L. PRICE

TABLE OF CONTENTS

DEDICATION

My parents, for putting up with me.

My guild, Sunless, for helping me make decisions.

My readers, for being freaking awesome.

My writing groups, for keeping me *somewhat* sane.

FOREWORD

Thank you so much for picking up the first book in my debut series, *Of Astral and Umbral!*

The images above, paired with the voice of the chapter, will be your guide to perspective in this book.

I've been working with this world, and these characters, for a long time. They have been my passion for many years now and I finally found a story that does them the justice they deserve!

I hope that you enjoy yourself as you delve into your first taste of my world, Avrirsa.

CHAPTER ONE
Birth of a Deity

"We are taking you with us." The gold-robed Elder God reached for Arianna.

I gripped Arianna by her wrist and took off at a run for the door. Darkness whipped around us as we both channeled power into our legs to increase our speed. The entire situation felt wrong.

Whether it was the Elder's suffocating power or something else I wasn't sure. All I knew was that my instincts screamed for me to get Arianna away from these people. I wouldn't let them take her. They frightened me more than any of the scum we had come across in our missions, and more than any of the monsters wandering the wilds between our respective kingdoms.

Men with feathered wings of varying colors appeared from golden portals and surrounded us. One of them shoved me out of the way and *another hit me upside the head with the flat of a gaudy silver sword, dazing me. I stumbled and turned to snap at the intruders but the pressure of the men's combined auras silenced me.*

'I-It's like the last time people tried to take her away.' *I swallowed hard, my hands trembled.* 'Except instead of Human slavers, these people... The Elders and their servants are supposed to be on our side! Why is this happening?!'

A female shriek snapped me to my senses. I looked to my right, where Arianna had been standing, and my heart sank. 'Where did she...?'

"Let me go!" *Arianna clawed at the hand gripping her curls and dug her heels into the floor.* "N-Nali!"

"Children who encroach upon the duties of gods will be punished." *The winged man sneered and jerked Arianna off her feet by her hair. Arianna landed hard on her rump and kicked her feet. The man seemed oblivious to her struggle and continued to drag her.*

"Unhand her!" *Lucifer roared, moving to storm past the Elder Gods.*

One of the Elder Gods blocked Lucifer's path, placing a hand on the king's shoulder. At first, the man spoke calmly. Lucifer refused to comply but, for all his strength, the Devillian king couldn't dislodge the Elder's grip from his shoulder. The distraught expression on Lucifer's face made reality crash around me. These people, the Elder Gods *and their servants, were intent on taking Arianna from us.*

'What are you waiting for, Nalithor?!' *A male voice growled, accompanied by a puff of violet smoke as Djialkan, Arianna's fae-dragon, appeared beside me.* 'I cannot interfere with the Elder Gods, but *you* can. Will you just let them take Arianna?'

When I didn't respond, the fae-dragon lashed his tail across my face and snarled. Snippets of memories flooded through my mind all at once. Humans in the Vorpmasian wilds had knocked Arianna unconscious and dragged her from our camp in the base of a tree while I was tending our horses. When I'd found her, they'd been arguing about who would get to "break her in" during the return trip. Others knew who she was and wanted to slay her. My Arianna, they had wanted to kill her.

'Just like these bastards do.' *The thought turned my blood to ice.*

More Angels filed out of the glowing gateways as I turned to chase after Arianna and her captor. I sped past several while shoving others out of my way with darkness. They couldn't take her away. I wouldn't let them. I didn't give a damn if the Elder Gods had given the order or not; they didn't have the right to punish her.

"Don't take her away from me!" *I screamed with enough force that my voice cracked and my lungs burned.*

The Angel ignored me and continued yanking Arianna across the throne room towards the exit. Arianna clawed at the bastard's hand and wrist, unable to reach his wings—but he didn't seem to care, even when the princess gouged his arm open. I called out to Arianna, extending a hand towards her. 'Not close enough yet. I have to be faster!'

"Nali, my sword! Where is—?" *Arianna yelped in pain when the Angel yanked her long hair again.*

I managed to close the distance and grasp Arianna's hand. She gripped back tight enough to make my joints creak, and I felt a sense of relief. The moment was short-lived. The Angel ripped Arianna upward and out of my grasp, making me lose my balance and fall to my knees. I glared up at the Angel when he dangled Arianna above my head like bait. A sneer stretched across the Angel's face, taunting me as I growled.

Before I could spout off at the winged bastard, a silver blade blossomed out the front of Arianna's chest. Black blood dripped from the point of the blade and down to the floor between us. Her eyes went wide as she coughed up blood. Something reflected with light as it fell from her chest, and seconds later I felt it land in my lap. Shaking, I pocketed it as I tried to process what to do. How could I help her? How could I get the Angel away from her?

My world ground to a halt when I shifted a glare towards the Angel and then looked back at Arianna. She…wasn't breathing.

A sound between a scream and a roar left me. Hatred, loss, and terror ripped through every fiber of my being. She couldn't be dead, it wasn't possible! The bastards would pay for harming her. I would make them pay with their lives, and then Arianna and I could continue on as normal…right?

'Right, Ari?' I reached out tentatively but was met with no response.

The Angel laughed and slung Arianna's limp body over his shoulder, leaving the ornate sword lodged in place. Silver filigree, two sapphires set in the crossguard and pommel. The sword looked familiar but I was too disturbed to place it. Instead, I committed the sword to memory.

I would remember that sword, I would remember it and I would use it to slay every last one of the Angels and the Elder Gods if the opportunity *arose.*

'But if I can take it from him now...' *I snarled, my gaze honing in on the Angel and his cocky stride.*

Opaque darkness, black lightning, pale blue flames, and chunks of torn earth formed a deadly maelstrom around me when I charged after the laughing Angel. My power shredded everything in my path, leaving gouges inches deep in the granite and cleaving the Elder's auras from the air.

A small tremble of something that felt like Arianna passed through me but no words accompanied it. My imagination? Most likely. She wasn't breathing, so it couldn't possibly have been her. 'Not...breathing...'

My vision blurred with tears. I couldn't shelve my despair but I still tried to reach her. A dark rip appeared in the air before the Angel. He turned to sneer at me again before stepping through it, disappearing with Arianna still slung over his shoulder. Djialkan barreled through the portal after them both but it closed before I could leap in.

I slowed to a stop, at a loss for what to do. Nor did I know how to even begin *processing what just happened. My tears blinded me as my power vibrated and warped, threatening to break from my control. I felt my knees hit the floor again as I collapsed in place. My entire body felt numb, but it was as if a storm raged inside of me. Something pulsed with warm power from within my pocket, releasing what should have been a comforting aura and scent.* Her *scent,* her *power.*

"Sh-she's gone." *I gasped, pulling the warm item from my pocket. The clear crystal was shaped like a lotus and danced with the colors of darkness, cobalt flames, pale wind, and ice. My eyes widened and horror lanced through me in recognition as the heartbeat-like pulse of the crystal continued.* "Th-this is...?"

Vaguely, I was aware of panicked shouting somewhere behind me, and a massive surge of power from the gods. I didn't care. The crystalline object I was holding—I knew what it was. The heart of a deity. Arianna's heart. That meant the sword that pierced her had to have been a Godslayer. That's why it seemed familiar. Her heart should have shattered upon coming into contact with it. She should have died instantly. But it didn't, and she hadn't.

'Why, why is it still beating?'

Power pulsed through me as I lost control over my power and emotions both. A primal wail ripped from me as my power split the palace apart like an egg around me. Arianna, my Arianna, my partner of the last ten years. It had been so difficult to get her to open up, to stop being shy or scared of me. Now I would never see her again. The Elders, and the Angels, had taken her from me.

'I will kill them all!' *My blinding fury and grief fought for dominance as I slammed my free hand into the floor.* 'I...failed to save her, but I can still destroy them for what they've done!'

"Rely'ric?" a vaguely familiar voice called. "Hey, wake up!"

I opened my eyes in unease, adopting a passive expression as my gaze fell on a nude woman with jet black hair. Arcane sigils of lavender twinkled along her ashen gray skin, identifying her as a Jrachra—a Devillian race with close ties to the magical arts. Her pupilless silver eyes were open wide with both concern and an all-too-familiar reverence.

"Why are you still here?" I asked with a sigh, raising a hand to my head and pushing my hair back between my horns. *'Honestly. Why must food always invite itself to stay?'*

"Night terrors?" The Jrachra ignored my question and leaned forward. "I thought your powers were going to tear the room apart, Rely'ric! If you wish, I can try some of my people's spells for soothing night terrors."

"Unnecessary." I sat up in bed, the satin sheets drifting down my own nude body. "I have a meeting with the emperor to prepare for. You should leave."

The woman didn't budge. Instead, she stared up at me with a mindless reverence that I couldn't stand. The once-proud Jrachra woman was now spellbound by my power as an Adinvyr. My position within Lucifer's court had only made situations like this more frequent.

Adinvyr like myself had to feed periodically on sexual energy. We could draw it from active brothels, through blood or other bodily fluids, or through participating in sex itself.

Nature made certain that it wasn't difficult for us to find "food." Our individual powers attracted willing sources to us *constantly*. The more hungry we were, the stronger our pull.

Prey like the woman in my bed were especially common in the streets of Dauthrmir. I couldn't go anywhere without men and women offering themselves to me. Even the rare individuals who weren't drawn by my power as an Adinvyr still sought me for my rank in Lucifer's empire.

"Humph, so it's true then," the woman snorted as I strode past her. "You're still caught up on that princess after a hundred and eighty years? Something must be wrong with you. But I'm sure I can fix it. *She* was just a child, but *I'm* a *woman*. I can make sure your needs—"

"Enough." I kept my voice calm and pivoted to look at the woman. The magelights in the room flickered and then flared bright in response to my free-flowing power. The Jrachra woman froze like a deer, her eyes wide.

"B-but…" She flinched and shrank back. "Her Highness is just a ghost of the past! Why do you let her haunt you? Why do you let her keep you from finding—"

"Her Highness is the only reason we aren't all slaves to the Vunsori by now." I directed tendrils of darkness towards the woman and lifted her off the floor by her throat. "*You* are *food*. A means to an end. That is it. You knew this when you offered yourself to me, and you should know that it is terribly rude of you to invite yourself to stay in an Adinvyr's bed.

"*Leave.* If you are not gone by the time I return from my bath I will have the guards remove you by force."

I dropped the woman to the floor next to her discarded clothing and then turned to leave. She directed a bolt of lightning towards me from her hands but I squashed it beneath my power. I shot her a glare over my shoulder when I sensed her building power around herself again. I strode across the room while shrugging on a robe and stifled her power beneath mine.

"You were both mere children, yet you act like you loved her!" the woman snapped. "All the girls in town talk about it, you know. How 'The Black Dragon has been driven mad by a shadow from the past.' Lucifer must be mad too if he lets you serve him!"

"Mad?" I asked, turning to arch an eyebrow at the angry woman. "Tell me, how would *you* feel if the person you cared most for was murdered right before your eyes? If you were so close to rescuing them, only to be bathed in their blood as a blade plunged through their heart?

"What I may have felt for Her Highness is a very small part of the matter, *girl*."

The woman spouted off something unintelligible and I sighed. It seemed as if my allure as an Adinvyr grew stronger by the day. She was beyond reasoning with and her eyes still held unyielding reverence, yet she acted like a scorned lover, not like proper food. The growing pool of urine beneath her suggested that, somewhere under that reverent façade, she understood that I could end her life with a mere thought if she pushed me further.

'Tch. Perhaps I will return to drawing energy exclusively from the brothels.' I grimaced as the Jrachra's screeching followed me down the hallway. *'Removing food is so much more hassle than it's worth...'*

One of the palace servants shot me a knowing, sympathetic look before bowing to me and scurrying past—likely to fetch the guards and towels. The palace staff was well-accustomed to situations such as this by now. Adinvyr, myself included, expected our food to leave after being fed upon. It was the socially acceptable thing to do back in Draemir.

Unfortunately, the commonfolk of Dauthrmir were slow to understand this.

'Still, using Her Highness as a way to jab at me?' I sighed as I passed granite pillars and silver sconces, then slipped into the large bathroom at the end of the hall. *'They're becoming more problematic than normal. I haven't done anything different or changed my routine… Is my power growing as well?'*

I raised a hand and summoned darkness above my palm, attempting to gauge if anything about my power had changed. The darkness drifted over my palm like smoke, spilling over the sides of my hand and dripping down towards the floor like water.

There didn't seem to be anything different about it.

Sighing, I dismissed the darkness and shed my robe before walking towards the bath. The steaming water was a welcome sensation against my skin. I waded into the room-sized bath and passed several more pillars. Once I managed to free my waist-length white hair from its braid, I waded into deeper waters and then sat with my back against the tiled edge.

'Arianna…' I pursed my lips and then raised a hand to my chest. When I withdrew it, a crystalline lotus hovered above my palm. Whenever I looked at it, I never knew what to think.

Everything I had ever been taught stated that the Godslayer should have shattered her heart. It should have stopped pulsing with aether and grown dim, yet the powers of darkness, wind, fire, and ice still swirled within the crystal petals in their endless, lazy dance.

'It has grown.' A small frown tugged at my lips. I reached out with a small drop of my own power and hesitated before prodding at the crystal. The lotus grew warmer in my hand and pulsed faster for a moment before returning to its usual rhythm. The elements themselves seemed unfazed and continued in their arcing paths.

The heart of a goddess, separated from its owner, and yet it still beat on as if she was still alive. I didn't know what to believe anymore; the Elder Gods, or the heart I'd kept with me for the past 180 years. Shaking my head, I let the crystal lotus sink back into my chest before I slumped back against the bath's edge and stared blankly at the water.

That heart, Arianna's heart, was the only reason I was still alive. There had been many times, especially during a Devillian's equivalent to teenage years, where I had considered ending everything. Sometimes it was because I wanted the chance to see Arianna again, sometimes it was for other foolish or selfish reasons.

Regardless of my reasoning, soothing warmth would radiate from Arianna's heart and calm me. Even in some of my darkest or most distraught moments, it had made me stop and reconsider what I was doing.

"Jich!" I cursed, batting at the water. "It has been a long time. Maybe I truly have gone mad."

I glanced to the side at a clock and then grimaced. The Court was expecting me to show up today, and making Lucifer angry with me was one of the last things I needed. That Lucifer hadn't slain me as punishment for being unable to protect his daughter was a minor miracle as far as I was concerned.

Soon enough I found myself sweeping through the hallways of the Dauthrmiran palace. Something about the air gave me the feeling that the Jrachra strumpet's rudeness was going to be the least of my headaches for the day. Everything crackled with a vaguely familiar energy that made my skin crawl.

I paid little mind to the decorations of the palace as I honed my senses and attempted to identify the source of my displeasure. If the servants milling through the hallways called greetings to me, I didn't hear them. The power I sensed felt similar to that of the Elders responsible for taking Arianna away from us. Nowhere near as suffocating, but still too similar for me to ignore.

"General Vraelimir, they're expecting you." A guard bowed deeply to me as I approached a pair of large doors.

I glanced up at the intricately carved ebony doors before turning to acknowledge the guard, taking note of his uneasy shifting. The Imperial Guard weren't known for being easy to rattle. *Something* within the throne room had managed to perturb them. *'So, I wasn't imagining that presence.'*

I pushed my way into the palace's secondary throne room and glanced around quickly, taking stock of everyone's locations. The original throne room, which I had destroyed in my grief, had been left in ruins. Lucifer kept it sealed off in remembrance of that day and wouldn't let anyone inside—not even me.

The new throne room looked drastically different compared to the old one. Although both were made of granite and obsidian—like everything else in the palace—this room was decorated with dark and grim paintings and artifacts while the original throne room had been a colorful, cheerful place.

This room, however, housed the spoils of war. There were bloodstained banners, confiscated weaponry and armor from defeated foes, and even the skeletal heads of some of Lucifer's enemies. After the deaths of his heirs, the enraged then-king had gone on a bloody rampage. He had conquered the last of the surrounding Devillian tribes, the wilds between them, and the border with the Suthsul Desert. The death of his children became the birth of the Vorpmasian Empire.

Although he claimed it was for both the children he lost that day, we knew it was more for Arianna than it was for her twin brother. Darius had been raised by his mother, an Angel, far away from Dauthrmir and its Devillian influence.

The guards *insisted* that both of Lucifer's children had been in the throne room on that day…but I couldn't remember seeing the boy.

How I had wished I was old enough to participate in the wars alongside Lucifer and my father, Lysander. But no, I had to stay behind with my mother and younger siblings. Even if I had been old enough at the time, I doubted they would have let me go. In hindsight, I wasn't in the right frame of mind for battle.

"You all look absolutely livid," I commented once closer to the dais at the back of the room. I examined the gathered Royal Families and several dignitaries I didn't recognize before asking, "What happened?"

"*You* tell *us*, Nalithor." Lucifer's tone was firm. His arms were crossed his arms over his chest and his mismatched emerald green and electric blue eyes settled on me in an intense glare. "The Elder Gods have formally requested *your* presence."

"The Elder…?" I trailed off into a scowl, turning my attention to the trio in plain white cloaks. "Unless you're here to tell me that I can execute the bastard that took Her Highness and her brother away from us, I have no interest in speaking with you."

The smallest of the three Elders approached me as my bloodlust rose to near intolerable levels. I wanted to shred the gods before me with claw and blade alike. I wanted nothing more than to drench the throne room in their blood. Even if it didn't kill them, it would certainly have made me feel better.

"*You have sensed it, have you not?*" the female of the trio inquired with a smile as she lowered her hood, revealing delicate features, blonde hair, and solid golden eyes that were void of sclerae or pupils. "*She was not meant to die, therefore she did not.*

"*You have kept her heart, yes? It still beats within you. I can hear it.*"

My scowl deepened as the female Elder circled me in silence. Her warm expression only made me want to destroy her even more. However, she seemed more interested in examining the dark Brands of Divinity that covered the right side of my body from my throat and down. She looked intrigued, and I felt her poking and prodding at my magic with her own.

That the woman would taunt us in such a way infuriated me.

'Claiming that Her Highness isn't dead? I should rip these bastards apart for expecting me to believe such a farce.' I had witnessed Arianna stop breathing with my own eyes, seen the amount of blood that spilled from her wound and mouth alike. There was no way she could have lived through it.

"You already know that only deities have crystalline hearts, yes?" one of the male Elders inquired. I nodded my reply in silence.

"We would speak with you, and you alone, about the events that transpired that day," the other male Elder continued. *"What we have to say is of no concern to the Lesser, Middle, or Upper Gods, but it will be of great concern to you."*

I frowned deeply at the Elders. *'What could they possibly have to say to me that they don't want the gods to know of?'*

Before I could question them aloud, blinding light engulfed us. When we reappeared, I found myself under a brilliant blue sky and with plush green grass below my feet. Wherever we were, it certainly wasn't within the Vorpmasian Empire. It seemed as if that small strip of land was levitating in the sky, but I couldn't be certain—and I wasn't prepared to show the Elders my back so I could check for supports beneath.

"The twins were meant to compete over the role of Balance," the female began as I prodded at the ground beneath us with my power.

"You worked closely with the girl, so I am sure you noticed the way she seemed to 'sense' things that were wrong in the world. Things that should have been beyond a child's knowledge."

'The Elder isn't wrong. Arianna truly did sense strange things, and she was never mistaken,' I thought begrudgingly. Arianna had been my partner in play, training, and in work. She had always been unusually aware of the events of the world despite her lack of interest in political lessons. *'But…it is supposedly for that very reason that the Elders deigned it necessary to execute her.'*

My frown deepened. That wasn't quite right. It was an Angel that had run Arianna through, not the Elders. The Elder Gods had simply said they were taking Arianna with them—they never said what their intentions were. *'Even so, their intentions couldn't have been good. Not when they were exerting their combined auras in such a way.'*

I glanced to the side at the Elders and took in what I could of their individual forms. Their robes did not glow, none of them wore a gold robe, and one was a woman. The Elders that had appeared on that day in Dauthrmir were all male. Their attire had been fancier, and their power stronger. I scented the air discreetly and bit back a grimace. They still smelled unpleasant.

"The Middle and Upper Gods have become too unruly. They spend their time bickering amongst themselves and looking for mortal toys," the Elder continued as if she hadn't heard my thoughts. *"Balance's role is to manage the Upper Gods, particularly Good and Evil, so that they can all function properly in their roles."*

I furrowed my brow and crossed my arms over my chest, waiting for the Elder to continue. My scaled tail twitched in agitation while I tried to rein in my thoughts and focus on the problem at hand. This woman hadn't even bothered to mention the Lesser Gods, such as Lucifer or my parents. Arianna had been concerned with the dealings between Lesser Gods—also known as Racial Gods—when we were young.

The Middle Gods ruled over, and represented, lesser archetypes. Those deities were the ones that the commonfolk worshiped on a day-to-day basis. Deities of fishing, hunting, foraging—if you desired a boon for your work, you would likely ask a Middle God for help.

Upper Gods, however, represented major concepts. Good, evil, chaos, tranquility, time, war, individual emotions, and much more. Those deities tended to be more removed from society, influencing the world through their followers or their Chosen who tended temples and shrines throughout Avrirsa.

'Why would they be speaking to me *about these matters instead of someone more qualified?'* I tapped my claws against my forearm as I thought. *'I am a demigod, but my parents are only Lesser Gods—the God and Goddess of the Adinvyr. If the Elders want a demigod for something, there are many others to choose from.*

'Although…we are not supposed to be privy to the workings of deities.'

"*Our intention was for one of our candidates to become the God or Goddess of Balance, while the others would be freed from the responsibility.*" The shortest male Elder made subtle motions as he spoke. *"I won't go into the details of our selection process—we have not the time for such a lengthy discussion."*

"In short, a divide has formed amongst the Elder Gods. Several of them rebelled against the plan to find a deity of Balance," the female stated. A sad expression formed on her face as the others fell silent. *"Our former allies chose to eliminate the dozens of candidates that we and our allies had selected."*

'Dozens of candidates?' I stared at the Elders in disbelief.

What they had said to me thus far made sense—that the Middle and Upper Gods had been neglecting their duties was something that neither mortals nor Lesser Gods had missed. It seemed logical that there would be someone to keep those deities in line. However, I had always thought that job fell to the Elder Gods.

'A rift between the Elders. That is disconcerting.' I glanced between the Elders and then down at the grass as I thought. It never even occurred to me that what happened to Arianna may have happened to other people—likely to other children. Why would the other Elders have taken such a drastic measure? Furthermore, which Elders were the rebellious ones: the ones before me or the ones that had Arianna taken away?

"You mean to tell me the other Elders went as far as to kill *dozens* of children who could have become Balance? Not just Arianna and Darius?" I shot the female a pointed look, watching as she gave me a sad smile and nodded in reply.

"We thought that all was lost…but it would seem that Arianna's heart

has changed you, has it not?" The taller of the two male Elders motioned at my chest. *"You have begun to sense things the way she did. Perhaps not as strongly, but you sense them all the same."*

"I don't like where this is going," I muttered, settling a glare on the Elders. "You couldn't possibly expect *me* to take on the role of a god in her place."

'What are they thinking?!' I gritted my teeth, attempting to keep my outward appearance calm. *'A role as they have described would lie between an Upper and Elder God in the hierarchy! How could they even insinuate that I should take on such a role?'*

I dug my claws into my forearms and attempted to calm my racing thoughts. Even if Arianna's heart had changed me in some way, that hardly made me qualified to bear such a heavy burden. I couldn't deny that, over the past few decades, I had begun to see the world in a different way. It wasn't a conscious thing and it was separate from just growing older. At times, I just *knew* where there was a problem—and how to fix it.

"We desperately need your help with the things that are about to happen to this world." The female Elder sighed heavily. *"We will need your help to fix Avrirsa and its deities."*

"Even *if* I did agree to help you, I do not see any upsides to this," I stated flatly, maintaining my glare. My tail thrashed with irritation as I continued, "How could you expect me to—?"

"We are not giving you a choice in this matter, Adinvyr," one of the males interjected plainly. He lifted a hand and summoned a prison of

golden light around me. *"As mortals say, desperate times call for desperate measures. You are the only one left who shares the instincts* she *possessed.*

"You are the only one that can truly save her and we need your help fixing what is to come."

"Save…" I trailed off and attempted to process the notion before gripping the bars of my cage, snarling. "You're telling me she's *alive*?!"

'They…they weren't simply taunting me?' I attempted to swallow my panic.

How could she have survived such an injury? Did they simply mean that they had reincarnated her soul? Or, had the other Elders lied when they claimed Arianna and Darius had both perished? It had always struck me as strange that they refused to give us anything to bury. Was she a prisoner somewhere? Did she remember what happened?

'Does she…remember me?'

I staggered back against the bars and lifted a hand over my face, struggling to process the information. Somehow, the notion that Arianna had been alive all this time was more painful than believing she was dead. She had been everything to me. I would never have left her somewhere willingly. *'But…does she know that?'*

"Sit down and listen, boy," the female ordered, ignoring the threatening look I shot her. *"We have much to disclose to you and precious little time to do it. You need to know the rules of being a God without a Goddess, the rules of Balance, and the risks we are all taking.*

"After that, then *we will tell you of your precious princess and what*

has become of her."

I shot them another begrudging glare before nodding my head sharply to indicate my compliance. I wanted nothing more than to rip all of the Elders and the Angels apart for what had happened so many years ago. But, if she was still alive, then perhaps there was a faint sliver of hope left. For the moment, I would shelve my whirlwind of questions and emotions so that I could listen to what the Elders had to say to me. Only by listening would I determine who needed to pay for the harm that had come to Arianna.

After 180 years, all I could do was hope that no one had made her suffer.

⚙

CHAPTER TWO
Nalithor Vraelimir

Twenty years later…

I stared up at the stars in silence and rested with my back against Dauthrmir's outer wall. Below me was a drop of a thousand feet, perhaps more. That precarious place in the Sapphire Quarter—sandwiched between the Nobles District and The Ruling Quarter—had always been Arianna's favorite hiding place.

When I was a child it had scared the hells out of me. Only a few yards of turf separated the wall from the drop off into the lake below. I had always worried Arianna would fall.

Yet there I was, in the place that once terrified me, alone with my thoughts and several bottles of strong liquor. There wasn't anywhere else in the empire I would have been on this day of the year.

As of today, two hundred years had passed since Arianna was taken from us.

She had been very much alive when I found her in Limbo despite the horrifying state she was in. The torture she endured still made my blood boil even though years had passed.

I couldn't fathom how she had survived it. Even the fae-dragons, Djialkan and Fraelfnir, didn't have the power to heal such horrendous wounds or stop that much bleeding.

For some reason, Arianna took on the torture meant for both her and her brother. They were raised apart from each other and, as such, had never grown close. Yet she still chose to protect him. I couldn't understand it. Although it appeared that the bastard Angels had held their end of the bargain, I couldn't be sure.

Limbo was a place of stasis where time didn't flow, a place meant to imprison Exiled Gods and their monstrous creations: the Chaos Beasts.

Normally Limbo was governed by the God of Time but I hadn't found a trace of him or his faithful while there. It was as if the Elders and Angels had repurposed Limbo for their own agenda and thrown the God of Time from his own realm.

"I knew we'd find you here." A voice sighed. "Come on, Nali. If we're going to get drunk, let's at least go to a bar."

I turned my head and watched my two closest friends step through the crack in the wall. The tallest of the pair was Eyrian Il'thar, a

Draekin demigod and the First Prince of Gron'kial. His blue and aqua mane looked even more disheveled than usual, and his seafoam green eyes held a hint of concern. We had both been friends with the princess, and studied with her, as children. We *might* have even fought over her a few times.

The second man was Xander Leukos—my adopted brother. He hadn't known Arianna for as long as Eyrian and I had, but he was still saddened by her death. Xander was now a Vampire, but when I first met him he had been a Vunsori—a Desert Elf. He still had the caramel-colored skin and glossy black hair of his original race. His eyes were a rich yet pale shade of blue, and were one of the reasons his tribe cast him out as a child.

During an undercover mission to the Desert Elf capital, V'frul, Arianna and I had discovered the nobles were trafficking slaves— Devillian slaves in particular. Xander, a child at the time, had been amongst the "cargo" and Arianna had rescued him.

I later discovered that Xander was terrified of Arianna when he first met her, but it came as no surprise. Before finding him, she had slaughtered everyone in attendance at the auction. To say she was blood-soaked didn't quite do her enraged visage justice.

"A bar is the last place I want to go." I shook my head before leaning back against the wall once more. "I don't think I have to explain to you what will happen if one of the wenches offers me 'comfort' for my sorrows."

They both grimaced but it was Xander that spoke, "I hope you have enough varikna for the three of us, then."

"I'm not sure if there's enough in the entire damned city for the three of us," I snorted in reply. "Not with everyone using the day of remembrance as an excuse to go out and party like it's Groslturvir!"

I snarled curses under my breath when my glass of liquor shattered in my hand and the shards lacerated my palm. The bastards in the city were drinking and eating as if it were a day of celebration, not a day of mourning. Regardless of which language I used I had no word strong enough to describe the fury I felt.

Keeping to myself was the only way to get through the day without killing anyone.

They may have been our people, but they didn't understand. Lucifer, Eyrian, Xander, and my parents were the closest to understanding how I felt, but even they didn't quite get it.

As the God of Balance I wasn't supposed to speak with anyone about what happened when the Elders sent me to Limbo. I had found loopholes in the Elders' rules, of course, so that I could let Lucifer know. He was her father; he needed to know.

However, neither of us knew how to handle what had happened. Arianna's memories being stolen from her was already a dagger through our hearts. That the Elders claimed *I* was the reason she died outside of Limbo was a whole other matter entirely.

I had carried her bloodied, unconscious body out of Limbo myself and Djialkan had accompanied me. Afterward, I had returned to fetch Darius and his Guardian, Fraelfnir. When I returned to where the

Elders were waiting, Arianna and Djialkan were gone. The Elders claimed that the trauma of moving between Limbo and our world was too strenuous for her—and that she had passed.

When I demanded to see her body as proof, they declined and told me that they had wiped her soul clean of memories of her life and of Limbo so they could safely reincarnate her. Then, they claimed that they had already disposed of her body and could not give it to me or to Lucifer for burial purposes. *Again.*

I had healed her completely before leaving Limbo. I had taken my time to mend her wounds, made sure that her blood was returned to her, and *then* I took her back to our world. All under Djialkan's supervision. Aside from Lucifer and myself, I knew of no one who had ever been as protective of Arianna as Djialkan was. Certainly it was his job as her Guardian, but it went beyond that. Before I came along, he was the only one she would speak to aside from her father and brother.

"I think he's going to need something stronger than varikna," Xander stated, interrupting my thoughts and earning him a glare. "You can't hide the fact that you're troubled from us, Nali. We've known you too long for that."

"You're not allowed to talk about it?" Eyrian crossed his arms and arched an eyebrow.

"No."

My friends sighed and then sat down on either side of me, moving the bottles of varikna out of their way. It was like a ritual. On the same day every year, I would go to the same spot and waste the day away drinking. Eventually, Eyrian and Xander would show up to keep an eye on me—and drink with me. Perhaps they were concerned that I would leap off the ledge, or perhaps they thought their company would lend me some form of comfort.

'I should find a better place to hide…but there is no other place fitting.' I grimaced and then summoned darkness around my bleeding hand to heal the wound. "Suffice to say it's something I can't drown out with work or with liquor."

"And there's nothing we can do to help?" Xander shook his head and then continued, "I won't pry, but we *know* you, Nalithor. It has to be something serious, and it has to be something about Arianna-jiss, if you're sulking about it this much."

"He's right you know." Eyrian jabbed a thumb in Xander's direction. "If you think of a way we can help, just say the word."

"Well, if you two know how to slay the Elder Gods that would be a good start," I muttered. "I—"

Pain lanced through the left side of my chest, forcing me to cut myself off with a groan. I clutched my chest and bared my fangs in a poor attempt to contain myself. Both of the crystalline hearts in my chest beat wildly and burned with unbridled fury and hatred. My breath came in short gasps and my hands shook as I tried to stifle the overwhelming power and emotions pouring from Arianna's heart.

Such attacks first started a few months after the Elders claimed they were going to reincarnate Arianna. Over the past few years, the attacks had become frequent—and often crippling.

"Her heart again?" Eyrian frowned at me after exchanging a look with Xander. "Shouldn't that mean…"

"It should have shattered if the Elders were telling the truth about her death," I snarled through gritted teeth. "I've searched Limbo several times over to see if they moved her somewhere else within it. She's not there."

"So, they moved her somewhere out of reach?" Xander murmured. "Well, they *are* Elders. I suppose they could stash her anywhere they wanted, couldn't they?"

"They said they reincarnated her," I replied with a tetchy huff once the pain had subsided to a dull ache. "If they were telling the truth about her…death, it is possible her heart remained. *If* they moved her soul to a new body immediately—but it's a stretch."

"A 'stretch' is too generous." Eyrian rolled his eyes. "At this point I don't think it's too 'hopeful' or 'naive' of us to think she's alive somewhere. Reincarnated or not, she's still attached to that heart of hers. If you're sensing things through it, she has to be in Avrirsa somewhere, right?"

"Why else do you think Lucifer decided to fund the expedition to the Nrae'lmar Continent?" I pointed out. "He's determined to find her, and he has more reach to do so than I do at the moment. Whether it's her or not is another matter entirely. Wherever she is…it can't be good. Not if it causes her this much pain and hatred."

"The Elders are claiming it's a fake—or a copy—connected to her heart." Lucifer appeared in an explosion of shadow in front of us, causing Xander and Eyrian to rush to their feet to salute the emperor. "Tch. Enough of the stuffy antics, boys. You're making me feel old. Sit down before you fall down."

Lucifer shot Eyrian and Xander both a sharp look before shifting his attention to me. Although my rank among the gods was higher than his, Lucifer's gaze still had a way of making me squirm.

The emperor was pale with messy dark brown curls, which hung even more disheveled than usual. Silver horns twisted back from above his temples, and a black-scaled tail swung lazily behind him.

However, it was his eyes that set Lucifer apart from other Devillians. His left eye was a brilliant electric blue, but his right eye was chartreuse green and gradated to yellow at its center. Both of his pupils were slits, but unlike most Devillian races, his sclerae were not black.

'Arianna really did take after him.' I pursed my lips and picked up a new bottle of varikna. *'The hair, the skin, blue of her eyes… I wouldn't have been surprised if her horns and tail grew to match those of her father as well.'*

"*We* haven't started drinking yet!" Xander huffed, motioning between Eyrian and himself.

"A fake?" I looked up at Lucifer again once I'd pried the cork from the bottle. "And what is their reasoning behind that one?"

"The Exiles," Lucifer spat, his lips curling into a scowl. "We already know that the Exiled Gods have been trying to create replicas of demigods and deities to further their schemes. The Elders claim that the Exiles have had their first success—and that her 'copy' is somehow bound to her heart."

"Even the First Exile shouldn't have that much power." I frowned, considering it. *'Granted, he shouldn't have had the power to create a new race either.'*

"Either way, that isn't what I came to talk to you three about." Lucifer crossed his arms and narrowed his eyes at us. "One of our scout ships found something strange in the skies above the lands to the far west, beyond Falrrsald. They described it as 'a flying island with a violet sky and no sun'—they're landing to investigate."

"We've flown west before and never found anything," Eyrian pointed out as he sat back with his own bottle of varikna.

"The island isn't anchored like other airborne landmasses we've found," Lucifer offered in response. "It seems that it orbits Avrirsa, not unlike one of the moons, but its speed is closer to the rotation of our planet. A few of the scholars are staying with the ship so they can get a grasp of its pattern.

"The others have gone to survey the land. They said they saw what looks like *X'shmir* on the eastern half of the island and the Sihix Forest to the north."

"X'shmir?" Xander asked in disbelief. "That country has been missing for years! Have you notified the rest of the Rilzaan Alliance about this, Your Excellence?"

"That's why I was looking for you as well; *you* can relay it to the Beshulthien Empire," Lucifer replied, waving one hand dismissively.

"Several Beshulthiens are on board as well but they said they're unable to reach your capital. You'll need to relay the information to your Emperor yourself."

"I'll wait until we have more to go by." Xander tilted his head in thought. "If they've been stuck in the sky for this long, I doubt they need to be suddenly swarmed by a bunch of outsiders."

"I will want to go to the Sihix Forest," I spoke up, drawing the Emperor's attention. "They're more likely to tell us what happened to X'shmir than the Humans are. The people of X'shmir were never very friendly, if I recall."

"Eyrian, you and your men are going up there tomorrow morning," Lucifer stated, giving the Draekin a firm look when he opened his mouth to protest. "Fear not, I've already informed them. You're free to drown yourself in alcohol for the rest of the night if that's what you really want to do.

"Nalithor and I will have to wait before venturing there. We need to make sure that magical power doesn't make the inhabitants *too* skittish."

"You honestly think there are still people living there?" I arched an eyebrow. "That place was never meant to be a flying island, unlike Tulja or Juln."

"The city *is* active and there's precious little else outside of it." Lucifer conjured a stack of parchment and tossed it me. "These are the readings the scholars have taken thus far. They've requested you compare them to your findings with the Ceilail and Xiinsha Forests."

I looked down at the first page and frowned while skimming over the data. It made no sense. The amount of aether was far too high for the size of the island. *This much aether should have made anyone, and anything, living there ill.'*

"How much of the island is covered by the Sihix Forest?" I asked after rifling through the stack of papers and finding no answers.

"You'll have to ask them yourself. They didn't say." Lucifer shrugged. "I want you to look into the data and then take updated readings from Ceilail and Xiinsha Forests as soon as possible. In the off chance that place is where the Elders took Arianna, I want to make sure one of us gets there first."

'She can't be alive.' I kept the thought to myself and slumped against the wall, closing my eyes. I wanted to believe that Arianna was still alive but at the same time it was a frightening thought. Upon leaving Limbo she had reverted to the form of a child, looking much as she had the day she was taken from Dauthrmir.

She hadn't remembered anything prior to being taken from the Dauthrmiran palace—would she even remember *that* now? If the Elders had tampered with her again there was no telling who or what she was now.

A bottle of varikna groaned and cracked in my hand but I eased my grip before it could fully break. The cold liquor soaked my hand, seeping from the fractures in the glass.

I sighed deeply—I had to keep that place from my mind. I doubted I would ever find out how Arianna didn't go insane while trapped there. If she truly was alive somewhere she deserved a quiet, peaceful existence after all that she endured in Limbo.

'If she is still alive, I can't let her grow close to me—and I can't grow close to her.' I clenched my teeth. *'I can't let her suffer the responsibility of this role. Balance is the role of a monster.'*

A monster. For a moment I thought my heart would stop. Arianna probably wouldn't even want anything to do with a monster like me. She would hate and loathe me, despite all I had done to save her. Despite all we had done together as children. None of that would matter—she would just see a foul creature that had to keep the balance through *any* means necessary.

Ahhnn, but isn't it so wonderful to be like a monster?

I frowned when warmth radiated from Arianna's heart to soothe me. It was a strange phrase, one that she had uttered in Limbo. At first I hadn't thought much of it. Not until I later searched her memories and discovered who she was. Now those words seemed to follow me.

'She always was a strange one…' I took a swig of alcohol, oblivious to the other three men talking. *'Just how connected to this role was she?'*

"It's growing chill. We should find some fiirzik to drink or head inside." Eyrian jabbed me hard with his elbow to get my attention.

"Then let's go inside. I want to start working on this data." I rose to my feet. *'Real or fake, I will find her. If it is a fake…* I will end whoever is responsible. I don't care if it's the Exiles or the Elders, they will die.'

CHAPTER THREE
Arianna Jade Black

The brilliant violet sky surrounding my homeland stretched before me like a sea. Floating above me was what looked like a rip in the sky itself. Within that jagged tear rested an orb that rippled like water and shone with pale lavender light. Its position in the sky told me it was close to midday.

No one would expect me for several hours yet.

'Not that my presence is welcome,' I mused while swinging my legs back and forth over the edge of the flying island.

A cool autumn breeze drifted by me, carrying the scents of fallen leaves, pine needles, and churned dirt. It was a familiar smell—the smell of the forest surrounding X'shmir's one and only city. Anything was an improvement over the stench of the city for me, but the smell of wilderness was especially enticing.

Well over two hundred years had passed since X'shmir rose from the world Below and into the sky to become one of Avrirsa's many flying islands. During my admittedly limited studies I had been unable to ascertain *why* or *how* our city-state left its original place in Avrirsa.

All-in-all, the why and how didn't matter. What mattered was that my people had been cut off completely from the other species—and other Humans—in the rest of Avrirsa. We had even lost contact with *all* of the gods. Lesser, Middle, Upper, or Elder—it didn't matter the rank. The faithful's prayers had been left unheard for two centuries because we could no longer commune with any deity.

Of course, we had plenty of stories about how we ended up there. Our citizens passed on tale after tale by word of mouth. We had a limited number of books available in X'shmir, and even fewer were available to the commoners. They had to entertain themselves somehow.

According to the most popular story, the second King and Queen of X'shmir had received a vision of the Elder Gods stripping humankind of access to magic. Fearing that our race would become little more than livestock to the more powerful species of the world, the king and queen devised a plan to strike back at the immortals.

However, something went awry. Humanity lost its access to magic and our flying island was engulfed in a sickly violet mist soon after.

None of the city's current occupants had ever seen the *real* sky. All we knew was the endless violet expanse that we called "the Mists."

There was nothing in the sky around X'shmir aside from the Mists and the liquid-filled tear that tracked through the sky during the day.

I would have loved to see the real sky at least once. Some of my books described the day and nighttime skies as such beautiful things. They seemed fantastical to me.

'*Moons and stars. I wonder—*' An angered, gurgling roar echoed through the forest and sent a shiver of excitement down my spine, drawing my thoughts towards *it* instead. '*Beasts? What are they doing so close to the city? It isn't even winter yet!*'

My back groaned and strained in protest as I rose to my feet. The pain of my stretching wounds almost knocked the wind from my lungs. I gritted my teeth, inhaled a deep breath, mentally shelved the pain, and then sighed. After 20 years in that horrible place, I'd grown accustomed to working and fighting whilst wounded.

'*Now then, the Chaos Beasts,*' I tugged the hems of my gloves and turned my back to my cliff perch. '*Humph, the work of an Umbral Mage is never over, is it?*'

Darkness bloomed around my feet and rose halfway up my legs moments before I broke into a sprint. Without magic to aid me, I would have died to the beasts or succumbed to my wounds long ago.

The wilderness of X'shmir was a harsh place and, as such, our people had retreated behind the city's crumbling walls.

Men, women, children, and livestock all lived within the city itself. Our farmlands were abandoned; we no longer had hunters or foragers willing to brave even our immediate surroundings. There were a few men who still went to the western lake in search of fish but it was a dangerous task.

'There it is,' I smirked within my hood when I caught movement to the north of me.

The Chaos Beast was an amalgamation of mismatched limbs and hides. It staggered through the forest on six legs. Oil-like blood seeped from the sections where foreign parts had been fused together. Its breath came in ragged gasps and its featureless head twitched as it swiveled around in search of...something. It seemed oblivious to the forest's canopy scraping the top of its already-bleeding skull.

I grimaced at the familiar scents of rotting flesh, dirty fur, and the acrid smell of venom.

'Starting with the venomous ones already, are we?' I made an upwards motion with my left hand, summoning an array of sharp icicles over my shoulder. *'I don't see any barbs or spines that could be the source of venom. So, it either has fangs or claws?'*

Falling still, I listened for a moment. The forest floor crunched and groaned beneath the massive creature's feet. Birds called warnings in the distance and rodents fled from the Chaos Beast in every direction. What I didn't hear, however, was the sizzle of venom eating at the leaves or roots of the forest floor.

'Fangs then.' I nodded to myself.

The ground shook beneath my feet when the beast roared again. I steadied myself against a tree trunk and summoned several more blades of ice. With my back wounded as it was I couldn't risk getting close to the beast. Swinging weapons around was my last option.

'It needs to die.*'* I shivered as excitement threatened to overtake me. *'Filthy, corrupt monstrosity! Where the fuck do they keep coming from?'*

I sent my darkness rushing towards the beast and then smiled when the creature screamed in terror. It turned to face me with its eyeless head and then charged, tearing across the forest floor. It stumbled over its own mismatched limbs in its haste. How the damned thing could run on six limbs of varying lengths was beyond me.

A subtle motion of my hand sent the first half of my icy blades soaring through the air and into the beast's pelt. Blood sprayed into the air around the beast but it continued its charge, painting the trees in the color of oil as it passed.

'That won't do.' I frowned and shadow-stepped away, bringing my blades of ice with me.

The next array of blades sunk deeper into the beast's patchy flesh, earning yowls of pain and anger. Yet it didn't slow. Instead, it turned toward my new location and barreled towards me once more. This time I sent a single blade at it and tore its throat open. A torrent of blood spilled to the ground but the beast came at me again.

'Are you playing with your prey again, Arianna?' an exasperated voice rumbled.

A black dragon no larger than a house cat appeared from a puff of dark purple smoke beside me, a look of disapproval on his draconic maw. Black smoke poured from his nostrils as he looked from me to the rampaging beast and back with annoyance.

"I'm not playing with it—it's being stubborn about dying," I retorted, motioning loosely at the beast to unleash the remainder of my blades. "Djialkan, aren't you supposed to be in the castle helping your brother teach Darius?"

"Your brother has already 'dismissed' us for the day," Djialkan muttered as he came to perch on my shoulder. *"Hmm, I see. It is a resistant one. How are your wounds?"*

"I can't risk getting close to it." I shadow-stepped away from the beast again. "They usually don't get this close to the city. Has something happened?"

"Fraelfnir and I agreed that the Mists have smelled different for the past fortnight." Djialkan shrugged his wings. *"Perhaps the change has agitated some of the younger beasts. After all, this one is much smaller than the ones you have been dealing with as of late."*

I ignored the fae-dragon for the moment and focused my attention on the clumsy beast, taking in the damage it sustained from my blades thus far. The flow of blood had slowed to a trickle but, unlike other types of beasts, its wounds weren't closing. It seemed as if it didn't know how to do anything beyond roaring and charging.

'Well, if it's a stupid one, I should be able to end this quickly.' I summoned several orbs of cobalt fire and spun them above my palm. "Djialkan, after I kill it we should go back to the castle. I'm going to need you and Fraelfnir to reseal my wounds."

"Blast it, girl!" Djialkan snapped at me. *"You have torn them open already? I thought you said you were going to be careful!"*

I sent my orbs of fire arcing towards the Chaos Beast and slammed them into its open wounds. Pillars of brilliant blue fire exploded from each of the holes. The beast came to an abrupt stop and slumped in place, lifeless.

"I was careful." I flicked Djialkan's nose with my free hand. "Unless I lay facedown in bed all day I'm going to end up reopening some of the wounds. There's no *reasonable* way to keep from moving!"

"We cannot afford to have you testing your wounds, Arianna!" Djialkan butted my cheek with his forehead. *"If you find yourself bedridden or worse, fall, there will be no one left to take care of—"*

"I know, Djialkan, I know." I sighed at him and turned to begin the walk back to the city. "First things first—let's get back to the castle so you and Fraelfnir can take a look at my wounds."

"Afterward, Darius still wishes to have dinner with you," Djialkan informed me, earning a sour look. *"We need to determine if he, too, has sensed anything strange about the Mists. If he has noticed strange things as well, we can cross him off our list of possible causes."*

Djialkan was right but I still didn't want to have dinner with my brother. Despite what *I* wanted, Darius was an Astral Mage and I was an Umbral Mage. According to X'shmir's stupid laws, I had to obey.

'Fuck the X'shmirans and their superstitions.' I grimaced, conjured an ornate leather half-mask, and settled the eyeless contraption over the top half of my face.

Darius and I got along well enough but we both had our share of hardships in and out of the castle. We had our own unique problems to deal with and I preferred to work on my issues *away* from the city and my brother.

'Enough pouting.' Djialkan smacked me upside the head with his tail. *'He is the only real family that you have in this wretched place, and the same can be said for him.'*

'That doesn't mean I have to like it.' I glanced at Djialkan before settling my gaze on the growing shadow of the city before us. *'Darius and I are too different. I can only tolerate him in small doses, and those doses are becoming too frequent.'*

Djialkan and I fell into silence again as we neared the city gates. Sections of the wall surrounding the city were crumbling but that didn't keep my soldiers from guarding the gates or my archers from manning their posts along the wall.

Without magic these men stood no chance against the Chaos Beasts—so I had trained them to hold the creatures off instead. *If* the beasts grew brazen enough to venture close to the city, my men could protect X'shmir until I made it to the front lines myself.

"General Black." The guards saluted me as I passed them and entered the city.

I nodded to them and made my way along the damaged roads of X'shmir. Many of the houses were in ruin or on the verge of collapse. Men milled about the derelict buildings to collect materials they could repurpose for the farms on the far side of the city. The few who noticed me casted filthy scowls or spat in my direction.

Few citizens in X'shmir truly liked or respected me. My status as an Umbral Mage meant that most saw me as some sub-Human creature with little more rights than an animal. However, amidst all the scum in our city, there were still people who understood that I played a large role in why they were still alive.

"Your Highness," a woman called quietly, motioning me toward her. "Has something happened? All of the farm animals are behaving strange. We've spent all morning trying to calm them but they just…won't."

I parted my lips to speak but stopped myself and looked to Djialkan instead.

"Her Highness just slew a beast near the city walls," Djialkan offered with a tilt of his head. *"Perhaps the livestock sensed its approach?"*

"They've been like this for hours." The woman shook her head, frowning. "Even the birds are acting odd, Your Highness. We've never seen the animals act like this, not even when a beast broke into the city."

"They are not panicked?" Djialkan questioned.

"No, my lord." The woman shook her head again. "I don't know how to explain it. Whatever caused it, it can't be beasts."

"We will look into it," Djialkan declared before I could attempt to voice my opinion to him. *"If you will excuse us, we must attend to a matter in the castle first."*

The woman curtsied to us before scurrying off. I shot Djialkan an agitated look but my mask dampened the affect. He just laughed at me, so I began walking again—this time at a brisker pace.

'*Tomorrow we will begin our investigation,*' Djialkan informed me. '*If even the commoners have noticed strange happenings, we do not have much time before your parents, the nobles, or Darius notice.*'

'*You think this is related to whatever is going on with the Sihix Forest?*' I asked. When Djialkan nodded his response, I frowned and crossed my arms.

In all honesty, I didn't want more problems piling up on my plate. Soon autumn would turn into winter, X'shmir would be buried in snow, and the beasts would be more active than any other time of year. Chasing thin leads, beasts, and aetheric disturbances in the snow wasn't my idea of a good winter.

'*I just want to curl up by the fire with some tea...*' I thought. My shoulders slumped—and I immediately regretted the movement. My wounds pulled, and a moment later I felt hot blood leaking down my back. '*Ugh, have Fraelfnir meet us in my rooms, Djialkan.*'

'*Arianna?*' Djialkan nudged my cheek gently when I staggered and braced myself against a wall.

I clenched my teeth and shook my head in reply. Once I managed to regain some semblance of control I began walking again at a hurried pace. The fae-dragon brothers needed to see to my wounds as soon as possible. I couldn't have the damned things crippling my movements.

Several minutes later I stormed into my wing of the castle, down the hallway, and slammed my doors open. Two familiar scents, not one, greeted me as I entered my rooms. I released a growl under my breath before adopting a more neutral expression and then stalked towards the bedroom.

Sitting beside my bed I found my twin brother, Darius. Perched on top of my bed was Djialkan's brother—and Darius' Guardian—Fraelfnir. The white fae-dragon looked bored when he raised his head off the comforter and settled his golden eyes on me.

"You opened your wounds?" Fraelfnir grumbled, startling Darius out of whatever book he'd been reading.

"Ari!" Darius called cheerfully. "Whoa, you're more pale than usual. You okay?"

"Of course she is not 'okay!'" Fraelfnir hissed as he rounded on Darius. *"I told you we were coming here to further heal your sister's wounds, you fool. If she was doing well we would not have come in the first place. You will have to finish your studies after dinner tonight."*

"You two are still getting along well, I see," I commented dryly, removing my mask.

Darius shot me a concerned frown but I pretended to not see it. Instead, I moved towards the wardrobe adjacent to my room. As usual, my brother was dressed in gaudy white Astral Mage robes. The embroidery and his jewelry were both shining gold and followed the theme of suns, earth, water, and stags. His inner robes were alternating gold and jade green, matched by the jade and emerald stones set in his jewelry.

Because he was also the crown prince, Darius' attire was more regal and flamboyant than a lowborn Astral Mage's would have been. Since coming into our powers I never saw Darius wear anything other than his mages' finery. He always seemed to be clad in brilliant white clothing that followed the same theme.

I wasn't much better. As the outcast in the family, I had limited resources—including clothing. It was a good thing I liked black, seeing as that's all my wardrobe consisted of. Black and platinum clothing, sometimes lined with fur, with the occasional flash of sapphire blue.

"So why is Darius here for this, exactly?" I asked as I stepped out of my wardrobe in my bra and a pair of loose pants.

"It is high time he learned healing techniques—and I will need to borrow his power," Fraelfnir replied, narrowing his eyes at me as I approached. *"You are in quite a state. We took our time healing you last night. Did you pull your wounds whilst fighting beasts?"*

"Quite a state?" Darius yelped when I passed him. "A-Ari, your whole back is covered in blood!"

"I kept myself at range and used magic to kill the one beast I saw today," I replied before shooting Darius a look over my shoulder. "Do you listen to *anything* your Guardian tells you? Of course my back is covered in blood. I'm injured. You three are going to help heal me."

Djialkan and Fraelfnir sighed at each other before turning their attention to me. Deep purple smoke engulfed Djialkan whilst golden and white light swallowed Fraelfnir. When their respective powers dissipated, both had taken on the form of Devillian children.

Fraelfnir was pale with streaked white and gold hair. His horns, eyes, claws, and scaled tail were all golden like in his draconic form. By contrast his brother, Djialkan, had bright white hair, silver horns and claws, a black tail, and brilliant purple eyes.

'It's kind of scary how similar they look,' Darius commented. *'I'm kind of glad we don't look that much alike. It'd be kinda weird since you're a girl and I'm a boy.'*

I glanced to the side at my brother and then at the impatient-looking fae-dragons. Darius was right—Djialkan and Fraelfnir looked like they would have been identical twins were it not for their different colorings. It was a little unsettling to see them together in their Devillian forms. Thankfully, both of them preferred their fae-dragon forms as those were their true appearances.

Darius and I, on the other hand, were quite different. My brother had tan skin, golden brown hair, and chartreuse green eyes. In contrast, my skin was pale, wintry white and my eyes were electric blue. My hair was also much darker than his.

The features we did share were our curly hair, height, slit pupils, and pointed ears. We were a little strange-looking for Humans, but our parents and their advisors insisted we were the "next step" in Human evolution. Some sort of blessing upon X'shmir—or at least, my brother was.

I was just a curse.

"H-how am I supposed to help with wounds like that?" Darius' nervous gulp was audible, making me shift to look at him again. "Those are ch-chains, right? How are we supposed to take them out of your back without making things worse?"

"We have to leave them there." Djialkan curled his lip into a scowl

as he looked up at Darius. "*Fraelfnir and I removed the chains from her once, back when your parents first gave the order for Arianna to be tortured.*"

"Leave them there...? Why?!" Darius exclaimed, looking a tad green as he raised a hand over his mouth. "Isn't that dangerous? Won't her body try to fight them off?"

"If they're removed, the torturers notice," I began as I laid on the bed stomach-down, "and if they notice, they add more—and they make it more painful than they usually do. Which, in turn, means that Djialkan and Fraelfnir have to expend more power to heal me."

"More? But there's already so many!" Darius exclaimed. "How can you even move?"

"*Are you ready?*" Djialkan asked me with a concerned frown.

"As ready as I can be," I replied, pulling a pillow to my chest and wrapping both my arms around it. "How bad is it?"

"Isn't...isn't that light magic?" Darius took several steps toward the bed and wrung his hands. "They're torturing you with *light*? B-but how is that possible? You and I are the only mages in X'shmir!"

"*Not all of the Royal Family's allies are Human, Darius,*" Fraelfnir stated before pointing for my brother to sit down. "*You do not have the skill to mend wounds such as this. Stay there and allow me to draw power from you. Djialkan's power and mine combined is not enough for this task, as I feared.*"

I twitched and swallowed a growl as Djialkan unhooked my bra and peeled it away from my back. Both fae-dragons muttered to each other in the draconic language as they examined my maimed back. I did my best not to fidget, and they tried to be gentle, but the wounds were utter agony.

A knot formed in my throat when I sensed more light emitting from the chains followed by a searing sensation through my torso.

'Fucking hells!' I dug my fingers into the pillow and attempted to stay still. *'Djialkan, can't you drown out that accursed light?!'*

Djialkan shushed me before returning to his work. Fraelfnir's power joined with his brother's darkness as they attempted to mend my back and suppress the power held within the chains. I wasn't sure what the damned things were made of but I knew they were engraved with runes in the Angelic language.

The fae-dragons had convinced me to keep the origins of the chains from my brother for the time being. We weren't certain how he'd react to the fact that *Angels* were the ones responsible for cursing and torturing me. Personally, I was pretty sure Darius already knew. Both of us had a penchant for sneaking around the castle and finding places we weren't supposed to be.

'Ari? You still awake?' Darius prodded at my thoughts.

'I was just thinking,' I muttered, glancing to the side at him as a new round of pain lanced down my back. *'How did your studies with Fraelfnir go today?'*

'Terrible! I can't concentrate.' Darius sighed, slumping back in his seat. *'It's like the water and the earth are restless. They seem different. I thought it was just my imagination, but I heard from one of the servants*

that all the animals in and around the city are behaving strangely. Some of the people are beginning to act weird too.'

'*The wind is the same,*' I offered after a moment of thought. '*Djialkan and I intend to investigate tomorrow. We want to make sure nothing has happened to disturb X'shmir's natural aether.*'

'*Natural aether?*' Darius sounded confused. '*Isn't aether an element on its own? How would that be related to wind, water, or earth?*'

'*Do you listen to* anything *Fraelfnir teaches you?*' I shot him a sideways look. '*Aether and crystal both serve as conductors for the other eight elements. It's the reason X'shmir's soil is rich with wind, earth, and dark crystals.*'

'*No, he does not listen to anything I teach him,*' Fraelfnir snorted, flicking my long hair out of his way. '*Be still. We are moving on to the deeper wounds now.*'

Djialkan and Fraelfnir gave me a few moments to steel myself before beginning their work anew. My head spun in response to their poking and prodding. Before I could form a coherent thought my body went limp and my mind went blank as it was consumed by pain and loathing. I was vaguely aware of the fae-dragons and my brother discussing something but I was in another place now.

'*Light… Corrupted, filthy light.*' I twitched, feeling my anger rising. '*Someone needs to snuff it out. Every. Last. Particle. Why is something so corrupt allowed to exist? If I could just reach it… I'd extinguish it myself!*'

I tried to move, summon my magic—anything—but was met with more pain. No matter what I tried, I seemed incapable of calling forth my elements or moving a part of my body. The light and darkness were still there, attempting to heal me. My disgust towards the light threatened to overwhelm me.

'*Don't take her away from me!*' The vaguely familiar voice of a boy screamed.

'*I…see. I'm going to have that nightmare again.*' My heart sunk as I felt myself being pulled to sleep. '*Just how many more times do I have to witness that poor boy break?*

'*His name, what was it… Nali?*'

CHAPTER FOUR
X'shmiran Beasts

'N-Nali it's okay, I'm still alive! Nali, please, don't cry! I can't bear that look on your face... Please—'

The sound of something hard hitting my windows jolted me awake, out of bed, and scrambling to the floor for cover.

I summoned a sword of ice in my left hand and prepared to defend against whatever was trying to break through my windows. This time, dozens of objects rattled the panes of weather-worn glass. Groggy, I moved to charge at the windows but was halted by Djialkan. He looked even grumpier than I felt.

"Calm yourself, Arianna, lest you give the peasants a show." Djialkan snorted darkness from his nose at me. *"At least dress yourself before ripping into them. Judging by their shouting, something must have*

happened."

"Shouting?" I paused to listen. "What in the hells are they doing near *my* wing of the castle?"

"Get dressed and find out." Djialkan leapt towards the windows and then nosed the door to the balcony open so that he could yell down into the courtyard. *"Give Her Highness the time to get dressed you bloody scoundrels! Do you* want *to see the face and body of an Umbral Mage?!"*

'Gee, thanks Djialkan.' I rolled my eyes as I stalked towards the wardrobe. *'As if they need to be any more frightened by me.'*

'Something must have frightened them more than you do for them to encroach upon your territory,' Djialkan countered.

The fae-dragon had a point, so I relented. I rifled through the contents of the wardrobe and yanked a set of mage robes over a pair of leggings and a blouse. Once the heavily embellished robe was settled into place I pulled my nearly knee-length curls into a bun, flipped up my deep hood, and then placed a half-mask over the top half of my face to obscure my eyes from view.

'How are your wounds?' Djialkan asked with a hint of worry.

I grimaced at myself in the mirror and did a few tentative stretches to test my mangled back and my range of movement.

'I should be able to fight as I please, but my skin feels a bit…tight,' I answered while pulling on my boots, followed by a pair of black leather gloves. *'Are the commoners still blubbering?'*

'I have never seen the X'shmiran people this frightened.' Djialkan sounded unusually concerned for them. *'They keep rambling on about*

demons but I cannot make out what they are attempting to convey.'

'Demons?' I arched an eyebrow behind my mask as I walked towards the balcony. *'You'll need to speak for me, you know. Do* try *not to make me sound like the kingdom's biggest asshole?'*

'No promises.' Djialkan perched on my left shoulder once I stepped onto the balcony. *"By the gods, one at a time! What, pray tell, possessed you to throw rocks at Her Highness' room?!"*

The commoners below fell silent and shrank back when I rested my hands on the railing so that I could look down at them. Farmers, soldiers, shopkeepers, smithies, masons, men, women, and children were all gathered below me.

There must have been at least forty of them and they all bore expressions of sheer terror. For once, those expressions were not because of my status as an Umbral Mage. No, their fear was directed somewhere outside the city. I could smell it.

"Y-Your Highness." A man with greasy blond hair stepped forward and bowed. "Demons have appeared by the lake south of that accursed forest! Our fishermen had to leave their posts and flee for the city!"

"Demons?" Djialkan rumbled. *"You mean beasts?"*

Djialkan's question was answered with a wave of no's, shaken heads, and whimpers of fear. "Demons." We both knew what the X'shmirans were talking about—Devillians. Why the Humans of X'shmir called Devillians *demons* was beyond me, but that wasn't what I found bothersome.

Aside from those who were bound to the Sihix Forest there were no Devillians in X'shmir. This country had been airborne, and isolated from the rest of Avrirsa, for well over two hundred years.

However, beings bound to the Sihix Forest couldn't live without the dark-aspect aether of Sihix to safeguard them against other elements. The lake covered a large portion of X'shmir, but our fishing shacks were set up at least a three-hour walk away from the forest's edge. Sihix's people would die before getting that far. The Guardians could make it, perhaps, but they were not Devillian.

'The winds have *changed these last few months,'* I muttered, glancing to the side at Djialkan. *'Do you think that outsiders have found us?'*

'It is more likely a new type of Chaos Beast.' Djialkan frowned. "*Yes, yes. Demons, scary things, blah blah blah. You have not stated your reason for coming to the castle and waking my ward!*"

"Who else in the kingdom could we go to?" A woman's panicked shriek rung louder than the men around her. "If she can slaughter the beasts, then she can protect us from the demons as well!"

A small frown tugged at my lips. One of the men lifted a hand to strike the woman for speaking out of turn, but a second man caught his arm and shook his head. Normally the woman would have been slapped, if not beaten, for acting as such. Yet most of the men present were nodding their agreement to her response.

'They're more terrified than I thought. Djialkan, I'm going to go on ahead. Once you've filled Fraelfnir and Darius in, join me.'

"Y-Your Highness?" a man stuttered as I leapt over the balcony and landed in front of the crowd. "P-please, those creatures can only bring horrors upon us! It's your duty to—"

"You're in my way," I stated quietly, pointing towards the path leading out of the courtyard. "Do you want me to deal with them or not?"

I suppressed a grimace as scalding hot pressure squeezed around my throat. Thankfully, the peasants and soldiers parted to let me through—I wouldn't need to risk talking to them any further.

Once I was past them, I raised a hand to my throat and rubbed the pain away. The curses placed on me for being an Umbral Mage seemed like they were activating faster and faster as of late. Perhaps I needed to be more careful about speaking aloud.

'But I can't rely on Djialkan to speak for me all the time...' I swallowed my sigh and picked up my pace.

Umbral Mages were abhorred in X'shmir, while Astral Mages like my twin brother were revered. We were the only—and probably the last—mages in this country but superstition far outweighed our "rarity."

When Humans still had access to magic, it was very rare that one had an affinity for light or darkness. Humans usually had a natural affinity for earth or water but it wasn't unheard of for them to align with lightning, wind, fire, or ice either.

Astrals were seen as heavens-sent blessings from the Elder Gods. The people of X'shmir believed that not only should their ruler be an Astral Mage, but also that an Astral Mage had the ability to conquer the entirety of Avrirsa and claim it as his own. My brother was revered, even worshiped, despite being born after me.

Originally, I had been heir to the X'shmiran throne because I had been born first. That changed when my brother and I turned six and came into our individual powers.

By law, an Umbral Mage could not inherit the throne, nor could they wed into a noble or royal family. I was stripped of my titles, my right to the throne, and most of my rights as a living being due to the fact I was X'shmiran *and* an Umbral Mage.

To hear an Umbral Mage speak was to be cursed. To see an Umbral Mage's face was to be turned into stone. To lay with an Umbral Mage was to be turned into a "demon." Superstitions, the lot of it, but X'shmirans were devout in their beliefs. With no access to the outside world, they had no reason to question their views.

My role was simple. Keep our precious Astral Mage alive, keep the kingdom safe, and train our military. Having to sneak food from sympathetic citizens, castle staff, or outright steal it from the kitchens made things more difficult on some days.

'I guess word of the "demons" has spread through the city already.' I pursed my lips as I walked down the crumbling cobblestone streets. *'Shops closed, no one in the streets… The ones who came to the castle were the only ones with the balls to venture outside their homes, huh?'*

"General Black!" a voice called to me from ahead. "You're going to fight the demons? Let me join you!"

"It would be best for you to stay here, Matthew." I shook my head and approached the young soldier. "If any beasts wander close while

I'm gone you will need to give the command to activate the defenses."

"They haven't come close in *years*!" Matthew protested. "I want the chance to see you fight!"

"You can't run as fast as I can," I yanked the visor of his helm down over his face. "*Stay here*. That's an order. Something strikes me as strange about this situation. I don't want to take any risks. I'll be gone for several hours. Someone has to protect my brother while I'm not here. Got it?"

"Fine…" Matthew whined. "I'll make sure the men are watching for him. We don't need the prince sneaking off to follow you again."

That was something I could agree with at least. My brother wasn't skilled enough with a bow to be of any use outside the city's walls and he probably wasn't fast enough to keep up with me on the way to the lake either. Until he started taking Djialkan and Fraelfnir's lessons seriously, Darius was useless as a mage as well.

I took off at a run through the forest surrounding X'shmir's only city. Although it was mostly coniferous, there were occasionally smaller deciduous trees peppered throughout. They were easy to pick out due to their glossy red, orange, yellow, and sometimes purple leaves. Soon enough those leaves would fall, leaving only the larger, denser trees to protect X'shmir from the winter storms.

Demons. Even if Djialkan thought it unlikely, my instincts told me it wasn't some type of Chaos Beast I'd be facing off against. There *were* unfamiliar presences emanating subtle magic from somewhere on our flying island, but it was nothing like the foul aura of beasts. It wasn't like the power of Sihix either. Something foreign had come to X'shmir, somehow, and I needed to determine if it was a threat.

'Where are the beasts?' I scented the air as I ran, finding it unusually void of the creature's foul smell. *'Tch. Those fools' magic must've drawn the damn things to them!'*

I channeled wind and darkness around my legs, increasing my speed further. Had I been walking at a normal pace, it would have taken hours to traverse the forest and reach the barren plateau beyond. Instead, it took a matter of minutes.

Once I reached my destination I slowed my pace to a walk. I spread tendrils of darkness outward from my location in search of beasts, intruders, and the fishermen—anything of note.

'So I passed the fishermen in the forest somewhere.' I looked over my shoulder briefly and then up at the violet sky. *'The birds are absent. Beasts must have passed through recently.'*

The plateau was unusually still as I tread across it. No animals, no beasts—not even a breeze. I didn't like it. This place was chaotic more often than not. Being quiet like this made my skin crawl. Perhaps something wasn't right, but I didn't sense anything "off" in the immediate area.

"Humph, you already came this far?" Djialkan appeared in a puff of smoke and hovered beside me. *"Impatient for a fight as always."*

"I don't think there's going to be a fight," I tapped the small dragon's scaled nose before adding. "Well... Not unless they're here to conquer us or something anyways."

Djialkan fell silent for several minutes as we walked but he was anything but passive. His power swirled around us and across the wilds, probing at anything and everything it came into contact with. The black crystalline trees of the Sihix Forest to our north pulsed and glowed in response to the touch of his power, whilst the wind and earth crystals that littered X'shmir's soil dimmed in reply.

To me, Sihix was beautiful. To the X'shmirans, it was an evil and terrifying place they dared not wander near. Its trees rose hundreds of feet into the air, dwarfing the royal castle I had grown up in. The translucent black trees glowed with mingled violet, deep blue, and black energies. All of the flora and fauna native to the forest, or corrupted by it, were a glossy black, deep purple, blue, or some mixture of the three. In spring, brilliant flowers bloomed in scarlet, amethyst, and sapphire.

Sihix was one of the ten Aledacian Forests, known by many as the "Cursed Forests of Avrirsa." Each of these forests was the embodiment of a single element and, as the Forest of Darkness, Sihix was the most feared. Regardless of element, exposure to such pure elemental power corrupted whatever it touched. Because of this elemental corruption, people considered the forests cursed.

What many didn't realize was that the forests were sentient. They could choose whether or not to corrupt things that wandered into it. For me, Sihix was more my home than X'shmir could ever hope to be.

'Home.' I pursed my lips, thinking back to the nightmare the peasants had interrupted. *That boy kind of smelled like home for some*

reason. He seemed like more than "just a dream."'

Djialkan butted my cheek and shot me a knowing look. "*This is not the time for you to dwell on such matters.*"

"I wouldn't have to dwell on 'such matters' if you would just tell me the story behind that nightmare."

"*You would dwell on it more if I did tell you.*" Djialkan whacked me with his tail. "*Without a way for us to return Below—or regain your stolen memories—it is best for you not to know.*"

"So you tell me. Constantly." I rolled my eyes behind my eyeless mask, but Djialkan knew me too well and smacked me with his tail again. "Fine. I'll focus on the matter at hand.

"Our visitors seem like they don't know to hide their power or their auras from beasts."

"*It is possible that our beasts are unique to our territory,*" Djialkan suggested. "*We never encountered beasts obsessed with magical power when we lived Below.*"

The corner of my eye twitched. "When we lived Below." How could I *possibly* have lived Below at some point? I was only twenty-five. Over two centuries had passed since X'shmir rose into the clouds! Sure, I didn't look very Human…but…

"*You should don one of your X'shmiran-made masks instead of that one,*" Djialkan murmured. "*You are correct that we have visitors. I would rather not explain to them how you acquired a Magitech mask. At least not until we have determined where these people came from and what their intentions are.*"

"You're sure?" I waited until Djialkan nodded before reaching up to remove the platinum-adorned leather mask. Without it, I would have to rely on my ability to see aether in order to get around.

Masks for Umbral Mages were solid with no holes for the eyes. It made it impossible for us to see, but made the citizens feel safe because there was no risk of being turned to stone.

'Damned superstitions.' I dismissed the Magitech mask into my shrizar—essentially a magical pocket removed from our dimension—and summoned a X'shmiran one from within. The leatherwork, platinum edges and embroidery were beautiful. However, I was sick and tired of having to hide my face all the time.

"Enough pouting." Djialkan nudged my cheek with his nose. *"It will be some time yet before Darius has the power to change the laws of X'shmir."*

"I have no reason to believe he will change them at all," I replied, pulling on the mask as I spoke. "After all, *he* is the one that forbade me from speaking to anyone other than you, the soldiers, and the people of Sihix."

"Given their superstitions, you are lucky he has allowed you even that much," Djialkan grumbled. *"We must be patient for now. Darius should soon realize that his attempts and methods at keeping you safe are both misguided and unhelpful. You should have more faith in his intelligence."*

"I'll have more faith in his intelligence when he stops thinking with his manhood," I snorted.

"He is young and male. You ask too much of him," Djialkan's tone

was dry but held a hint of his amusement.

Silence fell around us again as we neared the edge of the plateau. Most of the northeastern and northern borders of the lake were walled in by the Sihix Forest. The rest of its shores were abandoned farmland and a forest not unlike the one surrounding X'shmir's capital.

Although the fishermen were willing to risk running into beasts, our farmers and hunters were not. Very few of our people wandered beyond the city walls, which meant we had to repurpose crumbled sections and the eastern half of the city into farmland.

I tapped my foot as I surveyed the lands and the lake far below me. Freshly churned earth hinted at the presence of beasts but it was their blood pooled on the ground that intrigued me most. Humans such as the X'shmirans were incapable of fighting against Chaos Beasts. They had no magic and were not fast enough to contend with the giant creatures. I could only assume the injuries were caused by our "guests."

"Devillians." Djialkan nodded his agreement. *"When we return to the city I will fill my brother in on the matter. We will begin searching for whatever has caused a breach in X'shmir's unnatural protection."*

"Better you than me. I don't think Fraelfnir likes me much," I murmured, pivoting to look at one of the few paths that led upwards from the lake below. "Would Devillians have wandered in the direction of an Aledacian Forest?"

"No, they will have gone south." Djialkan shook his wings and repositioned himself on my shoulder. *"If they are still fighting, they have likely led the beasts into the trees. That they are not near the shore means*

they must not have a mage with affinity for water with them.

"Either way, we should probably find and help them before interrogating them."

"Very well." I made an upwards motion with my left hand and summoned a series of pitch black platforms leading downward from the cliff's edge. "Let's go. I wouldn't want to miss out on a fight!"

Djialkan sighed as I leapt off the edge of the cliff and onto the nearest platform. *"That you have somehow not managed to wipe out the lot of them is concerning. There can only be so many left in such a secluded nation."*

"It isn't that impressive." I rolled my eyes. "Obviously the damned things are coming from somewhere. We just haven't been able to figure out from *where*."

"There should not be anyone in X'shmir capable of creating them," Djialkan retorted. *"If there were Exiled Gods here, we would have noticed their auras."*

"Perhaps an underground vault that we haven't found yet?" I offered as I landed on the ground at the base of the cliff. "It's not like there's many places to—"

The ground rumbled beneath my feet, followed by faint echoes of shouting. Earth-aspect aether glistened brighter in the soil before dimming once more. I grew still, sniffed at the air, and listened for further sounds of battle. They were still a long ways off if the scent of beasts was anything to judge by.

'Well, at least we don't have to deal with aquatic beasts.' I shifted my

attention towards the lake, searching for anything out of place amongst the blue-tinted aether.

Angered roars and panicked screams drew my attention away from the lake once more. Unfamiliar powers pulsed through the air briefly before disappearing altogether. I exchanged a glance with Djialkan and then took off at a brisk walk in the direction the roars were coming from.

'The Devillians' power seems weak.' I frowned and picked up my pace. *'I suppose a leisurely stroll by the lake isn't in the cards for today.'*

Traces of glowing aether arced through the air, hinting at the battle that had taken place here. Fire, earth, lightning, and wind appeared to be the only elements available to the mages in the party of foreigners.

I could only describe their aether as dim and stringy. It was similar to when Darius and I had first started learning magic. Our powers appeared similar to this when we were novices.

'Yet these Devillians are not novices.' Djialkan pointed his snout in the direction of muted black aether. *'They have drawn much blood from the Chaos Beasts. Novices would not be capable of such a feat.*

'Something else is causing them to struggle.'

"Let's hurry," I murmured, nudging Djialkan's shoulder. "I smell venom. They've drawn nasty ones to them."

Djialkan leapt from my shoulder and soared overhead as I took off at a run. I felt oddly compelled to save the Devillians from their monstrous pursuers.

Normally, I would want to sit back and watch the foreign beings work. That way I could learn about them, their approach to combat, and how much of a threat they were to Darius and myself.

A pulse of power rumbled through the forest ahead, causing the earth and water aether within the trees to flicker before settling back into their normal rhythm. Next came a clap of thunder, followed by the distant sound of shouting. The roar of beasts ahead shook the ground beneath me and made leaves fall from the canopy overhead.

'You will startle them into attacking you if you charge in like that,' Djialkan pointed out from somewhere above. 'I have spotted them. They are in the clearing to our southwest. It would seem they tried to retreat to their ship and are now trying to defend it.'

'Which of the Devillian languages are they speaking?' I slipped into the shadow of a nearby tree and conjured a fan of frozen swords.

Djialkan was silent for several moments before finally responding. 'They are communicating in Draemiran. Do you remember your lessons in the language?'

'I'm rusty but I can't speak with them anyway, remember?' I pursed my lips and then glanced down at my feet. 'I'm going to travel through the forest's shadows so that I get to the beasts quicker. Meet me there.'

I shut my eyes, concentrating for a moment, before letting myself turn into darkness and meld with the shadow of a tree. A sense of calm overcame me as the shadows embraced me. It was the closest to "home" as I could find. But I couldn't linger. There were beasts to kill and Devillians to rescue.

'And potentially execute,' I reminded myself as I propelled myself through the shadows of the forest.

The Chaos Beasts growled and snapped at the air in the clearing ahead, fighting each other for a better vantage point against the defending Devillians.

On the far side of the clearing, the Devillians conversed in rushed words and gestured at the deformed monstrosities. I couldn't make out what they were saying but they sounded perplexed.

I circled the clearing at a measured pace, taking in the positions of the beasts and Devillians alike. The Chaos Beasts had muted, sickly aether and their weight was distributed unevenly. Their forelegs were abnormally short and their hindquarters mismatched. The persistent strong acrid scent in the air told me that these beasts bore venomous barbs, talons, or fangs—potentially all three, if I was unlucky.

'Djialkan?' I questioned.

'I do not see barbs.' Djialkan's response was sufficient.

"We should just get in the ship and try to fly away!" a woman with what looked like aetheric tattoos argued with the man beside her. "We cannot take on Chaos Beasts of this size without a demigod on our side!"

"They will swipe us out of the air!" the largest of the men snapped back, the fiery aether in his chest, horns, tail, and claws flared brighter. "We have no choice but to fight. We will not be able to return to Dauthrmir just by running with our tails between our legs!"

'Dauthrmir…' I shook my head as I materialized behind a tree and spun my frozen swords before me. *'Djialkan, stifle their magic if they*

attempt to fire at me.'

Without waiting for the fae-dragon's reply, I stepped out from behind the tree and slashed open the heel of the nearest beast. Its pained cries made my ears ring, but I had no time to be disoriented. The damned things had to die first.

"Hold your fire!" one of the males roared at his comrades as I moved between them and the beast. "Lyur'zi, you cannot possibly take on the creature alone!"

"The X'shmiran Lyur'zi will be quite fine, I assure you," Djialkan spoke from overhead. *'Arianna, do not hold back. We do not have the luxury of playing with the beasts this day.'*

The beast closest to the shouting man turned and batted him clear across the clearing. I heard a sickening crack as the man collided with a tree and slumped to the ground. The scent of blood filled my senses, making me scowl and lunge for the beasts with greater speed.

'Djialkan, get started on healing him!' I called to the fae-dragon. *'I will take out the beasts. Make sure no one gets in my way.'*

I shifted my stance and made an upward motion with my left hand, summoning the shadows of the forest to my person. The darkness swirled around me like a vortex, pulling screams of terror from the Chaos Beasts. Both turned to flee but their uneven limbs and weight made them stumble over each other in their haste.

"Throstor," I muttered in Draemiran, sending the darkness rushing toward both beasts at once.

Their screams of terror were silenced in the instant the shadows carried dozens of hidden orbs of ice to the beasts. My ice tore through their bodies, opening pathways for my darkness to grip. With one final motion, I tore the beasts apart. The aether in the bodies went dim and motionless before sinking into the earth below as chunks of flesh and bone dropped to the ground.

Easy, and yet they had herded and wounded the Devillians with little trouble. I pivoted to look at the foreigners and then glanced back at what remained of the Chaos Beasts. The ground sizzled and melted beneath the beasts from where I had punctured their venom sacs. My stomach turned in reply to the smell—it was like rotting fruit.

'I thought Devillians were supposed to be incredible warriors?' I tugged at my gloves and glanced to the side, examining the group's aether again. *'They* do *have a lot of power…yet they managed so little against the beasts.*

'Is something wrong with them?'

CHAPTER FIVE
Demons? Devillians?

"Djialkan." I glanced over my shoulder, sensing the fae-dragon hovering behind me. *'Will their comrade be alright?'*

'I will need your assistance in healing him,' Djialkan answered as he landed on my shoulder. *'His arm is broken but aside from that he is fine—just unconscious.'*

'If we're going to stay and heal him...' I glanced off into the woods and then back at Djialkan. *'That thing is their ship, right? It is putting out too much aetheric energy. They're going to draw more beasts to us—I can't heal him and fight off the beasts all at once.'*

"Lord Djialkan, why are you in a place such as—" one of the men began, but cut himself off when the fae-dragon turned to look at him.

"You whelps will save your questions for later!" Djialkan spat black

smoke at the Devillians. *"Shut off your ship's engines and equipment immediately, lest you draw more beasts to us!"*

"More?" a petite woman whose head came just short of my shoulders asked, her eyes widening before she turned and rapped her knuckles against the side of their craft. "Rahel, do as Lord Djialkan says!"

"Venerated Lyur'zi," the fiery man bowed deeply as he turned to face me, "words cannot express my gratitude. Without your assistance we would have been but fodder for the beasts.

"What should we call you?"

'Venerated?' I arched an eyebrow behind my mask and then glanced at the snickering fae-dragon.

'Umbral Mages—"Lyur'zi" in Draemiran—have always been revered in Devillian culture, Arianna.' Djialkan laughed as he flew over to perch on my shoulder once more. *"X'shmiran ways are much different than those of Dauthrmir. You may continue to refer to her as Lyur'zi, Magus, or General."*

"General?" the woman with aetheric tattoos questioned.

"She is a general in the X'shmiran military." Djialkan nodded his head once. *"We were sent to investigate stories of 'demons' disturbing fishermen along the lake shore. Visitors from Below are the last thing we expected to find."*

"Demons?" a man with lightning aether running through him huffed with indignation. "What in the hells—"

"Your comrade needs treatment before we speak further," Djialkan

stated with a flip of his tail. *"I require the general's assistance to heal him—you should let her pass."*

I rolled my eyes behind my mask as the Devillians began arguing in Draemiran. They weren't sure whether to trust me, but they quite obviously didn't realize that I could understand every word they said. One of the women, at least, seemed insistent that my affiliation with Djialkan indicated I didn't mean them any harm.

"The longer you wait, the more likely it is he wakes up in agony!" I snapped at them, finally losing my patience. "Either move out of my way so that I can heal them, or I will *make* you move."

"*Make* us move?" the large man with fiery power demanded, rising to his full height to tower over me. "You don't even come up to my chin! How're you going to manage that, eh?"

"Given the state you are in, easily," Djialkan answered before I could spout off again. *'Arianna, control yourself. We do not need your bindings forcing you to collapse.'*

I lifted a hand and made a sideways motion, shoving the fiery Devillian out of my way with a burst of darkness. Without pause, I strode across the clearing and towards their injured comrade. His arm was bent at an atrocious angle and bone poked out from his skin. Pitch black blood oozed from the wound and from several gashes on his head and body.

'Lend me your power. I will heal him myself.' Djialkan flitted off my shoulder and then shifted to the form of a boy, kneeling beside the unconscious man. *'We should not yet let them know that you are capable*

of both healing and combat.'

'Fine,' I replied, lowering my mental barriers enough for Djialkan to draw upon my power.

One of the Devillians growled at me, causing me to turn my head and examine the group again. Even with them all in one place the magic emanating from them was pitiful. It didn't match the glowing power held within their bodies whatsoever. Several attempted to spread power through the area or towards me but their aether dissipated after moving a few feet.

I pursed my lips and shifted my gaze past them. Dim but dark aether staggered through the forest on the opposite side of the ship. The number of shapes was growing, and several stood at least ten stories high. They hadn't begun making noise yet, but I could tell by their movements that they were searching.

"Djialkan, there's more." I shifted to look down at the fae-dragon, finding that he'd already healed the man's broken arm and had moved on to the head wounds. "We need to decide if we're staying or if we're leaving."

"Already?" Djialkan sighed heavily and rose to his feet before shifting back to his draconic form. *"What if we have them land their ship on the plateau? You will be able to defend easier from there."*

I nodded my reply, noting the shifting and exchanged glances among the foreigners. They seemed uncomfortable and I got the feeling it was due to my unwillingness to address them directly. After all, if they considered me a "venerated Umbral Mage" it was unlikely they shared the X'shmiran's superstitions.

"Board your ship and fly east," Djialkan ordered the Devillians, his tone sharp enough to make several flinch. *"General Black will be able to fight the beasts better in open terrain. I will cover you from any flying Chaos Beasts that might wander near."*

"You two will not be boarding?" one of the women asked with concern.

"I will fly and the general will traverse the shadows," Djialkan answered. *"Do not waste time with pointless questions! The less time your ship runs, the better."*

Once the Devillians disappeared into their sleek obsidian ship, Djialkan left my shoulder and took to the air. I tugged at the hems of my gloves and looked around the forest, searching for nearby beasts. Once I confirmed none were close, I vanished into the shadows and made a beeline for the plateau.

The darkness soothed my unease for the few minutes it took me to reach the surface of the plateau. If nothing else, perhaps the calming effect of the shadows would keep me from pelting the Devillians with questions. I wanted to ask them about the world Below, about their kind, their empire…but I couldn't. The risks of my curse were too high. I'd already pushed my luck with what I'd said so far.

'I wonder how well they can fight.' I shifted to look up at the violet sky and watched the strange contraption's approach. *'Well, I suppose if they mean ill we're about to find out.'*

Blinding blue-green aether billowed from slats along the side of the craft as it drifted through the air. The hum of its engines and the sheer amount of magical power made my joints rattle and my head ache. I would be happy when the damn thing shut down. Even if the beasts hadn't been attracted to the aether, it was much too noisy and bright for me to tolerate.

'Speaking of beasts...' I shifted my attention away from the ship, straining to hear the distant howls. Dark shapes moved in the forest between us and X'shmir, but they didn't appear to be moving for the ship.

"Now then, what's this about shutting off our ship?" a man with an unfamiliar accent demanded from the top of their ship's ramp.

'No horns, no tail... Human or Elf?' I prodded Djialkan with my thoughts.

'Elf. I did not spot or smell any Humans in their party.' Djialkan drifted down to perch on me once more. *"Your ship is to beasts as a flame is to moths. It is neither our desire nor our duty to remain here and protect your party.*

"It has been centuries since foreigners stepped foot on X'shmiran soil. Why are you here? Why now?"

"This...is really X'shmir?" the fiery man from before asked, pushing the Elven man out of his way so he could descend the ramp. "We thought it had been destroyed! All that's left of X'shmir in Falrrsald is a crater."

"Well, now we can understand why the crater is so vast," the short woman spoke with a catlike purr to her words. "My name is Nys'tur.

I'm in charge of this expedition." She paused to motion widely at the ship. "We are mostly scholars. Our job is to map Avrirsa and chart aetheric currents. Finding a previously undiscovered flying island was...unexpected."

"We do not have the authority to handle political matters like this, Nys'tur," the Elf spoke again, his tone harsh. "None in our group qualifies as an ambassador of the Rilzaan Alliance. It would be best for us to send a message back to them and—"

"And draw more of the lurking beasts?" Djialkan rumbled, pointing his snout in the direction of the eastern forest. *"The people of X'shmir have not seen someone of non-Human descent in their lifetimes. This goes far beyond whether or not you and yours are 'qualified' to speak with us."*

"None? None at all?" Nys'tur frowned. "We wouldn't want to cause unrest—as I stated, our mission is one of cartography. However, we've found our instruments incapable of navigating the skies around this place. We keep being led in circles."

"We already contacted the Vorpmasian Emperor, but we have been unable to contact the Emperor of Beshulthien," the fiery man stated. "I don't want to draw more beasts to our location, especially not without a plan of escape."

"The 'Vorpmasian' Emperor?'" Djialkan asked incredulously. *"Lucifer is an Emperor now?"*

"We could have them—" I began, but a familiar honeysuckle scent in the air made me cut myself off with a scowl. *'For fuck's sake! I thought they were going to keep Darius within the city?!'*

"Lyur'zi?" one of the Devillians asked as I turned to stalk across the plateau.

"*Your Highness*, you were meant to stay in the castle!" I snapped, summoning a wave of darkness and pushing it across the "empty" plateau before me. "And *you*, Fraelfnir, *you* should not encourage him!"

Fraelfnir's power flickered and shone bright blue-white before peeling away to reveal my brother. I hated it when they did this. Whether or not the beasts could *see* Darius didn't matter. No amount of warping light or other forms of camouflage could hide my twin's unruly aether from the beasts. Now our time for dealing with the foreigners was even shorter.

"Oh it's *fine*!" Darius laughed, his eyes twinkling with delight as he turned to look at the Devillians. "So it's true then? We have guests from Below?" He stood a little straighter and adjusted his robes. "I am Darius Raisur Black, Prince of X'shmir and heir to the throne. I also serve as—"

'*—as a massive pain in my side,*' I thought, listening to Darius ramble off a list of titles and roles. '*It didn't even occur to him that they might not even speak our language, did it?*'

'*Far be it from your brother to use his brain,*' Djialkan snorted. '*They do understand, at least some of them do, but it is quite arrogant for him to assume as such.*'

A new wave of roars shook the plateau, sending pebbles skittering across the surface. Darius flinched and ducked, while I simply shifted to search the aether for the beastly forms. They were still quite a ways off, but they were all now moving in our direction. I cursed and turned to look at the group of Devillians, Djialkan, Fraelfnir, and my brother.

'Darius, we need to return to the city,' I stated, pulling at my sleeves and shifting back and forth on the balls of my feet. *'Bringing them to X'shmir probably wouldn't be—'*

"Let's get back to the city before the beasts swarm us!" Darius declared with a cheerful grin. "I'm sure we can have rooms prepared for our guests at the castle. Will your ship be okay left unprotected?"

'Darius, that's not a good idea. The citizens will—' I started to protest but my brother ignored me entirely. Sighing, I pressed my fingers to my temples and then summoned a broadsword of ice. Once the heavy blade was balanced against my shoulder, I snatched Darius' robes with my free hand. "Are we *moving* or are we going to stay here *talking*?"

"Ah…ha ha ha…" Darius' tanned cheeks reddened. "My Umbral Mage is right. We can talk at length once we're at the palace." He shifted his gaze to me questioningly. "If they bring their equipment from their ship and to the city, can they use it there without causing problems?"

"That depends on how much aether it emits." I tilted my head in thought. "If it's less than a person's aura, it should be fine. Otherwise, we'd need something to shield or dampen the effect."

"We should be able to direct the aetheric output into storage devices, but we can also dampen it if there are no other options," Nys'tur stated in Draemiran, narrowing her eyes at me when my attention shifted to her. "You understand me but the boy does not. Why do you not speak to us?"

"*She is a Lyur'zi. She is not allowed to speak unless the Chrot'zi permits it,*" Djialkan answered, tapping my back with his tail. "*Even speaking to the prince and I whilst in your presence is a risk she should be avoiding.*"

"Tch, the Old Ways," Nys'tur spat. "I understand. I will not press it, but I have to report this to His Excellency."

"*Do as you must.*" Djialkan shrugged. "*Send the King—rather, the Emperor—my regards.*"

'*I don't like this,*' I muttered, gripping the hilt of my frozen blade tighter. '*Our people aren't going to accept* Devillians *in the city. The nobles are going to raise a fuss even* if *Darius convinces our parents this is the right course to take.*'

'*Darius is giving us little choice in the matter.*' Djialkan sighed.

'*Scholars and explorers from other lands cannot hope to protect themselves from the beasts in X'shmir,*' Fraelfnir intruded, casting us both a glance over Darius' shoulder. '*Leaving them on their lonesome is not an option. Should they fall prey to beasts or the Sihix Forest the result would be the same: potential issues with the Rilzaan Alliance.*'

I bristled as the small crew of Devillians and Elves trickled past me to follow Darius. This wasn't a good idea. Not at all. My brother had to be out of his mind to bring them to speak with our parents. I *thought* Darius was aware of just how corrupt our parents' views were, but his decision regarding the foreigners made me think otherwise.

A few of the Devillians cast glances at me over their shoulder, but the lack of aether condensed in their faces made it impossible for me to gauge their expressions. All I could tell was that they were tense, wary, and confused.

'It's like the Mists are conflicting with their powers.' I examined the erratic movements of aether around each of the men and women. *'Djialkan, are you sure they're not just poorly trained?'*

'Lucifer is strict,' Djialkan snorted, shaking his head. *'He would not let weak, untrained, or poorly trained mages take on an assignment such as this.'*

'Djialkan and I will begin our investigations immediately upon our return,' Fraelfnir added. *'We have close ties with multiple Devillian territories. If they have truly forged an alliance, then the two of us should be able to draw information from them.'*

'Be discreet. I don't want them getting the wrong impression from your inquiries.' I looked between the fae-dragon brothers. *'Even if their magic is limited, their physical strength is not. I won't be able to deal with them on my own if the situation turns sour.'*

By the time we reached the city it was dusk and a frosty chill hung in the air. The Devillians, my brother, and our fae-dragons had grown more relaxed during our long trek. I envied them for their attitudes. My muscles were tense and the hilt of my frozen sword had cracked so many times beneath my grip that I ended up discarding it.

I braced myself as we passed the city gates. The guards on duty stood in stunned silence before brandishing their weapons and shooting glances in my direction. I shook my head at them, but they still hesitated to sheathe their swords.

"Not only did you fail to keep His Highness' from sneaking out of the city, you are also pointing weapons at His Highness' guests." I swept around the foreigners and came to stand in front of my men with my arms crossed. "Go back to your posts or I will remove you from them."

"Y-Your Highness?" one of the guards stuttered, looking to my brother. "Demons? As guests? The king and queen will—"

"They'll understand!" Darius interrupted with a bright smile. "This is an excellent opportunity for X'shmir. We've been isolated for far too long. There are so many things we could gain from forming ties with the uh... What was it called again?"

"The Rilzaan Alliance," I answered, the corner of my eye twitching. *'You're not going to convince anyone if you can't even remember the names of the political power you're trying to form a relationship with!'*

"Demons?" the fiery Devillian growled. "We are called *Devillians*!"

"Demons are what Humans used to call the creatures in the Vorpmasian wilds," one of the Elven women stated, placing a hand on the fiery man's chest. "Calling Devillians 'demons' is like if I were to call you 'dogs' instead of 'Human.'"

"Ye implying somethin', woman?" one of the guards snapped, leveling his sword with the Elf's throat. "Say it again ye pointy-eared bitch. I'll show ye what 'appens to—"

My shin connected with the guard's throat, knocking him clean off his feet and onto his back. He tried to get up but I shoved my booted heel into his collarbone.

"You will treat His Highness' guests with the respect afforded to foreign dignitaries." I spoke in a frigid tone that matched the glare hidden by my mask. "Need I remind you of who you'll answer to if you disregard the prince's wishes?"

The guard stopped struggling and his face grew pale. He opened and closed his mouth a few times to speak, but no words came out. Finally, he slumped and closed his eyes, nodding his understanding. I removed my foot from his chest and offered him a hand back to his feet. He hesitated before accepting it, and then muttered his thanks before returning to his post.

'The citizens won't be as easy to contain as the guards are, Darius.' I glanced toward my smiling brother. *'How are you going to convince the nobles in the castle, let alone the commoners, that you haven't lost your mind?*

'You do realize I can't help you verbally anymore, right?'

'It'll be fine, Ari,. Darius' grin broadened and my heart sank. *'They won't act against me because I'm the Astral Mage! And, if they try to hurt our guests, you'll just kick their asses.'*

All I could do was sigh. My brother just didn't get it. Our people had been raised to think that Devillians were monsters. Monsters created to lure Humans into sin and despair. Beliefs like that couldn't change overnight, yet my brother seemed to think those beliefs would be altered in a matter of minutes.

"Lyur'zi," Nys'tur fell into step with me and spoke in Draemiran, her voice low. "The prince—he is a Chrot'zi, yes? Human?"

"That is correct," Djialkan murmured the reply on my behalf.

"But…his ears are like an Elf's!" Nys'tur protested, barely keeping her voice down. "And his eyes are like mine—or like any of the other Devillians in our expedition! Humans have not had magic in centuries. This does not make sense."

"Both the prince and princess do not look like normal Humans," Djialkan answered. *"They are believed to be a new step in Human evolution—a new mutation perhaps. If the Human God and Goddess have not exhibited these changes, I advise not speaking of the matter with the X'shmirans."*

"And you, Lyur'zi, you may not speak to us?" Concern touched Nys'tur's voice. "Even if you pretend that you are telling your companion what to say?"

"She is at her limit and the X'shmiran Chrot'zi will not lift the restriction," Djialkan spat flame-tinged darkness from his maw. *"I must insist your party comes to me if they require something. Our Lyur'zi is not in a position to assist you directly."*

"Djialkan seems like he enjoys having someone to practice his languages with!" Darius grinned, popping up beside us. "What language is that? Nys'tur, you are a Sundreht, right?"

"You know of my people?" Nys'tur sounded skeptical, bordering on suspicious, as she turned her attention to my brother.

"Fraelfnir and Djialkan have taught me some things about the different Devillian races," Darius replied cheerfully. "You have ears and a tail like a cat, so you must be Sundreht. The scary one over there is an Akor, right?"

Darius motioned at the fiery man from before.

"We're content with being called Vorpmasians," Nys'tur shook her head at Darius. "Vorpmasia, on the Continent of Rilzaan, is where we are from. The pale and tan Elves in our group are from the Beshulthien Empire to the southeast of Vorpmasia.

"The Elves with skin like stone are Kelsviir; they hail from Vorpmasia."

I turned my attention away from my curious brother and the weary "Sundreht" woman. The peasants of X'shmir were already crowding around and following us through the city. Darius seemed oblivious to the dozens of questions the people were pelting him with. Several of the foreigners kept their hands on the hilts of their weapons. Their backs were drawn taut and their tails snapped behind them in agitation.

The Elves seemed calmer, but the intensity of aether within their bodies was growing brighter. It was like they were preparing to defend themselves.

'Darius,' I called. When there was no response, I poured more power into the thought and practically screamed his name at him. He flinched and whipped his head around to look at me with wide eyes. Satisfied that I had his attention, I spoke again. *'The citizens are closing in and putting your guests on edge. At this rate I will have to subdue both*

the people and your guests.'

"Your Highness, what are these creatures doing here?!" a man nearby spoke, before pointing his finger at me. "*You!* You were meant to deal with the demons, not bring them to our doorstep!"

"The general has done as her Astral Mage commanded of her!" Fraelfnir roared, taking on the form of a horse-sized drake and leveling his face with the angry Human man. *"Would you have the Umbral Mage disregard her orders?"*

"But they're demons!" a woman shrieked, her eyes glassy with tears, her face and neck red with panic. "They'll kill us all, take our children and rape them, destroy our city!"

"You think we'll *what?*" the fiery man snapped, taking a step forward and then stopping when I stepped in front of him. "Lyur'zi, Chrot'zi, I can't simply—"

"Settle down!" Darius called to the crowd in a warm, cheerful tone. "They are not demons! They are Devillians and Elves, and they are here on behalf of the Beshulthien and Vorpmasian Empires!" My brother paused to flash a bright white grin at our people, revealing his slender fangs. "It has been centuries since we have had the opportunity for trade relations—this is an auspicious occasion!

"General Black and I will see to it that nothing happens to our people, our city, *or our guests.* We have much to learn from the world which we have been cut off from for so long! Please, set aside your assumptions so that we may pass."

"But, Your Highness…" the protests continued in a quieter tone as the peasants backed off to a more comfortable distance, letting us resume our trek through the city.

"This all appears to be remnants of a much more advanced city." The fiery man looked down at me as we walked through the streets of X'shmir. "I see ruined Magitech, collapsed aqueducts… Have you no way of repairing the damage?"

"If we ever owned texts outlining how to maintain them, they have been lost to time," Djialkan answered after a few nudges on my part. *"X'shmir's access to knowledge is limited. It is one of the reasons His Highness is so insistent on making friends with you—with or without your prior interest."*

"He does seem pushy," the man snorted, shaking his head before offering me a hand. "I failed to introduce myself properly. My name is Nizar; I am one of the Archmagi in service of the Vorpmasian Empire."

'Archmagi?' I arched an eyebrow as I accepted his handshake, noting the flare of fire within his palm as he gripped my hand a little tighter than I was expecting. I got the feeling Nizar was trying to startle me with the heat of his flames, but I answered with a small smile and a flare of my own flames in response.

"Not one to be intimidated? Good!" Nizar released a throaty laugh. "You will get along with Devillians just fine. Can't say the same for your Astral Mage over there, but he seems like the more…*political*…type."

"An accurate assessment," Djialkan answered dryly. *"I am afraid that I may not tell you the Lyur'zi's name. What did Nys'tur call it…? 'The*

Old Ways?'"

"I see, that's a shame." Nizar's frown was audible as he looked down at me. "If you think of some way we might help, Lord Djialkan, do not hesitate to let me know."

"We're here!" Darius called from ahead, waving his arms frantically. "Oh, you silly guards! Put your weapons down! These are our guests!"

We barely made it into the castle's entry hall before being confronted by our parents and several noble families—all of which were fuming. Djialkan's claws dug into my shoulder as I bit back both my distaste and a growl. The bastards needed to die…but if I slew them, Darius and I would die as well.

My curse would see to that.

CHAPTER SIX
Lurking in the Mists

I frowned at the stack of reports before me and nudged through them with one hand. Our expedition had been silent for several days before contacting us again, but the news that accompanied their stacks upon stacks of data made my stomach turn.

Beasts, something called "the Mists," remnants of run-down Magitech—and that was just scratching the surface of their findings.

Eyrian would soon arrive in X'shmir with a company of men, including other demigods. With them they had several of Dauthrmir's large, battle-class airships. He had told me he wanted to be prepared for both the beasts and for any unrest among the locals. Skimming through the stack of reports before me, however, I got the feeling the beasts would be the larger problem.

"*Archmagus?*" a sharp female voice called. "Are you even paying attention?"

"I don't recall inviting you in." I shifted to look at the irritated Rylthra woman. "What does an Oracle want with me?"

The Rylthra hissed at me and laid her vulpine ears back flat against her head. "I don't *need* your invitation to enter academy grounds!"

"Still, you are in *my* office." I shot the strawberry blonde woman a glare. "I am busy. What do you want, Oracle?"

The Oracle stalked towards me and shoved a sheet of parchment in my face. Her mouth was set in a snarl, and the fur on her tails was bristled. However, it didn't appear that *I* was the one she was angry with. Rage rippled off of her in waves, accompanied by a slight tremble in the hand that was holding out parchment.

"Mages. *X'shmiran* mages." The Oracle waved the paper in my face again for emphasis.

"Aren't the X'shmirans Human?" I frowned and took the paper from the agitated Rylthra. Skimming the document, my disbelief was soon overcome with shock. After reading it several times over to be certain, I looked back to the Oracle and spoke, "An Astral Mage and an Umbral Mage, accompanied by Fraelfnir and Djialkan, respectively? Is Nys'tur certain?"

"The X'shmiran Lyur'zi and Djialkan saved the members of the expedition." The Oracle sighed and took a seat across from me. "From what I understand, two Dux-class beasts were bearing down on our people and their ship. The Lyur'zi 'appeared out of the shadows and slew both beasts.'

"One of the men was injured; Djialkan healed him while the Lyur'zi executed the beasts. A few days later another one of our men attempted to do a supply run to the expeditionary ship on his own. He was cut down by a beast…and the Lyur'zi healed him herself. She fell unconscious afterward."

"Unconscious?" I frowned. "Did she overuse her magic?"

The Oracle hesitated before answering with a reluctant expression, "X'shmir practices the Old Ways, Nalithor. The Lyur'zi is not allowed to speak…but she disregarded those rules in order to calm our man down."

"The Old Ways?" I snarled and slammed my fist against my desk. "How is that possible? X'shmir vanished before the countries mistreating Umbral Mages were even discovered! If they have truly been isolated all this time—"

"In the reports Nys'tur sent me," the Oracle interrupted me and conjured another sheet of paper, "she stated that the Magitech instruments and the buildings of X'shmir have atrophied more than they should have in two hundred years. We have to suspect that the X'shmirans weren't completely cut off—or that they were affected by the World Split."

"The World Split?" I sighed, shaking my head. "It wouldn't be terribly surprising, but we should have found X'shmir long before now. I think it's safe to assume something else is going on with that place. The readings our people took of 'the Mists' are strange.

"What of the X'shmiran Royal Family?"

"The Chrot'zi is the crown prince of X'shmir and...he does not look Human." The Oracle shifted through a few papers and then nodded to herself. "Nizar and Nys'tur both reported that the prince looks more like a half-Elf half-Devillian. No one has met the princess as of yet, and the Lyur'zi is not allowed to show anything beyond the lower half of her face."

"And the king and queen?" I probed, watching the Rylthra's face twist in disgust.

"They are proving difficult to work with," the Oracle spat. "The X'shmiran Royal Family and their people do not know the difference between a demon and a Devillian. They fear magic, fear non-Humans... The Chrot'zi is the one convincing them to work with the Empire.

"After Eyrian arrives in X'shmir we should hear if the X'shmirans are willing to discuss joining the Rilzaan Alliance."

"Lucifer is already considering inviting them?" I frowned, crossed my arms, and settled back in my seat. "Why isn't he planning to conquer them? If they follow the Old Ways, then it would make more sense for Lucifer to take the country for himself."

"You haven't gotten very far through the reports, have you?" The Oracle's ears perked forward as she broke into a toothy grin. "The God of Balance is neglecting his duties? Tsk, tsk, tsk! This is unlike you, Nalithor!

"Page four hundred twenty-three. Go take a look."

I shot her a foul look before picking up the stack of reports and rifling through them. Once I found page 423, I split the stack and set the first half aside before skimming the document. My irritation turned to a mingled sense of unease and curiosity as I studied the graphs on the page. The only time I ever saw aether behave like *that* was when mages attempted to dampen each other's power.

"Our men and women aren't able to fight properly in X'shmir?" I questioned, glancing over the next page and then the one after that. "The expedition members believe this is the fault of 'the Mists?'"

"Aye, they all reported the feeling of something watching and suffocating them whenever they tried to use their powers." The Oracle nodded as she pulled a pipe out of her robes. "The two X'shmiran mages seem unaffected by it, but the boy is a novice. His power is wild and unruly; Fraelfnir appears responsible for keeping it in check."

"And the girl?"

"They compared the girl to an Archmagus like you or I. Aside from the beasts, she's the most dangerous thing they've found in X'shmir."

Before I could comment, there was a knock at the door and, a moment later, Xander strode through it. His mouth was drawn taut, his eyes flicked around the room, and his hands clenched and unclenched at his sides. He stopped once he reached my desk but didn't even look down at the Oracle before speaking.

"Lucifer wants the three of us to be prepared to go to X'shmir," Xander announced with a grimace. "Nali, have you read the reports about X'shmiran beasts yet?"

"I've read part of the reports." I nodded. "The only types of beasts our people have seen up there so far are Dux-class, right?"

"Both our emperors want us to put together a selection of demigods who can handle the damned things." Xander's shoulders slumped as he ran a hand through his hair. "You're to put together a complement of Astral and Umbral Mages, demigods, and Archmagi to escort Vorpmasian scholars.

"I'm to do the same with Beshulthien Archmagi and scholars. The Elves won't spare any of their demigods, so I'll be going to X'shmir to fill the role personally."

"And me?" The Oracle frowned.

"Lucifer wants you to bring one or two other Oracles with you." Xander finally glanced down at the Rylthra, his eyes immediately going to her bust. "He's hoping that Oracles can read the minds of the X'shmiran people—or that you won't be affected by the Mists in the same way.

"No one's been able to get information out of either of the mage— Ow! What was that for?!"

"Stop staring at my tits!" the Oracle demanded, hitting Xander with her tails.

"What do you expect when your robes barely even cover them?!" Xander snapped back at her. "One wrong shift and all of Avrirsa would see your nipples."

"That doesn't mean you can stare!" The Oracle huffed, crossing her arms in such a way that made her breasts look larger.

"You should know by now that she's doing it on purpose." I shot Xander a look when he opened his mouth to argue. "It will be fine. She can't dress like that for much longer anyway. Winter is only a few weeks off.

"Now, when does Lucifer want us to be ready?"

"He wants us to be ready to leave at any time." Xander stuck his tongue out at the Oracle before shifting to look at me. "If the X'shmirans are open to working with us, we'll have to determine what their terms for visitation are. At the very least, we can assume they will expect our Umbral Mages to abide by their rules."

"We will need to have Magitech masks made for everyone in both our parties then," I murmured, tapping my claws on the armrest of my chair. "When you speak with Eyrian, have him find out how cold the winters of X'shmir are. If we are going to that wretched place we will need to be prepared for both the beasts and the climate."

"Nizar told me that it's already beginning to snow there," the Oracle offered. "He said that the Chrot'zi and Lyur'zi are wearing fur-lined attire already, and the Chrot'zi in particular is wearing many layers.

"The forest around the Humans' city is dense but the plateau we've been told to land our ships on is bare. At the very least we can expect to deal with the full brunt of winter winds and deep drifts of snow."

"See if the X'shmiran Lyur'zi is willing to help the scholars with mapping the region of the plateau, forest, and city," I ordered after a brief pause for thought. "We need to know exactly where to land our ships, what the terrain is like, and what parts of the forest we can use to our advantage.

"I don't want the members of the Alliance to take any risks against the beasts. We need to make sure that our men and women study the area and are capable of protecting any dignitaries we may send to X'shmir."

"Djialkan and Fraelfnir have proven very helpful so far," the Oracle remarked, stroking her chin. "Nys'tur said in the report that the X'shmiran Lyur'zi seems like she wants to help; she keeps trying to talk but catches herself before she says too much."

"The Beshulthien members of the expedition had similar things to say," Xander agreed.

"I'll consult the other Oracles and see if we can think of some way to help the Lyur'zi without angering the X'shmiran royals." The Oracle rose to her feet and nudged Xander out of her way. "If she's truly capable of taking on Dux-class beasts by herself, we're going to want to speak with her."

"Not to mention the fact Fraelfnir and Djialkan are with them," Xander pointed out. "I know it's too soon to tell, but, the last time anyone saw those two, their wards were Lucifer's children."

"We need to tread carefully." I nodded. "Whether it's *them* or not, we know the Elders will be watching. Regardless of whom their wards are, fae-dragons still report to the Elder Gods directly.

"I, for one, do not want to be on the receiving end of Djialkan's wrath if something happens to his ward. It doesn't matter if it's someone he chose or someone he was assigned; he will be very protective of his ward. That's just how he is."

"With any luck I'll be able to speak with him or Fraelfnir." The Oracle shrugged as she made her way to the door. "We both serve the Elder Gods—even if he does not trust the Rilzaan Alliance for some reason, he should be able to trust me."

'I wouldn't be so sure about that.' I kept the thought to myself as the woman and her vulpine tails disappeared through the door.

"Nali," Xander stated, earning a glance from me. "Something seems off about the reports I received. What about yours?"

"They're withholding information." I nodded. "They didn't mention the names of anyone in X'shmir aside from the fae-dragons. Not even their 'savior.' Aside from the readings and graphs they sent us, their reports themselves were vague."

"They must believe they're being watched." Xander crossed his arms. "Nalithor... Do you think we've actually found *them*? I mean an Astral Mage and an Umbral Mage, both the wards of Fraelfnir and Djialkan. It's—"

"It's unlikely." I shot the Vampire a sharp look. "We need to be careful what we say, Xander, whether it's in private or otherwise. As far as we know, the Chrot'zi and Lyur'zi are not related. Unless we find out otherwise, we should operate under the assumption that something else is going on in X'shmir.

"After all, the Sihix Forest covers a great portion of the island. It isn't unreasonable to think the X'shmirans might have stolen children from the forest."

"It's true—if there are any non-Human people living in X'shmir, we're likely to find them there." Xander shrugged, shook his head, and then looked at me with a more pleasant expression on his face. "My work for the day is done, so I'm going to head down to the Merchant's District for some food and booze. Wanna join me?"

"I still have work to finish." I grimaced, motioning at the papers on my desk. "I have to compile and sort the information we received so that our scholars can begin analyzing it. They're going to run some experiments with crystallized aether."

"You think Sihix might be part of whatever is causing 'the Mists?'" Xander arched an eyebrow. "Send me a copy of the compiled info too will you? I can have our Archmagi look into it as well."

"Have them join my subordinates here at the academy then," I offered. "The more eyes we have on this the better—especially if some of us are getting dragged up to that damned place."

"You sure you don't wanna join me for a night out?" Xander grinned. "It's been what, a century, since you've been laid?"

"A century by your terms maybe," I replied with a glare. "Honestly. I do not need to feed for another week or two at least—nor am I in the mood for the noise of the city streets.

"Go on without me. We can have a drink some other time."

"Sourpuss," Xander snorted before sticking his tongue out at me and leaving my office as well.

'Now then...' I sighed, shaking my head as I looked at the papers

strewn all over my desk. *'Honestly, the Old Ways? Dux-class beasts? The X'shmirans should be dead if that's the case.'*

After a few minutes of rifling through hundreds of pages I lifted the entire stack and carried it over to one of the two sofas in my office. It would take me all night to go through the data and separate it accordingly, so I chose to be comfortable while doing so. I skimmed through the information for the umpteenth time, taking in the varied reports on X'shmir, its beasts, its people, the Mists, and the presence of the Sihix Forest.

Finally, I turned my attention to the smattering of pages that spoke of the crown prince and his Umbral Mage. The prince was described as young, a novice, immature, and overly cheerful. From what little the reports said of him, it sounded like he wasn't even trained well enough to be *called* a mage. He lacked the training to be given the title of "Astral Mage"—Chrot'zi in my own tongue—but the X'shmirans had given him the title regardless.

'Fraelfnir must *have taught the boy something.'* I gave the sheet another glance-over before picking up the thicker stack of reports. *'At any rate, it seems our expedition has much more to say about the girl.'*

Cold, powerful, controlled, silent. Those were but a few of the words used to define the Umbral Mage. No mention was made of her elements aside from darkness, but Nys'tur and Nizar seemed to have unending praise. Their report went into great detail about how she slew the beasts by their ship, and how she saved one of the expedition members from the brink of death days later.

'Djialkan speaks for her?' I arched an eyebrow and turned the page. "I can sense you standing there, Sebastian. What do you want?"

"Ahhh, and here I thought you were too absorbed!" The God of Chaos stepped into view and grinned, delight dancing in his violet eyes. "I hear interesting things are going on. Very interesting things indeed! How do you plan to keep this from the Elders, hmmm?"

"You know as well as I do that we won't be able to keep much from the Elders." I shot Sebastian a look. "Are you here for a reason, or just to annoy me?"

"I'm here because we have a problem." Sebastian shrugged before flopping onto the other end of the sofa.

"What now?" I muttered. "The Elders have already told us we're not allowed to do our duty for the foreseeable future. What more could they possibly have in mind?"

"It isn't about the Elders this time." Sebastian laughed and pulled his long black hair over his shoulder. "No, the 'problem' is the Exiles. They're starting to make noise again."

"Sebastian, you know as well as I do that the Elders forbade us from hunting down the Exiled Gods." I put my fingertips to my temples. "The Elders essentially have the Upper Gods on house arrest, and the Middle Gods haven't the power or the want to do anything about the Exiles being on the move."

"I'm not saying we need to move—I'm saying we need to let the Alliance know." Sebastian shook his head at me. "My Chosen have given me the reason to believe that the Exiles are targeting mortals and not gods or demigods this time."

"I will inform Lucifer the next time I see him," I murmured, setting my papers on my lap for the moment. "See if any of our allies have Chosen they can spare as spies in Dauthrmir and Beshulthien. This timing is a little too close to our discovery of X'shmir, and our defenses *are* noticeably weakening as we send more men and women to meet with the Humans there.

"If there's nothing else—"

"X'shmir," Sebastian interrupted. "Even from here we can't sense anything going on within that country, even if it's our *job* to know. It's like an empty hole. I sense nothing from it. Not a need for chaos, no need for tranquility—nothing."

"From what I understand, the people of X'shmir believe gods are a myth, a fairy tale." I motioned down at the hundreds of pages of reports. "There are some faithful people remaining in that country, but they have to hide their trinkets and their belief. Whatever is keeping us from sensing that place seems to be keeping the Humans—and the people of the Sihix Forest—from reaching out."

"I don't like it," Sebastian stated, his voice flat. "The Elders won't let any of us go there unless it is on a joint political mission with the Alliance or with the Elves of Suthsul."

"No one?" I questioned.

"Not even the gods pertaining to aspects of nature, or the gods who preside over forms of craftsmanship," Sebastian confirmed. "Lucifer or Rabere would have to directly hire the God of Carpentry to work in

X'shmir in order for the Elders to allow him there."

"What of the emperors or the kings and queens of the Alliance?" I offered. "They are all Lesser Gods. They usually are allowed to go and act as they please."

"Not allowed unless for solely political reasons." Sebastian shook his head. "Lucifer and Rabere have both been warned of how easy it would be for them to overstep. It's likely they will not go to X'shmir themselves due to how overbearing the Elders have become.

"The same warning has been issued to all of the Lesser Gods both in *and* outside of the Alliance."

"That must be why Lucifer wants me to prepare to go there." I grimaced. "Have you found out anything regarding that *other* matter?"

"Nay, still no sight." Sebastian shook his head once more. "No progress on either matter. Ceres has heard nothing from the trees, and my Chosen haven't been able to find any traces of that pesky item or its makers either.

"Now then, I really should be going. The wife will have my hide if I'm a moment later."

Sebastian disappeared off the couch in a puff of darkness, finally leaving me alone in my office once again. My desire to work had been soured, so I discarded the reports into my shrizar and then rose to my feet.

'Even Ceres' trees can't find the Godslayers?' I wondered as I shrugged on an overrobe. *'The weapons couldn't have just disappeared. They have to still exist somewhere. Perhaps the Elders took them all to their domain?'*

The Godslayers were meant for keeping the Lower, Middle, and Upper Gods in check. Being deities, it meant that we were close to immortal. We could still be killed, but it was difficult—and impossible for mortals. That is, unless they found themselves in possession of one of the Godslayers.

We knew several had been made by the Elders so that mortals, or even other gods, could execute rogue deities. If a god rebelled against the Elders, skewed the balance of power, or was an Exile, the Godslayer was meant to slay them.

Except, even though it was my duty to hunt down Exiled Gods, the Elders hadn't given me a Godslayer. At first, I thought perhaps the Elders were concerned I would turn the blade against them. After all, that was my intent for the past two centuries. However, it didn't make sense for the Elders to fear such a scenario. They were supposed to be immune to such weapons—slaying the creators of the universe was meant to be impossible.

'And yet they dodge my questions.' I swept through the academy halls, glancing occasionally at the moonslight filtering through windows. 'They are making it harder and harder to believe they are truly the Elder Gods. Even the other deities are growing suspicious...

'What were they thinking? Forcing me to become the God of Balance, and then subsequently keeping me from doing my job? Have they lost their minds? All that will do is make other deities wary of them.

'We need to deal with the Exiled Gods. They can't be allowed to continue creating Chaos Beasts. If they're going to start attacking *mortals...something will have to be done.'*

"Bad news?" A bronze-scaled guard smiled at me as I neared the academy's exit. "It's late, General Vraelimir. You look like you could use a glass of fiirzik and some sleep."

"And a bath." I chuckled. "Have you heard back from General Il'thar yet, Wyrvin?"

"Not yet, General." Wyrvin shook his head before glancing up at the starlit sky. "Judging by the readings the scholars aboard the expedition did, General Il'thar won't arrive for another few hours. We'll have to wait until at least tomorrow—er, later today—to hear from him."

"Is X'shmir not still above Falrrsald?" I asked with a small frown.

"It's closer to the Vorpmasian border now, sir." Wyrvin half-shrugged. "But General Il'thar took the biggest ship he could get his claws on."

"And thus the slowest one." I rolled my eyes and pressed my fingers to my temples briefly. "Sounds like Eyrian alright. Thank you for the information, Wyrvin."

"G'night, General Vraelimir," Wyrvin stated with a sharp salute. "Get some good rest, alright? Looks like you could use it."

"I will try," I replied dryly as I turned to walk in the direction of the palace. "Hundreds of pages of reports have a way of exhausting me."

By the time I found myself within the warmth of the Dauthrmiran palace, my exhaustion had finally caught up with me. A few servants cast me sympathetic glances before hurrying off towards the kitchens, mumbling something or other about bringing tea and dinner to my rooms. I was too tired to argue.

'A Human Lyur'zi and Chrot'zi...' I considered while taking my hot but quick bath. *'It's been well over two hundred years since the Elders stripped their race of power. The X'shmirans couldn't possibly have evaded the change.'*

When I returned to my suite, I found a cart with food, a pot of tea, and even a bottle of fiirzik—a type of hot liquor—waiting for me. After making sure the servants had truly left my rooms I sighed in relief, closed and locked the doors, and then made my way to the cart of foods.

'Too tired to eat?' I wondered for a moment, but a growl from my stomach answered the question for me. *'Tch, I suppose I can work while I dine. No one in their right mind will bother me here.'*

I searched through the reports again as I dined, reading and rereading the sections that related to the actions of both the Umbral and Astral Mages of X'shmir. Although I was grateful to her for saving the members of our expedition, I couldn't understand why she would have acted in our favor.

If she was truly bound by the Old Ways, her loyalty should have laid with X'shmir and its Astral Mage—the crown prince. The reports showed the fear and hatred of the Humans in great detail, and yet neither of the mages seemed to share the emotion with their people. It appeared that the boy was overly welcoming, whilst the woman seemed unfazed and disinterested.

Neither reaction was something I expected from isolated Humans.

'The woman must have some connection to the Sihix Forest.' I decided, skimming the details of her interactions. 'And the boy... He seems naive, but he is also a political figure. There must be something he wants out of us.'

X'shmir. It was a place that once had rich trade deals with both Elven and Devillian nations. Their mages once pursued perfection in the art of Magitech, and their lands had been rich with the crystallized aether needed to make such creations work. Both their creations and resources resulted in mutually excellent trade negotiations despite their distaste for the other races.

Even after the Elders chose to take magic from Humans, the resources available in X'shmiran lands—and the proximity of Aledacian Forests—meant that we had wanted to maintain relations with them. And yet...the nation had disappeared when I was a child. Several years ago, I had finally seen the crater left behind by X'shmir with my own eyes.

'The reports make it seem like the X'shmirans have lost more than just their magic.' I set aside the reports and rose from my seat. 'If their city, and the remaining Magitech, is crumbling down around them they will not survive much longer without outside assistance. Perhaps the prince realizes that despite his immaturity.

'I want see the state of affairs for myself. Beasts, the Old Ways...Human mages. Even if the Elders will not let me act in accordance *to my role, that's no excuse for staying uninformed.'*

CHAPTER SEVEN
A Familiar Scent

My wide yawn was interrupted by a stream of curses when I stubbed my toes into the foot of the bed. Djialkan cackled at me, and my glare only made him laugh harder. I huffed at him and then yanked a sheet over his head as I limped past.

"Have you and Fraelfnir made any progress?" I asked while adjusting my trousers and sword belt.

"We have not," Djialkan answered, wriggling out from beneath the sheet to snort darkness in my direction. *"Fraelfnir and I examined the Vorpmasian and Beshulthien ships. We did not find any indication of devices that allow them to pierce the Mists."*

"So something about the Mists—or X'shmir—has changed." I pursed my lips as I rifled through a drawer in search of my masks.

"That could be problematic. We still haven't addressed the problems with the Sihix Forest. I don't know if we can handle both matters at once."

Djialkan nodded his agreement and watched me carefully. Once I pulled on my hooded overrobe, an underbust corset, and my mask, the fae-dragon glided to my shoulder. His talons gripped my shoulder tighter than usual, giving me a hint of his unease.

"The Beshulthien and Vorpmasian Empires agreed to abide by our customs while visiting?" I inquired, nudging his cheek with one finger. Perhaps conversation would put him at ease.

"They are familiar with the 'Old Ways,' according to Fraelfnir," Djialkan spat, his tail snapping into my back with a dull thud. *"They are aware that they cannot make things change overnight. I am sure they will tread carefully whilst determining the extent of which X'shmir follows them."*

"So, they'll seal their power behind barriers before arriving and don masks and hoods…" I grimaced, stepping in front of a mirror to check that everything was in its proper place. "That's a shame. It won't be easy to determine who would be fun to fight!"

Djialkan laughed in response to my pouting, so I shot him a glare before turning to gather my belongings. I took one last glance in the mirror and admired the crest on the back of my robes before striding over to the wardrobe.

Each of my robes had the same crest emblazoned on the back—an iridescent black lotus with a white, nine-tailed fox poised in mid-pounce in the foreground. Vine-like platinum embroidery surrounded the crests, setting the black lotus apart from the black leather and cloth. The fox was a brilliant contrast with the rest of my attire and had blue eyes close to mine in color—not that anyone looking at me would know it.

"Let's go, Djialkan." I nudged him again. "I'll pack all of our things into my shrizar in case this meeting of mine goes the way I'm expecting."

Djialkan nuzzled my cheek, purred, and then curled around my shoulders. An amused smile touched my lips but disappeared the moment I began discarding items into my shrizar. The subtle pressure of our guests' magic gnawed at me and made me strain my senses in search of approaching beasts. Even though the emissaries, their guards, and the scholars were suppressing their own auras, the air in X'shmir shone with multicolored magics.

Every step I took felt like I was wading through honey. My heart raced within my chest, my mouth felt dry. A handful of the presences in the city were beyond anything I expected. They put the mages in the Sihix Forest to shame with their sheer power. I knew beforehand that some of our guests were supposed to be powerful…but no amount of verbal warnings could have prepared me for this much power in one place.

"You are taking everything?" Djialkan questioned as I pulled down a stack of blankets.

"I have a bad feeling about the meeting," I answered, opening a new shrizar and tossing the blankets into it. I watched them disappear into the dark void before turning to the closet that held pillows and linens. "I want to be ready in the event we need to flee."

A shrizar was essentially a magical cubbyhole that mages could utilize to carry their belongings, armor, weapons, and supplies while traveling. Some linked to a dead end of magic space like a true pocket, while others were linked to actual places—such as a wardrobe or an armory.

It made traveling easy because we could also use it to store food, drink, and medical supplies for extended absences. Personally, I didn't have any weapons or armor aside from what I was already wearing. Regardless, it was important to keep most of my things in a shrizar. If I didn't, my parent's loyal servants would destroy everything I owned whilst I was away.

Once satisfied that everything I owned was safely tucked away, I left my rooms and swept down the granite hallways of the castle. My wing of the castle, normally a quiet place, was alive with activity. Every Umbral Mage that had come to X'shmir with the Rilzaan Alliance was assigned to stay in what I considered *my* domain. The sconces that I usually left dark now shone with magelight but, aside from them, the walls were bare as ever.

'Hmmm? That smells like…the boy from my nightmares.' I paused in the middle of a hallway in the main entry of the castle, sniffing subtly at the air before my lips parted in surprise. *'I'm wide awake now. If I smell that…'*

The smell of sweet spices, musk, and undertones of sandalwood was unmistakable. It was so thick in the air that I felt like, if I squinted, I would be able to see it. Glancing around in search of the source, I only spotted servants and guards milling about on this floor. It was same in the entry hall below me. They carried stacks of firewood, blankets, and other necessities while preparing for the arrival of even more guests.

Clearly the scent wasn't strong enough for normal Humans to detect—or perhaps it just had a particular draw for me.

A melancholy sound drew my attention away from the foyer and to a nearby window. Pursing my lips, I slinked over to the window and glanced down into the courtyard's gardens below. X'shmir was too deep into winter now for the flowers and trees to be blooming…and yet everything around the Devillian man below me was verdant green and blossoming beneath the layers of snow.

The audible hum of his power as he played his violin accompanied and complimented his song in a strange but suiting way. Tendrils of pale blue magic spread from the man and through the garden, seeming to revive the slumbering plants and trees that had grown ill over the past several years.

Even though the garden was one of my favorite places in the castle, I had never seen the plants bloom like that before. They appeared to be drinking the Devillian's power with greedy abandon, growing larger and becoming more vibrant as they feasted.

The Devillian man was tall—I doubted my head even reached his collarbone. A long, black-scaled tail swayed lazily behind him as he played. Veins of platinum glinted in the pale lavender morning light, casting glints of silver on the castle walls. His tail was several feet longer than his legs. As it danced behind him, I realized that he was keeping it just above the frozen garden floor. His tail must have been like an extra limb if he was so physically aware of it.

The white hooded robes he wore both baffled and displeased me. His robes obscured his horns and hair from view, though I saw by his hands that he was very pale and had claws. Upon first glance I thought that he was an Astral Mage due to the color of his robes. However, a more thorough examination revealed the intricate platinum embroidery, jewelry, and other embellishments of an Umbral Mage.

Unlike the finer details of my attire, his bore the theme of dragons instead of foxes.

However, his white attire and unusual appearance were only a small portion of my confusion. On the back of his robes, displayed for all to see, was a crest too similar to mine to ignore. An opalescent white lotus stretched across his broad back, its shape matching the black one on my robes. A fearsome black dragon soared across the foreground of his crest, looking as if it was preparing to strike at something with its maw or breathe flames at an unseen enemy.

Blue topaz made up the dragon's eyes as well as adorned the Devillian man's jewelry. Pale aether drifted around each of the stones, indicating that their purpose wasn't purely for decoration. Taking in his appearance again, I decided he had to be high-ranking in

Vorpmasian society. The clothing and jewelry that other officials from the Alliance wore didn't even compare to his.

'The Vorpmasian Empire is taking these negotiations more seriously than I thought if he *is here,'* Djialkan commented from my shoulder, shifting to peer down at the violin-playing Devillian. *'Come. We should not be late to meet with your parents and Darius.'*

'He's…' My thoughts trailed off as the man's sleeve slipped down further, revealing Brands of Divinity on his arms and the backs of his hands. *'Black on his right, white on his left—and that scent. Is he…is he Nali? The same one who was so distraught when I was being taken away? The one that rescued me from Limbo?*

'That can't be right, can it? He's a deity. There's no reason for a deity to visit X'shmir in person.'

Djialkan nudged me to get my attention, so I nodded to him and turned away from the window. Making my way down the staircase, I passed several servants and guards who hurried to avert their gaze from me. The scent of their fear almost didn't register over the scent of that Devillian man. His spicy-sweet aroma hung over everything. It was oddly distracting, making me question if I could even think straight.

Despite the distracting scent, something about the song he was playing pulled at me more. I felt like I recognized it from somewhere but, no matter where I searched within the recesses of my mind, I couldn't place it.

"Ari?" Darius sounded curious as I slipped into the throne room, "You seem distracted."

'All that clothing looks stuffy...' I arched an eyebrow, counting at least five layers of silk and velvet robes on my twin and then watched as he sniffed the air in confusion. *'Ah, so he noticed that enticing scent as well.'*

"Not as distracted as you are, it would seem," I stated as Darius glanced around and tugged at the lobes of his own pointed ears. "Where should I—"

"Hmmm? No one told you?" Darius blinked at me and released his earlobe. My back tensed when I sensed the vile presence of our parents behind me, and my brother's face smoothed over into a neutral mask. "Your services aren't needed for the negotiations. The Vorpmasian and Beshulthien ambassadors have made it quite clear they don't mean to harm X'shmir."

'My "services" aren't needed?' I stared at my brother in astonishment. *'I would expect a phrase like that from our parents but...not from Darius...'*

"You heard your master!" our father snarled as he came to stand in front of me. Before I could spout off at him he punched me hard enough in the face to knock me off my feet. "Get the fuck out, trash!"

Djialkan hissed in displeasure and tensed on my shoulder before pivoting to nuzzle the cheek my father had struck. I bit back a feral snarl and reached up to make sure my hood was still in place. Our parents had haughty expressions on their faces but Darius just looked startled. Pulling myself to my feet, I brushed off my robes before shooting a glare at our father, directing my darkness toward him.

"I see that I should have removed *both* of your arms," I remarked, feeling ice forming around my feet in response to my anger. "Clearly, if you call that a punch, you are not deserving of your other limbs."

Without waiting for a response, I turned with a huff and stormed out of the throne room, making my way toward the castle doors. I was aware that I was leaving frozen footprints in my wake but I didn't care. Even as I neared the large wooden doors that would lead me into the frigid winter air, I heard Dilonu and Tyana's indignant shrieks and curses. Their fury was my victory even though it did little to quell my own anger.

It was a shame that I had missed my chance to kill them all those years ago when I first took the bastard's arm.

'Perhaps if I get another chance I should take the time to torture them,' I contemplated, heading for the gates that separated the castle from the rest of the cramped city. *'Although... It is difficult to think of appropriate punishments for the two of them. Hmmm.'*

"Is your cheek alright, Arianna?" Djialkan asked softly, nosing my skin again.

'I wonder how venom from the beasts would affect Human bodies in small quantities.' I grew closer to the city gates, ignoring passersby. *'Or perhaps I could dilute it with something? I wouldn't want them to die too quickly.'*

"General Black, w-where are you go—" a soldier started, but he yelped and shrank back when my attention turned to him.

"My presence in the city is apparently unwelcome!" I snapped. "I will be hunting beasts until our 'esteemed guests' have concluded their business with the Royal Family."

'Arianna...' Djialkan probed again, this time tapping my back with his tail.

'We can worry about it later,' I replied with a half-shrug before erecting a dim shield of magic around us. *'Ugh... The rats should learn to behave when I'm in such an obvious foul mood. Mmm...perhaps I can—'*

'You know you cannot destroy them just for their poor behavior,' Djialkan reprimanded me. *'Come. Let us get you out of the city before you disregard your restrictions.'*

I shivered as I considered tearing apart the nobles and commoners alike. They seemed intent on throwing things at us: rocks, spoiled foods, even a few weapons were thrown into the mix. Their aim was so terrible that I almost didn't even *need* to utilize a shield. Still, there were a handful of citizens "on my side" who offered murmured thanks or subtle bows to show their respect as I passed. A few went as far as to dissuade the rowdy ones but it didn't work. It never did.

'You did *notice that we are being followed, did you not?'* Djialkan snorted as we slipped out of the city and into the snow-blanketed forest.

'Yes. That Devillian mage from the courtyard seems to have been drawn by my brief spike of bloodlust,' I answered the fae-dragon as I shifted my head to scent the air. *'A few others seem like they've been drawn as well. Do you think they're going to follow us all the way to Sihix?'*

Drawing darkness around both of us, I ran through the forest with enhanced speed. I wanted to put as much distance between the filth of X'shmir and myself as I could. Otherwise I would probably return to destroy as many of them as possible before my curse ended me. Destroying the bastards would have been a delightful experience but it wasn't worth the price. For now.

'Unlikely. Our guests are not allowed within five miles of the Sihix Forest.' Djialkan nuzzled me again before continuing, *'You are lucky that the Mists are still strong enough to interfere with their senses. The deity should be capable of hearing your thoughts. Since he cannot…he is being more cautious than he would normally be.'*

'Humph. Djialkan still won't speak that one's *name,'* I observed from within my deeper barriers, glancing to the side at the fae-dragon before picking up my pace. *'Ahhhnnn… I smell a beast! Let's kill it!'*

Grinning wildly, I veered off in the direction of the monster's vile scent and giggled to myself. Destroying the monstrous creature would be a welcome albeit temporary relief for my rage. Since it was a beast and not a citizen I could rip it to shreds without fear of repercussions. Perfect.

'A-Ari?! You're not seriously returning to Sihix already are you?' Darius yelped, causing me to growl in response. *'What if beasts come close to the city? You're supposed to protect me* and *our people, remember?!'*

'I'm sure your "guests" can handle them!' I retorted hotly as I conjured a blade of ice and neared the putrid pile of flesh that was scooting across the forest floor. *'After all, you said it yourself, my services*

aren't required. *If you* do *happen to find something that I'm* "required for" *you can have Fraelfnir contact Djialkan.'*

I shut my brother out of my mind and leapt into the air. My blade tore deep into the Chaos Beast's stomach, spilling its internal organs and partially digested corpses of animals and Humans into the snow. A second strike was all it took for me to silence the beast's screaming. Oily-black blood billowed into the air and stained the snow around us. For a moment I contemplated ripping the beast into smaller chunks but a quick sniff of the air informed me that the Devillians were closing the distance between us. I didn't have time to enjoy myself.

With a displeased click of my tongue, I turned away from the corpse and wove through the trees with renewed speed. The beast had died too damned easily. I wanted more of a challenge and a longer, dragged-out fight. However, it was clear that I wasn't going to find such a fight any time soon. It wouldn't do for me to slaughter our guests in my rage, after all. Pity.

'You are letting your bloodlust run rampant,' Djialkan stated with a heavy sigh. *'Arianna, you will draw every Devillian mage and warrior in X'shmir to us at this rate. You need to calm yourself—or at least hide your desire to kill.'*

'Why?' I leapt out of the trees and landed in a crouch atop the snow-covered plateau, and surveyed the open expanse in search of a people-free route. I didn't feel like having to deal with any of the Beshulthien or Vorpmasian guards around the airships.

'The Devillians are like you,' Djialkan began in a dry tone,

whacking me in the shoulder with his tail several times. *'The prospect of a challenge—particularly in battle—excites them. Oftentimes, they will challenge people they believe close to them in power so that they may test themselves.*

'Vorpmasian culture is rooted in battle, magic, obtaining knowledge, and, above all, proving oneself.'

'Well, that is different than what the X'shmirans teach for sure,' I commented with an amused smile, casting a glance over my right shoulder. Several mages in black and silver robes filtered through the trees, closing the distance between us at a rapid pace. *'They are chasing me because they desire a fight then?'*

'The ones who are pursuing us are Adinvyr,' Djialkan replied with a bark of laughter, nodding his head once. *'They are the most warlike of the Devillian races. No doubt they noticed your abnormal level of bloodlust and desire to challenge you whilst you're angered. They should stop soon but he will most likely continue until we have entered Sihix itself.*

'As a deity, he has a little more freedom in X'shmir. That said, even he should know better than to follow you into an Aledacian Forest without invitation.'

I pursed my lips as I caught the scent of the god Djialkan was referring to. Sinking into a deep crouch, I summoned darkness so thick that it was opaque. In the next instant, I launched across the surface of the snow with greater speed than before and ran along the tree line to avoid confrontation with any of the visiting soldiers. My companion seemed amused by my desire to get away from the Devillian mages but

I tuned out his chuckling.

There was something terribly alluring about *that one* in particular, and finding anything or anyone appealing was *not* good for my longevity.

The deity appeared to be exercising caution as he pursued me, but by the way he reached out with his power I could tell he was unaccustomed to the presence of the Mists. He struggled more than he should have to locate me and seemed to be letting the weaker ones rush ahead while he took a more methodical approach.

'Following the trees at this speed should save me from confrontation of any kind at least.' I flicked my gaze to the forest and then to the dozens of airships lining the plateau.

Most of the strange contraptions were a deep pewter color and emblazoned with the Vorpmasian Empire's imperial sigil: three moons aligned vertically with a pair of white and black serpentine dragons intertwined around the lunar objects. Black, silver, and sapphire seemed to be a recurring theme amongst the soldier's armor and the plating on the ships.

The Beshulthien's, in contrast, bore a theme of gold, burgundy, and garnet. Their crest was a crystalline tower with an angered phoenix wrapped around it, its wings spread and head tilted back as if screeching—or roaring.

'Fraelfnir and I are still looking into the Beshulthien Empire,' Djialkan hissed in an unusually displeased tone. *'The species who founded that empire is…new. All we have been able to ascertain, thus far,*

is that they were created within the last few decades.

'The Vorpmasians appear to detest them yet still allied them out of necessity. The Chaos Beast threat Below has become quite troublesome from what I understand.'

Nearing the end of the forest surrounding X'shmir, I took a sharp turn to my left and bounded across the open surface of the snow. Sihix's translucent black trees towered hundreds of feet above the northwestern section of the plateau, casting deep shadows across the frozen expanse.

Winter thus far had been harsh and, despite the thick crystalline canopy, it was likely that snow coated some of Sihix's forest floor. Were it not for my magic, the snow on the plateau would have come several feet above my head.

"Wait!" The command came from surprisingly close behind me as I leapt onto one of the branches Sihix extended for me. I pivoted to look down at the Devillian deity in surprise as he continued, "You're the X'shmiran Lyur'zi, aren't you? I wish to speak to you about—"

"Djialkan," I commented quietly, prodding the begrudging fae-dragon's chin. "You may explain the situation to him if you like. I'm going to continue on ahead."

Glancing down at what was visible of the deity's face, I found a surprising expression set on his mouth—he appeared upset. I recognized that expression even though he was clearly an adult now and it was almost enough to make me linger. Almost. Shaking my head as if it would help push the man from my mind, I turned and darted into the forest in hopes of calming my racing heart.

Never in my life had I heard such a powerful voice, nor was his accent similar to any of the other Devillians I'd overheard conversing in the palace over the past few months. I didn't know how else to describe his accent other than as "warm" and "purring." He rolled most of his r's, but there was another odd sound to his pronunciation I couldn't quite place.

However, it was the sheer power in his words that made me nervous. Something about his commanding tone almost made me want to obey. An amused smirk formed on my face as I dropped from the branches and to the forest floor. *'I can't have that, now can I?'*

'His accent was like that boy in my nightmares,' I thought as I wove through the maze of crystalline trees. *'I'm pretty sure that was white hair spilling from his hood as well, but it was long. His scent…his voice…*

'I knew I shouldn't have doubted my instincts. That's the same Nali from my "dreams."

'So… Are they not just dreams?'

CHAPTER EIGHT
The Umbral Mage

I stared after the X'shmiran Umbral Mage and the stream of darkness she left trailing behind her. Bewildered, I watched as she bounded across the branches of the Sihix Forest and disappeared into its shadows. I thought of chasing after her but it was as if the forest sensed my thoughts. The branch Sihix had extended for the petite woman swayed upwards into its standard position far above my head, blocking out the violet sky.

If I wanted to follow her, I would have to brave unwelcoming territory with my own wings.

Her musky scent of jasmine and vanilla lingered in the air, disturbing my senses when I took a deep breath. How was I meant to calm myself after detecting such a familiar, and unmistakable, aroma?

It wasn't possible. I couldn't breathe without drowning myself in her scent and losing my focus all over again.

'I put so much power into my command.' I glanced down at the hand I had offered her. *'Yet she barely paused. How did she resist a command from an Adinvyr, let alone a deity?'*

'Does this accursed country truly interfere with my abilities to that extent?'

My heart felt as if it would leap out of my chest. The run from X'shmir to the Sihix Forest hadn't tired me—such a pace was trivial. Nor was the woman's desire to face off with a Chaos Beast the cause for my near-panicked state. A Human shouldn't have been able to take the creature on, let alone with such ease, but she had come out of it unscathed.

No, my state of mind was because of her scent. It had grabbed my attention the moment I arrived in the X'shmiran castle. No two people in our world shared a scent, and *that* one in particular had stopped me in my tracks. That Arianna might still be alive, even in a place like this, shook me to my core. I would have to be mad to leave the possibility alone.

I was of half a mind to disregard protocol and track her through the Sihix Forest despite the risks. *She* was far more important to me than Lucifer's negotiations with X'shmir could ever be.

When I first chose to follow her from the castle, I wasn't sure what to think. The iridescent black lotus of her crest on the back of her robes was like a dark twin to the opalescent white one on mine. Under other circumstances I could have written it off as coincidence. However, the shape and orientation were identical. Although her mage's refinery was distinctly vulpine and mine was draconic, the eyes of the fox on her crest stunned me. They were a sparkling electric blue, just as *her* eyes had been.

"Djialkan…" I began with a small sigh, shifting to watch the small fae-dragon drift downward to me. "That scent is unmistakable. Don't even *attempt* to tell me that wasn't Arianna."

'I'm not sure my hearts could take it right now,' I added to myself, clenching my hands into fists within my robes.

"The Royal Family made it clear that they do not require their Umbral Mage's services *for the remainder of their negotiations with foreign powers,"* Djialkan snapped in a formal yet bitter manner as he perched on my shoulder, his talons twitching tense. *"You…noticed the X'shmiran people's treatment of her as you followed us through the city, did you not?"*

"They seemed quite intent on throwing things at her," I answered softly, glancing to Djialkan and then to the looming crystalline trees before me. "You aren't concerned that Sihix will corrupt her?"

"She acts as a Guardian of Sihix. From the outside," Djialkan snorted in response, appearing oblivious to my startled expression. *"Need I remind you that no one from the Alliance is allowed within five miles of the forest, Nalithor? If you pursue her into Sihix without invitation you will risk her refocusing her wrath upon you instead of that bastard king."*

"You don't intend to tell me *anything*?" I demanded, crossed my arms, and cut deep trenches into the snow with my tail as it snapped back and forth in rage. "Djialkan, after I found the four of you in Limbo, the Elders told me Arianna *di*—" I shut my eyes in pain briefly. "They told me she was no longer with us, and that they were going to cleanse and reincarnate her soul.

"The same goes for Darius. They were quite clear that they intended to assign you and Fraelfnir new wards."

"That is what they said?" Djialkan tilted his head, his tone unreadable as the catlike swaying of his tail ceased. A moment later he flinched and looked towards the forest. *"Alas, I must calm my ward before she returns to the city to claim Dilonu's other arm. I will not have her risking her life over such an unworthy target."*

'Risking her life? She can slay a beast in two strikes. How could taking the king's arm possibly compare to facing a Dux-class beast without armor?' I stared blankly after the fae-dragon as he flew from my shoulder and into the forest to join his ward. The limbs of Sihix shifted to create a near-impenetrable wall of crystal in front of me. *'Is it trying to keep me out or her in?'*

Sensing Sihix and its guardians watching me from within the darkness, I cast my eyes to my right and caught movement. Several foxes made of opaque shadow watched me from their perches, their eyes of pale ice tracking me unblinkingly. The scent of the foxes was the same as the woman I had had chased; Arianna had made them.

'Arianna...' I sighed and covered my face with one hand, staggering back a step while I tried to regain control of my emotions.

'Am I already accepting that she must *be the same woman? There's still the possibility that the Exiled Gods are playing a cruel joke.*

'But…could they really duplicate her down to her very scent?'

Taking a deep breath to calm myself, I found her all-too-familiar aroma filling my senses again. It was of little help. Turning my back to the dark forest, I felt my shoulders drop as I examined the dissipating shadows Arianna had left in her wake. The shadows had taken on the form of foxes and were charging past me to catch up to their mistress. Several paused to stare at me, sending chills down my spine, before continuing on their way. Such mastery over her darkness was…worrisome.

'If the Elders truly did as they claimed, her scent should be different. Djialkan shouldn't be with her. She shouldn't be so in tune with her darkness.' I frowned, settling into a leisurely gait in X'shmir's direction. *'She always did like foxes, didn't she? As well as music and sweets of course.'*

Baring my fangs in irritation, I looked up as a large Chaos Beast swooped down from the sky above me on silent wings. As with every beast we'd seen in the damned country, it was unlike any of the ones documented on the Rilzaan Continent. Its visage was twisted and rotting. Looking at it, I couldn't fathom how the featherless being remained airborne on such misshapen wings. With little more than a flick of my finger I tore the creature asunder with darkness and flames, sending the foul-smelling creature tumbling into the snow behind me.

With a displeased click of my tongue, I picked up my pace and began placing seals over my power once more. Clearly, the X'shmirans had been quite serious when they stated the beasts here were drawn to magical power. It was no wonder that Arianna had her powers under such tight seals. Tight enough seals that I almost mistook her for a normal Human, at first.

'Human. Right.' I frowned, sifting back to my memories of her in Limbo. *'She was Human there as well. What happened to—?'*

"You should duck!" The female voice startled me out of my thoughts but I obliged. Her scent had caught my attention moments before being overwhelmed by the stench of yet another beast.

I staggered backwards when the snow several yards before me burst upwards, accompanied by earth and shattered rock. Another twisted monstrosity clawed its way to the surface, massive talons gouging through earth and snow with equal ease. The beast was almost as massive as one of our airships but it was the woman springing over my head who had my attention.

"Really! Do the Mists mess with your senses so badly that you couldn't sense *that* stalking you?!" Arianna chastised me as she summoned a massive scythe of ice in her hands. She twirled the weapon into an offensive stance as if it weighed nothing.

In the blink of an eye, she shadow-stepped toward the towering beast and severed its head from its shoulders without even the faintest hint of hesitation. I found myself staring after the petite Umbral Mage in sheer disbelief. Anyone other than a deity taking the head of a Dux-class beast in a single blow was unfathomable.

My disbelief gave way to utter shock the moment she ignited the corpse with cobalt flames. It was as if everything, including my pulse, stopped. There were only two people I knew of with flames that color. Emperor Lucifer Shujare was the first. The second was the Emperor's firstborn daughter: Arianna Jade Shujare. *'Can…can the Exiles even duplicate something like that?'*

"You could sense it?" I asked, watching as she turned to me and dismissed her scythe into frost and allowed the faint blue particles to mingle with the snow beneath us.

"I could *smell* the damnable thing." She retorted and crossed her arms, "*You* should return to the city before— H-hey, don't do that!"

Her panicked tone made me pause long enough for her to rush forward and grip both of my wrists to keep me from pulling my hood down. The Lyur'zi's grip was strong for someone who was *supposed* to be Human. Her hands couldn't even wrap around my wrists in full, yet she was able to exert enough physical strength to stop me.

Looking down at her from so close, I realized that she was tiny. In some strange way she had seemed much larger while fighting the beasts. Yet the top of her head just barely reached my collarbone. That said, the startled expression on the lower half of her face and the slight flush in her cheeks was adorable.

'I wonder what's behind that mask…' I tilted my head, examining the solid black leather mask that obscured the rest of her face.

"Lyur'zi are not allowed to remove their hoods or masks unless within Arianna's wing of the castle, or under the protection of Sihix's boughs," Djialkan huffed from Arianna's shoulder. *"They have their ways of*

knowing. To break this rule is a death sentence.

"*If you break it,* this one *is who will be ordered to take your head.*"

'*So her name* is *Arianna, then.*' I looked from the fae-dragon and back to the petite mage, examining her plump, scarlet-painted lips for a moment before shifting my gaze to her ornate mask again. '*They would force her to try and kill a* god? *What is wrong with this place? And where did she acquire a Magitech mask from?*'

"Just as *they* have their ways of determining you've wandered too close to Sihix," Arianna added as she released my wrists with an abrupt motion, pointed at the sky above with one finger, and then motioned at the monstrous forest behind me. "I would rather not receive orders to kill you. I recommend you return to the city immediately."

"You believe you could kill me?" I questioned, watching her expression fall slightly. She clenched her hands behind her back and shifted back and forth on the balls of her feet for a moment in silence.

"Whether I *can* doesn't matter..." Arianna shook her head. "I would be ordered to regardless. Failure to do so would be death. Disobedience would be death. Need I go on?"

Instead of waiting for my reply, Arianna strode past me across the snow. Her shoulders wilted as she made her way back towards the Sihix Forest. However, the slight wince that crossed her face when Djialkan nuzzled her cheek did not go unnoticed by me. The beast hadn't struck her—so who had?

I moved to follow her out of concern but Djialkan shot me a sharp look. Darkness poured from his nostrils and the massive trees of Sihix swayed into a threatening configuration.

"Very well. I will do as you suggest. For now," I called after her, watching her head shift slighting to acknowledge she had heard me. "Djialkan, I desire an audience with Sihix. Please inform me—or one of my men—if the forest decides to agree."

The fae-dragon nodded and, after a moment, the pair disappeared into the forest once more. I looked down at the corpse Arianna had left on the plateau, discovering that her cobalt flames had already eaten the creature away. Nothing but dust remained scattered across the surface of the snow. That her flames had not burned all the way to the ground below was testament to just how much snow had accumulated on the plateau.

'There wasn't even the slightest hint of magical power coming off of her, and yet...' I pursed my lips, thinking back on the corpse she had left near X'shmir. *'She left prints of ice from the castle and all the way to Sihix. She destroyed not one but* two *Dux-class Chaos Beasts: the first in two strikes, the second in one.*

'Even when Humans could still become mages they stood no chance against beasts of any class, let alone the Duxes that seem prevalent here in X'shmir.'

I looked up at the violet sky above me with unease as I neared the forest bordering the Human-city state. The X'shmiran sky and its sickly hue were so incredibly foreign. It had come as a shock to me when I had arrived early this morning—our men's reports did not do it justice.

How we couldn't see the shifting violet mists from the ground was beyond me. It had taken us so long to journey from the edge of "the Mists" to X'shmir that I had opted to sleep instead of watching the endless sea of violet.

Upon arrival, I had spoken with several of our soldiers that had been in X'shmir for almost two months. In all that time, they hadn't seen a single cloud, the sun, or any of Avrirsa's three moons. Even the stars and neighboring planets were all "missing" from the strange-colored sky. The only object in the sky was the strange rip and the orb of shimmering lavender-colored water that seemed like it was attempting to push through it. Apparently *that* was what took the place of the sun for X'shmirans.

Most unsettling was the feeling that the damned sky seemed to be watching me. And, unlike the Sihix Forest, it did not appear neutral or friendly in the slightest. There was a distinct maliciousness to its presence, and it was so palpable that our soldiers kept second-guessing their senses. Half the time they weren't sure if a Chaos Beast was near, or if the sky was at fault.

'Nali, where are you? Negotiations are about to start.' Eyrian's telepathic voice sounded hesitant as it reached for me, eliciting a sigh from me as I made my way through the coniferous forest. *'It's unusual for you of all people to wander off.'*

"I was attempting to acquire the X'shmiran Lyur'zi's cooperation,' I replied, sinking my hands into the pockets of my overrobes. *'However, it would appear she does not want anything to do with me. I will return*

shortly.'

My own words stung as I pondered them. The thought that Arianna didn't want to see or speak with me was maddening. In all honesty, I wasn't sure what I would say to her if she *did* choose to speak with me. However, the hollow feeling that had settled inside my chest after leaving her in Sihix didn't sit well with me. Emptiness like this wasn't something I had felt in at least a century. Yet, just like that, it was back again.

Her insistence that I leave and return to the city without her only made it worse.

I pulled one hand out of my pockets and rested my fingertips over the left half of my chest. The crystalline lotus that had once been *her* heart had grown hot upon arriving in X'shmir. Since then, it pulsated with energy stronger than it ever had before.

That had been my first clue that perhaps Arianna had been reborn in X'shmir, yet I had dismissed it as wishful thinking.

However, my second hint was when I caught her scent in the gardens. It was clear from the feel of her aura that my music had drawn her attention, and the reverberations of telepathy in the air told me she and Djialkan had discussed something while watching me. That I couldn't listen in on her thoughts infuriated me. I wasn't sure if it was the Mists at fault, or if the woman herself was shielding both her and Djialkan's thoughts from me.

'Music did always seem to draw her...'A small smile crept across my lips and I shook my head. *'That's right. She was so shy when we first met*

as children. I had to find a way to lure her out of hiding and only my violin ever seemed to do the trick.'

Despite her ability to shield her thoughts from me, *nothing* could have hidden the rage that emanated from her shortly before leaving the throne room. At first I had followed her because I thought her power was going to spiral out of control. Frozen footprints such as hers were typically the sign of an Ice Mage losing all control of their power, and usually resulted in the mage freezing themselves, their surroundings, or both, solid.

Contrary to my assumptions, however, the X'shmiran Lyur'zi had incredible control over her power. A Human shouldn't have had power to begin with, so discovering her mastery over ice came as a surprise. However, the appearance of shadows when she leapt into the forest came as an utter shock. Humans were notorious for their fear of darkness, yet she had calmed to some extent instead.

Umbral Mages such as her or myself always had power over darkness and at least one other element. That said, *Human* Umbrals were notorious for self-destructing due to their natural fear of darkness. Fearing one of your powers often meant death for a mage or for those around you. Often they killed someone important to them, and then slew themselves in grief.

Self-destruction was one of many reasons the Elders stripped Humans of magic.

CHAPTER NINE
Generosity

"General Vraelimir, this way please," a X'shmiran solder muttered. He shifted in unease as I approached the X'shmiran castle and kept his eyes focused away from me.

It was difficult to not wrinkle my nose in response to the unpleasant scent of these Humans. With any luck, perhaps one of our first "gifts" to these people would be a proper set of baths.

"Oh?" The mumble came from a young man in white and gold robes. His unmistakable eyes tracked my movements through the meeting room. "I wouldn't have sent Ari away if I'd known the Rilzaan Alliance was allowing their own Umbral Mages to attend...

"I'm Darius Raisur Black, Astral Mage and heir to the X'shmiran throne. It's a pleasure to meet all of you, I'm sure."

'Darius Raisur…' Stunned, my thoughts trailed off as I examined the young man's eyes again. *'Slit pupils? Yellow around the centers? Do these fools truly expect us to believe he's* Human?'

'Nali… Did he just say Raisur?' Eyrian questioned, earning a brief glance from me. *'I suddenly find myself liking this place a whole lot less.'*

'The princess isn't present?' I inquired after surveying the room once more, my unease mounting. *'What excuse did they give us, Eyrian?'*

'Nothing yet,' Eyrian answered with a discreet shake of his armored head. *'Darius here seems to be the only one that isn't frightened by Umbral Mages. The rest of the nobles haven't let our Umbrals speak, and the King and Queen haven't shown their faces yet.'*

I frowned and settled in to process the information. Darius Raisur *Shujare* had been Arianna's twin brother. Like this boy, his eyes had been chartreuse green with slit pupils and yellow at the center—like his father's right eye. His ears were pointed like an Elf's, and I caught glimpses of both upper and lower fangs as he spoke. His fangs were placed more like that of someone from my own race, an Adinvyr.

This Arianna had said nothing of being a princess, nor had she carried herself as one. Was it because of her status as an Umbral Mage? Alternatively, was I perhaps incorrect in my assumptions? Unlike this boy, *she* had been careful not to reveal anything physical that would have given her away as something other than Human.

'Now I understand why our men and women have been so careful with their information.' I sighed, shutting my eyes for a moment to still my thoughts. *'I knew something strange must have been going on in order for*

them—especially Eyrian—to withhold names and descriptions from their reports.'

"Your Highness, you said you're an Astral Mage?" a female voice inquired, drawing my attention to my least favorite strawberry blonde Oracle; she looked horribly displeased by something. "What training have you had?"

"Training?" Darius grinned, revealing his fangs in full as he motioned to his shoulder. "Just a little bit from Fraelfnir here."

Several of my fellow Vorpmasians grew still as the white fae-dragon with golden eyes and claws appeared on the boy's shoulders. We were all old enough to know just who used to be Fraelfnir's ward: Darius Raisur Shujare, our emperor's *deceased* son. Djialkan was the Guardian of Darius' twin sister. By the expressions on some of my comrades' faces, not everyone had been informed of Fraelfnir or Djialkan's presence.

I was uncertain what to think about the boy or that woman. My instincts screamed at me that they were Lucifer's children. However, my mind insisted that it was impossible. Why would the Elder Gods *lie* to me about something as important as that?

I crossed my arms and leaned back against a wall, attempting to quell my unease. Taking steady breaths, I examined the dignitaries from X'shmir and the Rilzaan Alliance alike. The more I studied them, the more troubled I grew. Darius' scent was weak enough that he could have passed as a Human if not for his fangs, ears, and eyes. He was faintly floral-smelling like the Darius I knew as a child but the cheerful façade he wore was new to me.

One of the most distinctive traits of Lucifer's children had been their eyes. Arianna's eyes had mirrored the color of her father's left eye, whilst Darius' eyes were the same as Lucifer's right eye. *This* Darius undoubtedly shared that trait. That woman, however, would be more difficult to deal with. Convincing her to remove her mask seemed unlikely.

'*When I saw her in Limbo I* thought *it was truly her,*' I contemplated in silence, my claws digging into my forearms. '*The Elders claimed she died when she was removed from Limbo. That nothing beyond her soul remained. My instincts screamed otherwise.*

'*Just…just what happened when I went back to retrieve her brother? What did the Elders* do?'

"Will the princess not be joining us?" Xander questioned. I glanced toward him and examined the expression on his face; I didn't even have to read his mind to know the Vampire bastard was thinking about taking the princess to his bed if he could find her.

"Hmmm?" Darius tilted his head, a doe-eyed expression on his face as he looked at Xander. "My sister is very ill. She probably won't be able to join us."

The prince looked unnerved by Xander's pale blue gaze and flushed whenever he looked at the Vampire. Whether the boy knew it or not, we could all hear his heartbeat quicken when he looked at Xander and a few other male delegates. Fear wasn't behind his racing pulse however. His desire was obvious. He was visibly attracted to the males present and paid no mind to the women whatsoever.

"What of the Umbral Mage then?" I spoke up coolly, ignoring the flinching X'shmiran nobles and focusing on Darius' uneasy shifting instead. "I was informed that if I wished to learn of the beasts plaguing X'shmir, speaking with her would be my best choice."

"I apologize. My parents believed her presence unnecessary." Darius sighed, his shoulders slumping as he ran a hand through his golden brown curls. "They gave me orders to send her away, and so she left. She stated that she would be hunting beasts until her presence is required."

'So they want us to believe the princess and the Umbral Mage are different people,' I observed as the prince turned from me and back to the other delegates. *'Eyrian, Xander, you both smell her don't you?'*

'So you did *notice,'* Xander remarked with a sigh and settled back in his chair, his eyes tracing Darius' form. *'We were starting to wonder if becoming a god made you lose your edge.'*

'I assume that's why you were late?' Eyrian questioned, shifting in his armor.

'She retreated into the Sihix Forest,' I stated, watching both my friends twitch. *'Djialkan was rather insistent that I shouldn't follow her— and that she would not be corrupted.'*

'You didn't get a chance to confirm her identity then, I take it?' the Oracle piped up, uninvited, her vulpine tails swishing behind her as she cast me a sideways glance. *'Nalithor, we need to test this boy that thinks he's a mage. I had hoped we could test the girl, too, but it looks like*

that will have to wait.

'Xander, you're an Archmagus. Initiate talks of the boy being invited to study at the academy. Then we'll be able to have Nalithor perform the tests without raising suspicion.'

"Your Highness, just what sort of mage do you wish to be?" Xander crooned. He leaned forward on his elbows and channeled Vampiric power into his words. His attempts to lull the boy into submission didn't appear to work but Darius still took the bait.

"What kind of…?" Darius blinked at Xander with blank eyes. "I'm an Astral Mage! What else is there besides Astral and Umbral Mages?"

I battled down my displeasure and listened to my comrades explain to the boy that there were *many* more types of mages. A type for every element and a type for almost every combination of elements. Mages who healed, mages who destroyed—Darius seemed fascinated by the concept.

'If he's the same Darius he should have known all of this already,' I thought to myself dejectedly, even as *her* heart grew hotter within my chest. *'Was I getting my hopes up too soon?*

'Ahhh… Fraelfnir has been teaching him, has he not? Did some problem arise during his schooling? I can't see either of the fae-dragons letting a ward remain this uneducated.'

"Oh in that case, I would like to be a healer," Darius commented after several long minutes, oblivious to the distasteful looks the X'shmiran nobles shot him. "My Umbral Mage already wreaks enough havoc without *me* adding to the mix! She hasn't been injured in a long time…but there's no one to heal her if she *does* get injured.

"Fraelfnir and Djialkan are powerful, but they can't heal the kinds of wounds those monsters make!"

"Your Highness, it is very inappropriate of you to be concerned about an Evil Mage's well-being!" one of the older nobles chastised. "She exists to live and die for you and for your country. Her life is of no consequence to you."

I bit back my growl of anger and watched as Darius' cheerful façade slipped to reveal a pained and furious expression. He gripped the arms of his chair until his knuckles grew white and his eyes burned with hatred. He didn't appear to share the views of his comrades but something kept him from saying as such. The X'shmiran nobles, however, appeared oblivious to the prince's frustration. *We* were much less dense.

"Should negotiations go smoothly," Xander spoke up to break the uneasy silence. "You and your Umbral Mage would both be welcome to receive training at the Dauthrmiran Academy of Martial Science.

"As you are aware, the Vorpmasian and Beshulthien Empires founded the Rilzaan Alliance in order to combat the growing threat that the Chaos Beasts pose. The Vorpmasian capital, Dauthrmir, is home to the most prestigious academy of the arcane. Everyone in the alliance goes there to study."

"As an ally of Vorpmasia, and of Beshulthien, anyone that requires physical or magical training would be welcome at either of the academies in Dauthrmir," Eyrian added from within his plate helmet.

His tail twitched when the prince began laughing. "You seem…amused, Your Highness."

"I apologize!" Darius gasped between fits of laughter. "It's just that our Umbral Mage does not require training. The idea of her attending classes is so comical that I couldn't help myself.

"In all seriousness, while I am thrilled by the offer, I would not be allowed to attend unless my Umbral Mage accompanies me Below. However, she is our only weapon against the Chaos Beasts. As such, she cannot leave."

"Yet she would not be permitted to stay behind without her Astral Master." One of the nobles hissed, earning an involuntary twitch and a glare from me. "Such an action would be treason against X'shmir."

'Her Master?' I bit back a furious snarl and reached out with tendrils of magic, prodding at Darius' mind. *'Tch. As if this* boy *is capable of being her Master!* She *had to shield* his *mind because he couldn't do it himself! She would never sink so low as to—'*

I closed my eyes and took a deep breath to calm my growing rage. I knew that X'shmiran culture was much different from my own, but for them to call Darius her *Master* infuriated me. If my hunch that they were siblings proved true…such a relationship between family members would be unforgivable if it was willing.

"And if we offered X'shmir military assistance for the duration of their training?" I inquired in a frigid tone, watching the nobles stiffen in response. "Surely you would find more use in a squadron of trained demigods than you would in a solitary, and untrained, Umbral Mage."

"She's not untrained!" Darius protested hotly, shooting me a scowl. "You've seen the beasts, haven't you?! She has been slaying them all by herself since she was a child!"

"While I question our guests' decision to permit an Umbral Mage to speak to my son," a new, slimy voice piped up, drawing my gaze to a man in his sixties or seventies as he wobbled into the room. A barely-clothed woman of the same age sashayed alongside him as he continued, "If Vorpmasia is willing to handle our beast problem, we will permit Darius and his bitch to travel Below."

'His...**what**?' I grit my teeth as my tail snapped into the stone wall behind me with a solid crack. My fury was joined by nausea the instant I realized what was so wrong about the king and queen before me.

'Nalithor...' Xander's voice was weary as he glanced toward me. 'That *level of rage is unusual for you. What's wrong?'*

'*The King and Queen are siblings,*' I spat, linking my hands together behind my back and clenching them tight. '*I have a bad feeling about these people. Do everything you can to have the prince, princess, and Umbral Mage sent to Dauthrmir for training—assuming they're even telling the truth about the princess and the mage being different people.*'

Remaining in X'shmir would be difficult for me. My instincts as an Adinvyr told me to slay King Dilonu and Queen Tyana on the spot for their incestuous relationship. Yet my instincts as a deity told me to wait. It wasn't yet time for their demise. I needed to exercise a level of patience I wasn't sure I had, in spite of my upbringing as an Adinvyr prince. Under any other circumstances, I would have slain them without hesitation.

"I apologize if we offended you, Your Majesty," Xander offered them a flamboyant bow as he rose from his seat. "Our customs regarding mages are much different than yours. As such, our Umbral Mages are struggling to adjust.

"If you will allow it, I would like to have some of our Mages and our Oracle run His Highness through some magical tests. We will need to gauge his aptitude if we are to submit his name to the roster of students."

"Human Mages are nonexistent on the surface, so we need a better understand of where His Highness' powers lay, Your Majesty," the Oracle added with a charming smile as the geezer stared down her cleavage.

"We would have liked to gauge the abilities of both the Umbral Mage and Her Highness, seeing as magical prowess tends to run within a family line," Xander commented with a frown, stroking his chin. "If Her Highness is ill, one of our healers would be happy to—"

"That won't be necessary, Lord Leukos," Tyana spoke up from her brother's arm. I bit back yet another scowl when her gaze shifted to me and she began examining me like a piece of meat. "If one of you can find the bitch in the wilds you can examine her as well.

"For now, just our son will suffice."

'Let's get this over with. Preferably before *I decide to tear this rock from the sky,'* I huffed in anger to my comrades, *'As if the King and Queen didn't make me ill enough on their own. The thoughts she is*

directing me are somehow worse!'

"We can test him now if it pleases you," Xander offered with another subservient bow. "It would do us both well if the examinations take place before my fellow Archmagi have to return to the surface and perform their academic duties."

"Very well, we'll allow it." Dilonu nodded. "Your Archmagi and who—Oracle can test Darius while the rest of us see to civilized business."

'Did that bastard just call me a whore?!' The Oracle shrieked as Eyrian, Xander, and I followed her and Darius out of the room.

"I apologize, Oracle, Nalithor." Fraelfnir sighed from Darius' shoulder, earning a questioning look from the prince. *"The King and Queen's manners are almost as vile as their relationship."*

"Uhm, I was wondering," Darius frowned up at me as we entered a large, plush room, "why are your robes white?

"I am a healer, therefore I wear white robes," I stated, watching as the boy's expression became more confused. "Both Light and Darkness have healing or destructive properties depending on how they are utilized."

"Nalithor is one of the professors at the academy," Eyrian offered as he removed his helm and then motioned at himself. "Like Nalithor, I'm both a General in the Vorpmasian Military *and* an Archmagus. I'm what we like to call a Maelstrom Mage."

"Let's start with the basics." I conjured a stack of forms in one hand and a pen in the other once I was seated. "How old are you?"

"Twenty-five!" Darius replied with a broad grin as he plopped down in a chair across from me. "Oh, how rude of me! What is your full name?"

'You're really going back down to the surface so soon after catching her scent?' the Oracle questioned as I began filling out the forms. *'I mean, I suppose someone has to tell Lucifer, but—'*

'I am not telling him yet. It's much too early to jump to such conclusions,' I interrupted her. *'If we give him reason to believe it's…them…we won't be able to keep him from sending the entire military to X'shmir in order to reclaim them.'*

"I'm Nalithor Vraelimir," I answered Darius, watching his eyes widen slightly. "First son of Lysander and Ellena Vraelimir—the God and Goddess of Adinvyr, respectively. General, Archmagus, Professor…the list goes on, as they say."

"Wow, *two* demigods in the same room as me?" Darius exclaimed. "This is unreal! Ari is going to be *so* cross that she missed out on this."

"Unlike you, your sister at least listens to our lessons!" Fraelfnir spat, glaring at his ward. *"Had you spent more time paying attention to our teachings instead of the false teachings of the Human scum, you wouldn't be so surprised!"*

I paused, staring at the white fae-dragon in disbelief. Fraelfnir had always been so calm and doting whenever our paths crossed in the past during Darius' brief visits to see his sister in Dauthrmir. Never before had I heard this particular fae-dragon raise his voice—unlike his dark, hotheaded brother.

It seemed as if my initial hunch about the prince's education was correct. For some reason, Darius appeared to value the Human teachings over those of his Guardian.

'It's a pity Fraelfnir detests those who are aligned with darkness...' I contemplated while examining the cranky fae-dragon. *'He's always been more informative than Djialkan, but I can't question him in front of Darius.'*

"You seem close to your sister," Eyrian remarked. His thoughts made me tense when they reached me; he was concerned that the prince and princess were to wed each other as their parents had.

"She's always been there for me." Darius nodded before frowning. "Unfortunately, she's *really* ill and there isn't anything I can do for her... Fraelfnir and Djialkan have tried but it isn't something they're capable of healing."

'I get the feeling he isn't lying.' I nudged the barriers around Darius' mind once more. *'Not directly, anyway. Just what kind of "ill" does he mean? Tch. The common tongue can be so confusing and indirect.*

'Alas, he didn't deny Eyrian's assumption. The princess and the mage are the same person, then? I can't imagine the boy is quite that *airheaded.'*

"Hmmm..." Darius' frown deepened before he nudged the fae-dragon on his shoulder. "Fraelfnir. Door and barrier, please, since *she* isn't here to do it.

"Nalithor, I would like you to take off your mask and hood, please. My people may be insistent on this outdated tradition, but I rather hate it."

The prince's sudden change in demeanor intrigued me, so I decided to relent out of pure curiosity. I simply dismissed my mask and overrobe into my shrizar and watched a stunned expression form on the boy's face. Darius stared at me for a moment before turning to his fae-dragon companion, visibly struggling to speak to the creature through telepathy.

'I think he recognized you,' the Oracle began slowly. *'The girl may not be here, but her shields on his mind are damned strong. I can't get through them.*

'Her shields shouldn't be this strong if she is all the way over in the Sihix Forest.'

'Either that, or whatever is in the sky is fucking with us,' Eyrian snorted his indignation. *'I'm not even the deity here and this shit is suspicious to me. Nalithor, just how bad of a situation have we found ourselves in?'*

'I can't determine,' I replied with a grimace, examining Darius and Fraelfnir again as they continued to speak to each other through telepathy. *'It's in our best interests—and theirs—to get them out of X'shmir as soon as possible. The boy is trying to hide it, but he is desperate to get away from here.*

'The Umbral Mage looked as if she's on the verge of defeat—a much different mindset than the reports described. I haven't seen such a hollow expression on a mage's face since...'

'Not since Vorpmasia rescued hundreds from the fringe countries over a hundred years ago?' The Oracle nodded and then took a puff of her

pipe. *'I sensed it when she got pissed off earlier. That initial bloodlust was aimed at the King and Queen—not the beasts. There was more behind her rage than just anger.'*

"Are there texts I can read regarding the Vorpmasians' treatment of Astral and Umbral Mages?" Darius leaned forward in his seat, his expression eager. "I want to find some way to change things here for my Umbral Mage, or at least find a loophole that will allow her to follow *your* ways while we attend the academy.

"She's really pretty, I'll have you know! Before she came into her powers everyone likened her to a porcelain doll. It's such a shame she has to hide how she looks all of the time."

"Even you can't order her to reveal her face?" My frown deepened when Darius shook his head in reply. "I apologize, that is very strange to me. We have experience with other countries that once followed similar ways to X'shmir. However, their Astral Mages could order the Umbrals to do...anything. In every capacity of the word."

"I would offer you books on the subject, but *she* has the only copies." Darius shrugged, his voice tinged with exasperation. "X'shmiran ways are extreme."

"I could always contact her," Fraelfnir snorted from the prince's shoulder, *"After you so rudely dismissed her, I doubt she would come back unless—"*

"I see Fraelfnir hasn't changed much," Eyrian remarked dryly, eyes focused on the tetchy white creature. "I'm assuming your brother hasn't changed much either has he, Fraelfnir?"

"He has grown worse!" Fraelfnir exclaimed. *"However, I cannot blame him with how his ward is treated in X'shmir. I am half a mind to devour these fools myself."*

'Even Fraelfnir wants them dead?' I shot the muttering dragon a skeptical glance. *'That can't be a good sign at all. A light-aspect Guardian doesn't often have such murderous desires.'*

"Before we wander farther off topic, Your Highness." I conjured a series of crystal orbs on the table between us. "Your test is simple; fill each of these with as much of your power as you can."

"That's it?" Darius asked with a delighted laugh. "Oh, that's so easy!"

Golden light, chunks of stone, clear water, and pale yellow lightning popped into existence inside the spheres, warping and twisting in their desire to free themselves. The boy placed no buffer between the water and lightning, forcing me to use my own power to prevent the explosion opposing elements would have caused.

It took only a matter of seconds for Darius' power to fizzle out, but he had a proud look on his face as if he expected us to praise him for "doing well."

"That's all; you can go back to the negotiations." The Oracle nodded as she shooed Darius off, causing the boy to pout at us before obliging.

"That was fucking terrible," Eyrian pointed out once he was certain the prince was beyond earshot. "Nonexistent control and stamina aside—*four* elements? Just how much power does he have?"

"More than he should." I glanced down at the device in my left hand and examined the readings wearily. "Compared to the pressure his Umbral Mage exerted whilst fighting, Darius feels powerless. Yet the Umbral Mage only revealed three elements. We should assume she has *at least* a fourth if they are indeed siblings."

"He has the power of an *Upper God*?!" The Oracle ripped the device from my hand and read it for herself. "That can't be right! Did you break your equipment while chasing that girl?"

"It was in my shrizar." I glared at the Oracle and then reclaimed the equipment, packing it away from whence it came. "With that much power and so little control, I'm surprised that he hasn't blown this rock out of the sky.

"I'm returning to Dauthrmir. See to it that they are both brought to the surface as soon as possible. You have three months. If you haven't succeeded in your negotiations with X'shmir by then, I will return and take them from here by force."

Before they could question me, I stormed out of the castle and into the frigid winter air outside, summoning my mask and cloak into place as I walked. I couldn't think straight in that place. Not with *her* scent clinging to everything. That intoxicating musky jasmine-vanilla scent permeated everything so thickly that I felt as if I wouldn't be able to cleanse it from my clothes and hair…and I wasn't sure anymore if I would want to.

'Still, they shouldn't be Lucifer's twins.' I fidgeted with my robes, restless, as I made my way to the western plateau and our waiting ships.

'I may not have gotten a good look at the Umbral Mage, but Darius is clearly Human aside from the fangs, ears, and slit pupils. Getting him away from the rest enough of the Humans was enough to prove that.

'Is my sanity finally slipping?'

I glanced up with a slight pause in my step as a thick wall of bloodlust hit me. That woman was killing something again and I could hear its screams all the way from the city's gates. Her fury was on par with what I would have expected from a scorned Adinvyr woman.

Despite breaking into a full run, Arianna and her Guardian had both disappeared back into the Sihix Forest before I could catch a glimpse of either of them.

"Rely'ric." A soldier bowed to me as I strode toward the minced remains of a Chaos Beast. "That woman *can't* be Human. I don't care what the X'shmirans claim."

"She did this?" I arched an eyebrow at the soldier, removed my mask, lowered my hood, and then crouched beside shards of splintered bone and chunks of putrid meat. "With *what*, exactly?"

"Her hands," a second soldier stated, throwing his hands into the air. "Coated her arms up to the elbow in ice and went to town ripping the damned thing apart. The fae-dragon used his power to keep the blood from touchin' her—so I guess we shouldn't worry about the beast's blood making her ill."

"Had a mighty bad bruise on her cheek though, the poor thing." A female soldier sighed. "In the shape of a fist, too. Someone punched her real hard."

'*Someone* punched *her?*' I asked myself in disbelief before glancing toward the Sihix forest and reaching out to her Guardian. '*Djialkan, who had the gall to hit her when she's capable of doing* this *to a beast?*'

'*The king.*' Djialkan chuckled when I bristled. '*You may have a fancy title now but you haven't changed at all, Nalithor.*

"*You are leaving already?*'

'*The boy's tests require further analysis so that I can determine if my equipment is broken,*' I spoke with displeasure and strode in the direction of my personal ship. The fae-dragon's knowing snicker made me twitch. '*Besides, your ward has made it clear she doesn't wish to speak with me. I wanted to learn of the X'shmiran beasts from her, but—*'

'You *are not the problem!*' Djialkan chortled, causing me to hesitate mid-stride. '*However, it is true that she is the one you must speak to for such information. I will give my recommendation to Darius. Having her ordered to share her knowledge with the Vorpmasians is a simple matter.*

'*Tread carefully, Nalithor. I am sure I do not have to explain to you why.*'

Djialkan was correct; he didn't need to explain the reasons why I should be careful. There were plenty of reasons for me to take care in my approach. Aside from her shaky mental state as a mage bound by Old Ways, her unknown identity posed other problems.

If she was truly the Arianna from my past, reincarnated into the present, she would have no memory of her previous life with me in Dauthrmir. Nor would she know of me rescuing her soul from Limbo.

If, for some reason, the Elders had lied to me and *this* Arianna was the same as the one from my past…that created even more problems. I wasn't sure which the worst option was: that, or the threat that she might be a "fake" created by the Exiled Gods.

'Have you already retreated too far into Sihix?' I hesitated, glancing toward the towering crystal trees to my northwest.

'You are not still *thinking of pursuing her through—'* Djialkan began in frustration.

'No, it isn't that,' I responded with a sad smile. *'I would like you to give her something for me.'*

'…fine. I will be there to fetch it in a moment.' Djialkan relented, much to my surprise.

I leaned back against the side of my airship and waited, ignoring the soldiers who questioned me. Djialkan sounded exasperated when he spoke, and he wasn't known for being "reasonable." *'He must care greatly for his ward if he's willing to cooperate with me.'*

Several minutes passed before the small black dragon appeared. Even for him he looked terribly grumpy. He frowned at me when I procured a large box from my shrizar, with a smaller box placed on top of it.

"What are you up to, Nalithor?" Djialkan asked as he floated closer and the grabbed the lid of the smaller box with his talons, lifting it so he could peer inside. *"Magitech? I do not recognize the design."*

"I get the feeling that her life as an Umbral Mage keeps her rather secluded," I replied with a slight shake of my head before motioning with my free hand at the box. "She doesn't get to listen to music much, does she? That box contains 'headphones.' They're for listening to recordings of music."

"*They are yours.*" Djialkan sniffed at the box and then closed the lid, sneezing.

"I can quite easily get another pair for myself when I return." I shrugged. "It is a very long trip to and from X'shmir, Djialkan. It is much simpler to give her mine."

"*The second box, then?*" Djialkan inquired after nodding his understanding and placing the smaller box into Arianna's *shrizar*.

'*He has access to her shrizar? Just how bad is her situation here? For her to believe it's necessary that someone else has access...*' I eyed the dark rift floating beside the fae-dragon and then shifted my attention to him when he coughed pointedly. "Medicinal supplies for her to share with the people of Sihix, along with instructions on how to use them. Darius-zir made a comment about Arianna being ill—but apparently the King and Queen don't think it's necessary for us to heal her."

"*Of course they don't.*" Djialkan's mutter dripped with venom. "*Has your role as a deity made you soft, Nalithor? I would have thought Vorpmasia sought to conquer this country.*"

'*He didn't deny that Arianna and the Umbral Mage are the same person.*' I narrowed my eyes at the fae-dragon.

Djialkan was intelligent; I was positive that he knew I was fishing for information, and yet he didn't play along with the theme the X'shmirans seemed determined to establish. Either he didn't know that the X'shmirans were trying to make the princess and the Umbral Mage seem like different people, or he was giving me subtle information.

"I won't deny that the King and Queen tempted me to rip X'shmir out of the sky," I growled, earning a chortle from Djialkan. "My instincts as a god are telling me to wait, so I am going to wait."

"You still have a soft spot for Arianna." Djialkan shook his head at me before shifting into the form of a small boy and reaching up for the box with an expectant expression on his face. *"Still, you look like you have something to ask. I will reward your generosity to my ward and to Sihix by answering one question."*

"The crest on her robes—whose doing was that?" I inquired, surprising a laugh from Djialkan. "Come now, Djialkan. I know there are some questions you *can't* answer *because* you're her Guardian."

"The High Priestess of Sihix designed Arianna's crest." Djialkan laughed, shook his head, and then grinned briefly before closing the shrizar and shifting back to his draconic form. *"We were both quite startled when we saw your crest, so I can understand your curiosity.*

"Ah—the High Priestess is an Oracle that once lived in Vorpmasia. The people of Sihix still worship the gods, even if the X'shmirans do not."

"Will *she* be alright?" I sighed and ran my hand through my bangs and back between my horns. "The Old Ways are notoriously—"

"As long as she does not run out of Chaos Beasts to kill she will be fine," Djialkan interjected dryly before glancing towards Sihix with a wistful expression. *"Killing beasts is the only time I've seen her happy in the past twenty or so years. Alas…flying through the Mists in my full dragon form is impossible. I am incapable of rescuing her from this place myself.*

"Again, thank you for your generosity, Nalithor. I will give her your gift when she wakes."

I nodded to the fae-dragon and then watched him twist through the air in the direction of the Sihix Forest. Djialkan's words concerned me, but, I knew there was nothing I could do right now. My role as a god meant I had to be cautious. I couldn't just go storming into an Aledacian Forest in search of a woman that *might* be Arianna.

Still, even if she wasn't the same woman, no Umbral Mage deserved the treatment these disgusting Humans seemed intent on bestowing.

'If it is *her...'* I thought with unease as I settled into a seat inside the airship. *'There are only so many reasons I can think of that would make her run from* me *of all people.*

'Does she think we abandoned her here?'

My heart ached at the thought. Finding her again in Limbo twenty years ago had been a painful experience. Her memories of our childhood together had been shattered and her head had been filled with false memories—some of which were little better than nightmares. Her captors had tried, and failed, to drive her mad. I had made sure to scrub the vile false memories from her soul before releasing her to the Elders. Something told me to keep that information from the Elder Gods, and so I had.

'Her memories were destroyed.' I paused, staring blankly at the violet sky beyond my window while letting the thought sink in. *'Ahhh... That* is *a problem now isn't it? If this is really the Arianna I knew, she* still

wouldn't remember anything before being taken from Lucifer and me.

'She may not even realize she was running from her former partner.

'She...probably doesn't even remember her time in Limbo, or me rescuing her. Though that may be for the best.'

CHAPTER TEN
Gifts

I failed to cover a wide yawn as I strode through a small town deep within the Sihix Forest, searching for something to do. The nightmares were becoming more frequent. I needed to distract myself somehow. Most of the villagers were busy with their daily tasks, leaving me with one option left: the summons to Sihix's temple that I had received.

Although X'shmir and the surrounding lands had been cut off for so long, the people in the Sihix Forest had never stopped worshiping the gods or leaving offerings at the temple. It might have even been the first building built in the small town known as Auvry'e, and it was certainly the oldest. The temple also served as home to Sihix's High Priestess and the forest's Guardians.

"You sent for me, Corentine?" I glanced to either side at the horse-sized foxes who were watching me. *'What in the hells? I smell* him *here, but it's faint. Did that fool disregard the Alliance's agreement with X'shmir?'*

Before I could slip away, the female fox, Shir, grabbed me by the back of my robes and lifted me clear off the ground. She warbled around the mouthful of leather and carried me through the temple's wooden hallways. Despite my protests, Shir refused to set me down. Gari's claws clicked along the floor somewhere behind us as he followed me and his mate. Clearly he wouldn't be of much help to me either.

I shot Corentine a filthy glare the moment Shir carried me into a room at the back of the temple. Embroidered cushions littered the floor and various potted plants from the forest outside sat on almost every surface aside from the seating area. The High Priestess looked quite pleased with herself. Her jet-black vulpine ears flicked forward as she shot me a grin and her twin fox tails flopped around behind her in excitement. A small motion from Corentine resulted in Shir dropping me unceremoniously onto a pile of cushions.

"Sit, Ari," Corentine stated with another grin, pointing at the cushions Shir had dropped me on. "Djialkan went back to X'shmir to speak with Fraelfnir, so you're all ours for a little while."

"What do you want? Why does it smell like *that one* in here?" I questioned, pouting as I pulled myself into a cross-legged position and grasped my ankles.

"Ah, Djialkan didn't leave you a note?" Corentine cocked her head at me as the Guardians laid down on either said of me. "Your deity friend saw fit to entrust Djialkan with gifts for you and for all of us here in Auvry'e. You probably smell the case that Djialkan left with me."

"Gifts?" I frowned before glancing to my sides at the foxes; they were staring at me in an expectant matter, and I couldn't quite understand why.

"Aye, *he* gifted us with all manner of medicines, bandages, and other such heal-y things." Corentine nodded a little too seriously before taking a puff from her long pipe. "Instructions on how to use all of it, too."

'Gifts, huh?' I glanced in the direction Corentine pointed, finding an unfamiliar box resting on a nearby shelf. *'I don't sense him on the island anymore. He seemed rather intent on gaining an audience with Sihix—and with me. So, why did he leave already?'*

"We need a favor out of you, Ari," Corentine spoke bluntly, drawing my attention back to her. "The supplies he gave us were very powerful. Everyone in the village wants to show him their gratitude— and send letters to the families they left behind when they became part of Sihix."

"You want me to play deliverywoman?" I sighed and reached out to scratch both Shir and Gari's cheeks. "What happened to keeping me trapped here until my rage subsided? You also mentioned something about a gift for me."

"Djialkan left it in your shrizar but that can wait." Corentine pointed her pipe at me. "The more immediate problem is what Sihix and I have Seen. You need to stay away from the city for the next several months, Ari."

"What about the beasts?" I pouted in irritation before looking down at Shir as she shifted to rest her massive head on my lap. "You know I have no qualms with staying in Sihix for extended periods. That said, I can see on your face that you're nervous about something else. Spit it out."

"It's about Aurelian, Elise, and Sebastian's gifts for you." Corentine sighed at me when I tensed and glared at her. "You need to accept their gifts and begin training with them as soon as possible. Djialkan told you how to open the case their gifts are stored in, didn't he?"

Aurelian and Elise, the God and Goddess of War, had entrusted a platinum case to Djialkan a long time ago. It was something I found myself disinclined to open. I wasn't sure *exactly* when they had given it to my companion for safekeeping, but I knew it was from some time before we arrived in X'shmir.

I knew very little about the contents of the smooth platinum box. Engraved on one side was a crest identical to the one on my robes and, for the life of me, I had no idea where the seam for the lid was. It may as well have been a solid ingot.

According to Djialkan and Corentine, inside of it were items Aurelian and Elise wanted me to have—likely weapons or armor, judging by the way Djialkan had spoken of the box in the past. That

Sebastian, the God of Chaos, chose to include something as well was what concerned me most.

"Training, you say?" I looked away from the foxes and back to Corentine, narrowing my eyes at her when she nodded. "You're saying that I have more fighting than usual to deal with soon, then?"

"You know I can't give you any precise details about my visions," Corentine began with an irritated huff. "Suffice to say that you will lose everything you care about if you are incapable of wielding the gifts the gods gave you."

"What about helping Sihix?" I countered as I leaned forward to argue. "I still haven't found a way to heal the forest, and I've lent Sihix so much of my own—!"

"After you've opened that box," Corentine interjected and raised a finger into the air, "*you* are taking back all of your power. We've already called your creations back to the village. They're assembling outside the temple.

"Don't worry about Sihix. Now, accept Aurelian, Elise, and Sebastian's gifts before I *make* you open it!"

I shot Corentine an irritated glare and then willed my shrizar open. With a resigned sigh, I reached into it with one hand and then pulled out the platinum case. A small grimace crossed my face when I felt the warm, smooth surface of the box. It always struck me as strange that the metal was warm—almost hot—to the touch. The damned thing hummed so loudly with magic that both Shir and Gari shook their heads in discomfort before inching several feet away from me. Both

Guardians kept their eyes trained on me as if they expected me to dart off when they weren't looking.

The box felt heavy in my lap. I couldn't keep the sour expression off my face as I examined the pair of lotus crests. Corentine's giggling didn't help matters. In the past, I had never paid much attention to the second crest but, now, after having crossed paths with that deity, I couldn't ignore it. With them etched side-by-side it was impossible to deny that the lotus portion of the crests were identical.

"Did Djialkan mention why *that one* left already?" I turned the platinum case over in my hands a few times, searching for any hint of a seam or opening mechanism.

"Something about needing to analyze magical aptitude tests they ran your brother through." Corentine half-shrugged. "Apparently he needs to determine if his equipment is broken.

"Djialkan also got the impression that our deity friend saw or heard something troubling while observing the negotiations."

'That doesn't exactly help. There's plenty of troubling matters in X'shmir,' I mused, running my fingers over the crests. *'Really though, did they have to make my crest so similar to his? Tch.'*

I continued grumbling my displeasure under my breath. With two simple motions I summoned darkness in my left hand and cobalt flames in my right. The draconic crest drank my shadows with startling fervor, causing me to raise an eyebrow at it—an expression Corentine seemed to find hilarious, judging by her cackling. By comparison, *my* crest was lazy in its consumption of flames.

"The crests are linked to us?" I looked at Corentine and then back at the engravings, watching as both shadow and fire mingled together. "I won't pretend to know much about deities, but should he really be *that* hungry?"

"Awww, you're so cute!" Corentine teased, reaching out to squeeze my cheeks. "Barely even remember him and you're already concerned about him? That's so sweet!"

"Don't make me regret cooperating with you." I growled at her. "*Stop squeezing me!*"

I scooted out of her reach and then glanced down when I heard an audible click from the platinum box. The lid slid open and, before I could even try to question its contents, everything contained within dissolved into opaque darkness and rushed up my arms to disappear beneath my robes. I yelped, tumbled backwards off my cushions, and swatted at different sections of my body. The darkness was hot to the touch and felt like it was latching into place around varying sections of my body: wrists, arms, fingers, ankles, and waist just to name a few.

"Eh? I jingle?" I paused mid-swat and looked down at my pale wrist. Several platinum bangles and delicate chain bracelets now hung from around my wrist, and I knew damn well they hadn't been there before. Sapphire-like crystals dotted each piece of jewelry and they hummed with aetheric power. I'd never been allowed to have much in the way of jewelry, let alone so many pieces of it, so it was a new sensation to me. "What...?"

"Now you look like a proper demigoddess!" Corentine grinned and clapped her hands together in delight. "Don't give me that look, Ari. You know as well as I do you aren't normal—in the best of ways of course, I assure you!

"Now then! Shir, Gari, let's make sure she takes back all her power, hmm?"

"Sh-Shir! I can *walk* you know!" I yelped as the enormous female fox grabbed the back of my coat again. "I'm not one of your kits! Put me down! I can—"

I shot Shir's mate a begging look as he passed us but he just warbled in response. He had a mirthful look in his lavender eyes which just made me pout and protest more. Corentine grinned and patted Shir's shoulder a few times, walking in stride with us as the Guardian hauled me outside.

A quick glance at the small cobblestone plaza outside showed me that many of the forests citizens were present. Not just the shadowy foxes I had conjured years ago.

"Oh good. You've all finished with your letters and the like?" Corentine questioned, motioning for Shir to drop me again. "I have something I want you to deliver too, Ari. First things first though— take your power back."

"All of it?" I shot her a begrudging pout and pulled myself to my feet. "You're certain Sihix will be fine without my help for a while?"

"He'll be *fine*, Ari." Corentine sighed in exasperation and nudged me toward the dozens of shadowy foxes. "As for the rest of you, let's get everything situated in something that'll fit in her shrizar. We don't want to trouble Arianna too much, hmm?"

I watched Corentine stride past me and toward the waiting villagers. A quick glance at the cheerful people of Sihix told me just how much that deity's gifts meant to them, and made it clear just how powerful the medicines he brought to us were. There were people present who I hadn't seen out of their beds in years. Everyone seemed fine, fit, and happy. They were chatting more cheerfully than I had seen in a long time—some because they were healed of their ailments and others because a god had paid attention to them after two centuries of silence.

The Devillians, in particular, seemed elated.

"Alright you lot…" I murmured and crouched among the pack of dark foxes. "Let's see what Corentine is on about."

It made me a little sad to see my vulpine creations disappear but I knew that Corentine must have Seen something worrisome if she insisted I needed to retrieve my power. The Sihix Forest had been losing its magic for centuries and I had patched the problem by lending it some of my power in the form of roaming foxes so that they could protect the forest and its people. Doing so gave me the time to look for what was stealing power from Sihix but thus far I'd been unsuccessful.

The people there believed that the sky was "eating" Sihix's power, and I couldn't deny their theory. Every time Sihix lost a little more of its magic the glowing energy from one of the dark crystalline trees shot into the sky and disappeared. It was nothing like the gradual fade of aether in other living things.

"Where do you want me to take all of this to?" I turned and strode toward Corentine, the villagers, and the Guardians before motioning at a massive wooden box someone had summoned. The villagers had almost filled to the brim already. "You said you didn't want me going back to the city, after all, so I'm assuming you have something else in mind."

"The Vorpmasian ships on the plateau." Corentine shrugged, opened her own shrizar, withdrew a dark crystal and then offered it to me. "You should find my sister there when you arrive. She's a Rylthra like me—except she's got strawberry blonde hair and fur. We have the same eyes and the same loud mouth though."

"So she should be easy to find," I commented with a crooked grin. "Very well, I'll come back when I'm done.

"You said I need to learn how to use these gifts? They're more than just jewelry then?"

I raised one hand and wriggled my fingers in front of Corentine's face, earning a laugh. The jewelry was eye-catching and I found the design was similar to what I had seen *him* wearing previously. Except mine was studded with sapphires that matched my eyes, and the overall design was much more feminine.

"Each of the crystals stores a different piece of armor or weapons forged by Aurelian and Elise." Corentine grasped my hand in hers and used her free hand to point at a large sapphire on my index finger. "You should be able to feel them out with your power while you head for the airships—I'm sure you've already noticed the hum of aether in them.

"Just be careful while you're outside of Sihix, okay? Don't let Darius lure you back to the city. We have important work to do when you get back."

"I'll be careful," I replied with a small tilt of my head, examining Corentine's concerned expression. "I'm still pissed off at Darius. I don't intend to contact him unless I have to."

Corentine nodded before releasing me and shooing me off. Shrugging, I moved between the villagers and confirmed that everyone had finished before dismissing the box of letters and trinkets into my shrizar. Shir and Gari trailed close behind me as I began walking away from the village and through the obsidian underbrush. A brief glance over my shoulder revealed stern expressions on both their faces. They were my escort to the forest's edge no doubt.

In many ways, Auvry'e was in a better state than the city I grew up in. X'shmir was crumbling, collapsed in places, with many more building threatening to topple. Without assistance from the Rilzaan Alliance, I doubted X'shmir would be inhabitable for much longer. Fifty years at best.

Auvry'e, on the other hand, was all new construction aside from the temple. My fights against the Chaos Beast beyond Sihix tended to be violent, and the beasts often tore up the earth or uprooted normal trees in their desperation to destroy me. As a child I had decided to bring such materials to the people of Sihix so they could build proper shelters. Due to their bond with the forest, they couldn't wander far enough from it to forage for materials themselves.

"Ah, before I forget..." I murmured, came to a stop, and looked at Gari when he nosed me. "Hold on, you two. I should really see what *his* gift for me is, shouldn't I? It would be quite rude if I was the only one that didn't offer my thanks."

The two foxes exchanged a look, huffed at me, and then laid down at my feet once I perched on a boulder. I bit back a yawn as I opened my shrizar and then began searching for anything that "felt" unfamiliar. It didn't take long; *his* scent clung so strongly to the box that my nose wrinkled in reply. While I found his scent pleasant, and oddly alluring, I wasn't the only one who found it strong. I couldn't help but laugh when Shir sneezed several times and then glared at the box.

"Hmm, what's this?" I questioned mostly to myself, lifting the lid off the box and then examining the foreign half-circle of black material. Baffled, I picked up a note that looked like it was scribbled by Djialkan. "Magitech? Called 'headphones?'"

Intrigued, I lifted the headphones from the box and ran my fingers over the inlays of variegated blue crystal, and then across the cushions at either end of the curved contraption. We had very little Magitech in X'shmir, and nothing looked like the "headphones." Everything we had was from long before X'shmir was cut off from the rest of Avrirsa.

The X'shmiran castle, for example, had functional Magitech lights that we could turn on with a brief touch. However, many of those lights had fallen into disrepair and were long since replaced with candles or oil lamps. The same went for the lights in the city proper— except almost none of those still functioned.

It was probably a minor miracle that any of the plumbing systems and kitchens in X'shmir still worked, honestly. Almost everyone in X'shmir, regardless of class or their opinions of non-Humans, hoped that our contact with foreign powers would allow us to repair or replace all of the dysfunctional Magitech.

"Recordings of music?" A slight frown formed on my lips as I looked over the smooth black band again before lifting it up and sniffing slightly. "Humph. He must've noticed us watching him play his violin after all.

"What do you think, Shir, Gari? They smell like him don't they?"

I dangled the headphones in front of the Guardian foxes, watching them sniff at it with curiosity. Their approving warbles, chirps, and excited flips of their tails made me raise an eyebrow at them. Shaking my head, I returned the headphones to my lap and then ran my fingers along the band again in search of a way to turn them on. I couldn't deny that I was curious despite *his* scent clinging to them and to the box that housed them. Anything that gave me access to music was a welcome addition to my small collection of belongings.

Mumbling to myself, I lifted them up until they were level with my face. I finally found the correct switch and flipped them on. The sudden blast of music that blared from the two ends startled me to the point I almost dropped the headphones on the ground, but I managed to catch them and then searched for a way to make them quieter.

After several more minutes of trial and error, I figured out what each of the buttons did and then draped the headphones around my neck. Curious, I searched the box again and found another slip of parchment; this one was *not* written by Djialkan.

The language written on the paper was Draemiran—the language of Adinvyr. Djialkan, Fraelfnir, and some of the female Adinvyr in the Sihix forest had taught me the language over the years, but many of the words on the slip of paper were unfamiliar to me. Pursing my lips, I ran a finger down the numbered list and examined the words. Some sounded like they were names or titles, whilst the strings of words on the right side were all phrases or single words that I could understand with ease.

"Number five hundred forty-seven..." I tilted my head again, aware the Guardians wouldn't or couldn't respond to me. "Those syllables are... Dra-tae-mir? That could mean 'city,' 'city of' or 'house of' depending on how it's enunciated—right?" I glanced at the foxes who, to my surprise, nodded. "Oh, maybe—"

I pulled the headphones from my neck again and prodded a section of crystal that seemed to cycle through songs. Once "547" was displayed on the right side of the headphones, I brought them up to my ears and listened. The song's lyrics were all in Draemiran and accompanied by instruments I didn't recognize. However, it wasn't long before I caught the word "Drataemir" sung by one of the male vocalists. I still didn't know what it meant, so I would have to pester someone in Sihix or perhaps Djialkan for information later.

"So, the left column must be the performers and the right column is the name of the song." I nodded to myself. "Well, that makes it simpler. Shir, Gari, do you mind waiting a moment so I can write my thanks?"

The pair shook their heads and then nuzzled my legs, so I settled the headphones behind my neck once more and then summoned a stack of parchment from my shrizar, followed by a pen. After brief consideration I dismissed the box and its accompanying notes before staring at the paper before me. I had no idea how to address *him*.

'Djialkan,' I reached out and mentally nudged the fae-dragon a few times, catching a hint of his grumpiness as soon as our minds touched. *'I take it you're dealing with both our brothers?'*

'It is a shame your twin does not have more meat on his bones,' Djialkan snarled. *'As much as I would like to devour him, I find myself doubting whether or not we could make a proper broth from his remains.'*

'Fraelfnir provides just as little,' I teased, earning a snort of laughter from Djialkan. *'Still, this provides me with an opportunity. I need Darius' permission to speak with the Vorpmasian men and women around the airships.*

'Corentine has me playing deliverywoman. I have a sizable crate of letters and gifts that the people of Sihix wish to send to their families in Vorpmasia—and to him.*'*

'Ah, yes I can see your dilemma,' Djialkan acknowledged with a chortle. *'You need permission to speak with them, and you need*

information on how to address "him," *then? If only your brother was so polite. One moment.'*

I twirled my pen around my fingers and waited for Djialkan to finish conversing with our brothers. The music from the headphones kept me from being too bored and I soon found myself tapping my foot in time with the beat.

Having to get Darius' permission to speak with others was an absolute pain in my ass. He seemed intent on only allowing me to speak with my soldiers, Djialkan, and people within the Sihix Forest. Originally, he had attempted to keep me from speaking with the people of Sihix as well, but Djialkan had thrown such a fit that my brother had been forced to relent.

In many ways, Sihix—and Auvry'e—were more my home than X'shmir had ever been. Although I loved my brother, it was next to impossible for me to deal with him. He was so fervent in his belief of the X'shmiran teachings that it made it near impossible for us to see eye-to-eye on most matters.

The X'shmiran Court saw me as Darius' bodyguard, not as his sister. My purpose was to keep Darius and our country safe—that was it. And that mindset was a large part of the overall problems we both had.

'You will not speak with Darius?' Djialkan asked a few minutes later, so I grumbled my confirmation. *'The Vorpmasians have offered for the both of you to attend the Dauthrmiran Academy of Martial Science.*

'Somehow Darius and Fraelfnir have convinced the King and Queen

to allow it—*if you agree to go with him and keep him safe from the perceived "foreign threats."'*

My lips parted in surprise and I dropped my pen. All I could do was blink a few times as I attempted to process what Djialkan said. We had a chance to go *Below*, and the King Bastard and the Queen Bitch were willing to allow it? Was this why Corentine insisted I remain in Sihix and train for the next few months?

'We would have access to the academy's library, right?' I questioned, continuing once Djialkan confirmed, *'In that case, I'd have to be a special level of foolish not to agree. You know as well as I do that we've exhausted our resources in X'shmir.*

'Tell my brother I accept. You can regale me with the details of "when" later.'

'He said you have permission to speak with the Vorpmasians around the airships,' Djialkan replied after a few more minutes of silence. *'He is quite miffed that you will not speak with him. Am I correct in assuming Corentine has something to do with this?'*

'Corentine Saw "something" and insisted that I shouldn't let Darius lure me back to the city,' I replied with distaste, earning a low growl from the fae-dragon. *'I intend to keep our connection cut off until it's "safe."*

'Now, as far as that *one goes—?'*

'Take a look through the letters that our comrades are sending,' Djialkan ordered in a contemplative tone. *'Let me know if you see any addressed with the honorifics of -y'ric or Rely'ric.'*

'Rely'ric, -y'ric...' I mumbled, summoning the crate and then digging through the pile of envelopes. "Rehl-yeer-ick. Yeer-ick. That is the equivalent of 'my lord,' right, Shir, Gari?"

Again the foxes warbled their confirmation and I grinned at their nodding heads. Not being able to speak with them mind-to-mind could be bothersome at times, but their attempts at miming their way through a conversation never ceased to amuse me. They were damned adorable even if they were the size of horses. I couldn't wait for Shir to have her second litter of kits—assuming she gave birth to them in my lifetime anyway.

'Vraelimir doesn't sound like a first name,' I called to Djialkan in a conversational tone, fanning a few letters out between my fingers. 'Isn't -y'ric usually used as a suffix-styled honorific, Djialkan? Tacked onto the first name, not the last?'

'Aye, the ones improperly labeled are probably from the non-Devillian citizens of Auvry'e,' Djialkan answered with a small huff. 'Do any of them use his first name? You should be able to figure that out, at least, since you know the first four characters of his name.'

I made a sour face in response to the unhelpful comment and blatant "hinting" before returning to my search through the pile of letters. 'All of them say Rely'ric, Vraelimir, or Vraelimir-y'ric.'

'Utilize one of those then. Corentine obviously informed the people who their "savior" was,' Djialkan stated, his voice dripping with sarcasm. 'We can't have him growing more suspicious of you after all. It would be a little strange if you called him "Nali" without him having remembered to *introduce himself.'*

'*Alright, thanks,'* I muttered and then picked up my pen. '*How are negotiations going anyway? I assume Darius has tortured you with the details* at least *four times by now.'*

'*The Vorpmasians are being unusually patient with the X'shmirans,'* Djialkan answered warily. '*I doubt two hundred years is enough to have tamed their tempers or their bloodlust. The way the nobles and royals are treating the non-Human visitors should have ended negotiations quite some time ago.'*

'*So you think they want or are looking for something in particular?'* I paused my writing. '*I wonder if it has anything to do with* his *desire to speak with Sihix. That was a pretty strange request.*

'*Will you be staying in X'shmir much longer, Djialkan? If not, I would like your assistance with Aurelian's rather shiny gifts. I sense a rather detestable item within one of the jewels.'*

'*You* finally *conceded!'* Djialkan sounded genuinely pleased. '*I will be along shortly. I had hoped to borrow some Vorpmasian texts from the boy here, but it would seem the X'shmirans still intend to keep him from such tomes.'*

I murmured my acknowledgment as the connection faded, then returned my attention to penning the letter of thanks. It ended up being several pages longer than expected but I decided to go with it. I conjured an envelope to slip the parchment into, sealed it, and then added it to the crate.

Shir and Gari leapt to their feet with eager chirps when I stood up.

Both of them started nuzzling me again while I attempted to pull a Magitech mask on.

"You're making this difficult you know!" I laughed at them when I nearly dropped the mask. "Stay a decent ways inside the forest, alright? I won't have any cheeky beasts snatching either of you two up."

They both nodded and fell into step with me as I raced through the underbrush anew. They followed me up through Sihix's massive boughs and towards the edge of the plateau. The wailing of a beast in pain caught my attention when I leapt higher into one of the trees. I crouched on the thick branch and grimaced at the near fifty feet of snow piled along the surface of the plateau. I would have to go higher to see the source of the wailing.

Shir and Gari obliged me and stayed at least a hundred feet away from the forest's edge as I scaled the tree. Once I was high enough, Sihix extended one of its branches toward the plateau so that I wouldn't have to attempt the long jump I had been considering. I mumbled my thanks to the forest and then dashed along the dimly glowing obsidian branch and onto the plateau. Crouching on the surface of the snow, I checked my surroundings again.

The sickening stench of decay drifted across my senses, causing my lips to pull into a scowl. In the distance, a pair of massive beasts attempted to encroach on the Vorpmasian ships. Another ship was trying to land, but the creatures held no fear—instead, they tried to snatch the contraption from the sky.

Grinning, I shifted my stance and then propelled myself across the surface of the snow at breakneck speed. I prodded around inside the shrizar-like crystals in my jewelry as I ran, searching for suitable weapons and armor. Somehow, I found the jingle of the small bells and charms pleasant. Pushing the thought from my mind, I reached a tendril of thought towards Djialkan—he was still in the city. But, these monsters needed to die.

I hoped that Aurelian's armor would protect me from the blood of the beasts at least.

CHAPTER ELEVEN
Necessity

"Get back!" I roared at the Vorpmasian soldiers. Darkness rippled around me and then solidified to form plate armor and a pair of bladed gauntlets. "Their spines are venomous—stay out of reach of their tails!"

I ignored the soldier's startled looks and leapt into the air to grab the arm of one of the massive monsters. My clawed gauntlet pierced the beast's flesh with a sickening squelch that was soon drowned out by the creature's snarl of pain.

Shadows whirled down my other arm, turning the beast's snarls into shrill screams. The beast I had latched onto tried to grab me but its other arms were too short to reach. Before it could try to shake me off, I plunged my darkness through the creature's shoulder and severed its arm from its body.

"Ma'am?!" a Vorpmasian soldier yelped, looking from me to the fountaining blood and back as I landed into a crouch near him and his men.

"Arianna will suffice." I grinned and then turned to look at the beast, watching its attempts at nursing the gaping wound. Shrugging, I turned to look at the soldier. "I'm the X'shmiran Umbral Mage—Lyur'zi—whatever you want to call me. Our beasts are rather susceptible to darkness. If you have any Shadow or Umbral Mages among your ranks, soldier, you should direct them to fight.

"I'll finish this one. I assume your mages can destroy the second?"

The soldier had a dumbfounded expression on his face as he nodded his confirmation. It was enough acknowledgment for me, so I leapt for the wounded beast again. My bladed gauntlets and darkness tore through the creature with ease, tearing off chunk after chunk of flesh.

Throughout the short-lived fight, I felt the Vorpmasians' eyes on my back. My skin crawled in reply. A few of them tried to steal a glance at my face perhaps, but the hooded cloak and my plate half-helm kept their prying eyes from finding anything. I didn't like the intensity of their stares but I was thankful that my new toys had options befitting a X'shmiran Umbral Mage. It would have been quite awkward if I had broken my own peoples' laws in my haste to arm myself.

"Fight me!" The demanding voice came from a redheaded Devillian male. Bronze horns protruded from above his temples and a matching tail whipped around behind him. He squared off with me, a broad grin set on his face as he raised his hands as if he intended to fistfight me.

"This is hardly the time, Sorr!" a new voice snapped, belonging to a rather distinctive strawberry blonde Rylthra woman. "Honestly! One of these days you Adinvyr need to learn the concept of *timing* when you challenge someone!"

"Sorr, is it?" I made a subtle motion with my index finger, lifted the redheaded Adinvyr off his feet, and then hung him upside down with my darkness. "Aw, you couldn't even sense that coming? You're no fun.

"You there, Rylthra. *You* must be Corentine's sister."

"Coren…" The Rylthra's vulpine ears flattened against her head. "Just what is your business here?"

"Quite simple, actually." I dropped Sorr into the snow and then dismissed my armor and gauntlets, returning to my less imposing mage attire. "The people of Auvry'e—the town within the Sihix Forest— want to express their thanks for the medicinal supplies that Vraelimir-y'ric entrusted to my companion, Djialkan.

"They've asked me to act on their behalf," I paused to summon the large wooden crate from my shrizar, "and they've included gifts they wish their families back in Vorpmasia to receive.

"Corentine is the High Priestess of Sihix now. *This* message is for you."

I pulled the dark crystal out of a second shrizar and then offered it to the startled Rylthra before me. Her two fox tails now hung limp among the folds of her robes, causing the white tips to disappear into the snow beneath us. Although Corentine's fur and hair were raven-colored, everything else about her and her sister was identical. Even their expressions and mannerisms were eerily similar.

"Call me Oracle," the Rylthra stated, finally reaching out to accept the crystal. "Vraelimir-y'ric though? Your pronunciation is perfect but that's his surname, not his—"

"He neglected to properly introduce himself and it's one of the reasons I didn't let him into Sihix," I commented dryly, cocking my head when the Oracle began laughing. "Your sister seemed disinclined to tell us anything beyond his family name."

"Ooh, so *that's* where his headphones went?" The Oracle reached out and tugged on one end of my headphones. "That's just like him though. He's always forgetting to introduce himself when something catches his interest. He didn't stray *too* far towards Sihix, I hope?"

"Bah! He chased me all the way to the edge of the plateau!" I waved a hand dismissively. "Two beasts and some pouting later, Djialkan and I were able to shoo him away. He seemed a little miffed."

"Lyur'zi, this is a lot of letters," a soldier exclaimed, leaning on one side of the crate. "Just how many people *live* in the forest?"

"We have a whole 'nother city's worth of people in Sihix." I shrugged. "Unfortunately, medicines and bandages are things we lack in both Sihix and in X'shmir. Some of the people that received treatment over the past two days hadn't been able to get out of bed in *years.*

"With that said, I'm sure you can imagine why they're this grateful—and insistent."

"I would like to speak with my sister directly," the Oracle stated, crossing her arms as if it would hide how white the knuckles on her crystal-holding hand had become. "Lord Vraelimir relayed to us what Djialkan said. *You* act as a Guardian of Sihix. I'm assuming that *you* are responsible for the five-mile rule."

"Lyur'zi, your crest is—" Another soldier flinched, cutting himself off when the Oracle glared at him.

"Aurelian and Corentine's doing, no doubt!" The Oracle sighed and examined me. "What'll it be, Arianna-tyir?"

'*-tyir?*' I kept my expression passive as I tried to remember the word's meaning, '*I think that's the equivalent of miss, mister... Right?*'

"We can't approach in a direct way." I sighed, tugging at my hood absentmindedly. "Hmmm...this would be much simpler if I could communicate with Shir and Gari."

"Shir and Gari?" the Oracle asked, making me realize I'd been muttering aloud.

"The *actual* Guardians of Sihix," I offered as I crossed my arms and began tapping my foot in thought. "I have an idea but we'll need Djialkan first."

"And where is he?" the Oracle asked, examining me yet again with a strange look on her face.

"On his way," I replied with a slight shake of my head. "He was in

X'shmir speaking with his brother. That said, your men look eager to pack up and leave."

"Due to X'shmir's current location, it will take us nearly a day to fly back to Vorpmasia." A soldier in elaborate plate armor pulled out a map and tapped a location over the blue expanse which took up almost two thirds of the parchment. "We're currently here. If we wait too long, we'll be over a particularly nasty section of the Nrae'lmar Continent when we try to leave—which is mostly unexplored by both the Vorpmasian and Beshulthien Empires.

"The winds over Nrae'lmar make it difficult for our ships to stay in the sky, so we're hoping to leave before that happens."

"Then this is the Rilzaan Continent?" I pointed at the left side of the map, unable to contain my curiosity. "I get the impression that Rilzaan beasts are rather different from X'shmiran ones—elsewise, I don't see why *that one* would have pursued me halfway across X'shmir at a full run just to talk about beasts."

"Just to talk about beasts, is it?" the Oracle asked with an indignant snort before shaking her head and then tapping a claw on my nose. "X'shmiran beasts are absolutely disgusting compared to the ones native to Rilzaan. The ones here are like...like a mish-mashed conglomeration of corpses.

"Rilzaan beasts are just as violent, certainly, but their construction makes more sense. They're like animals. *Really angry animals.* And they certainly aren't *rotting.*"

"*Arianna, wouldn't removing the damned thing's heart have been enough?"* Djialkan chastised me as he swooped down from the sky and landed on my shoulder. *"Ah, an Oracle. Lovely. As if Corentine wasn't enough of a hassle."*

"She would like to speak with her *sister*," I informed Djialkan, reaching up to scratch his chin. "You know as well as I do how we can get around the five-mile rule. However, *I* can't ask Sihix to refrain from corrupting her."

"Very well, I will speak with Sihix, Shir, and Gari." Djialkan sighed in irritation as the Oracle shot us both questioning glances. *"They will meet us where you were thinking of. We should get going lest this lot miss their window to leave."*

To my surprise, the Oracle gave the soldiers orders to remain with the airships before following me to a nearby cliff that dropped into violet nothingness. Djialkan's abrupt shift into a full-sized dragon caused the Oracle to yelp and scramble backwards, but I just hopped onto his back and then offered her a hand up into the conjured saddle.

"If he can fly, then why…?" The Oracle trailed off, uneasy.

"Once he reaches a certain distance from the island, the Mists summon strong gales to impede his flight," I answered as Djialkan dove over the edge of the cliff and past the crystal-rich earth and stone that made up X'shmir's base. "You said *that one* makes a habit of failing to introduce himself when 'something catches his interest?'"

"Truth be told, you caught everyone's interest with that rage and bloodlust you displayed." The Oracle laughed. "He thought you were going to self-destruct. Elemental footprints such as yours are never a good sign; usually it signifies someone losing all control of their power. *He* is quite powerful—he likely intended to stop you but, obviously, that wasn't necessary.

"Knowing him, he's probably curious about how a Human Umbral Mage has survived this long, especially in these conditions. Human Umbral Mages are notorious for self-destructing before making it to their twentieth year."

"Growing up around Corentine has a way of making one stubborn," I answered dryly. I turned my attention to Djialkan as he banked to the right and flew towards a land bridge that ran along X'shmir's underbelly. "Can you take us directly to the cave, Djialkan? I don't want to risk walking."

Djialkan nodded and then followed the path of the bridge directly into a massive dark cavern. Once he landed I slid out of the saddle and then offered the Oracle a helping hand. She accepted my hand without hesitation and mumbled her thanks before straightening her robes and glancing around the crystal-filled cavern. It was a little strange to be treated without fear or reverence but I wasn't going to complain.

"There you are!" Corentine grinned from where she leaned against a crystal nearly eight times her height. "Ari, you figured out how to work your jewelry already?"

"Well, I figured something forged by the gods should have protection against the beasts." I shrugged as Djialkan shrunk and then returned to his perch on my shoulder. "I'll leave you two to it. Djialkan, you don't mind flying our guest back to her ship once they're done, right?"

"You're not going anywhere." Corentine latched onto my arm and then pouted over my shoulder at her sister. "You 'read' my message, right?"

"Yes, but she seems *fine*." The Oracle crossed her arms, "Mother and Father are quite cross with you for disappearing without a word, you know. They're going to want a piece of your pelt when they find out you *willingly* offered yourself to an Aledacian Forest! All of Ee'nir was in an uproar over the vanishing act you pulled!

"I can't say I disagree with your reasoning, it was a potent vision, but—"

"We need to heal this one." Corentine squeezed my arm, earning a heavy sigh from me.

"Really, *that's* what this is about?" I didn't bother masking my irritation. "Then the reason you *really* insisted I shouldn't go back to the city is because—"

"You saw something that terrified you enough to heal the wounds the X'shmirans inflicted on Arianna?" Djialkan interrupted me with concern. *"Corentine, you know as well as I do that they will increase her punishment a hundred fold if she goes back to the city with her injuries mysteriously gone. We already had it happen before; we do not need them doubling the amount of chains that are currently there!"*

I sighed as the trio began arguing amongst themselves. Djialkan leapt from my shoulder and onto Corentine's. Shaking my head, I plopped down on the cave floor beside Shir and Gari. I stroked their fur and tuned out the arguing Rylthra sisters and Djialkan. At this point I was so used to my "punishment" that I had almost forgotten the chains fused with the flesh of my back. Most of my movements were practiced in such a way that wouldn't strain my scarred flesh.

X'shmiran tradition dictated that Umbral Mages should be punished and that Astral Mages should be worshiped. As such, I had been subject to torture for so long that I didn't really feel it anymore. Or perhaps I was just practiced at escaping. Either way, I couldn't deny the presence of my mangled back. Every movement made dozens of once-molten chains shift and groan under my skin.

Djialkan and Fraelfnir did their best to heal me after each session, but sometimes it took multiple rounds of healing to truly close the wounds. Combined with Corentine's help, they had the power to remove the chains and heal my back until it seemed as if nothing ever happened. But as Djialkan said, the X'shmirans were enraged by it.

The punishment was doubling the previous number of chains. In one sitting.

It was a crude, cruel practice—one that would have killed a normal Human long ago. That had been perhaps one of my first hints that the "nightmares" I experienced in my sleep were *memories* and not *dreams*.

If I fought back, the curse placed on me and tethered to my brother would execute us both. I wasn't yet desperate enough to end *both* of our lives just to get away from the pain.

"X'shmir really practices the Old Ways to the fullest extent then?" The Oracle's irritated hiss caught my attention, making me glance in her direction. "We had hoped it stopped at the masks and hoods, but..."

"So, Vorpmasia did find other countries that follow such vile practices?" Corentine had a deep frown on her face. "Well, you understand what I showed you? Will you help me heal her?"

"We certainly can't do it in this cave," the Oracle pointed out with a huff

"We're going to need a clean environment and more light than this."

"Not that I'm ungrateful, but is this really a good idea?" I finally asked, earning a glare from them both. "I know I'm supposed to be going Below with Darius. But when we return, I'll—"

"You need to learn to fight without restrictions. That includes movement." Corentine's voice was flat as she pointed a clawed finger at me. "Like I said, you're going to be training to use Aurelian and Elise's gifts for the next several months.

"Let's go. We can heal Arianna in the temple at Sihix's core. I'd like you to see why we're all so fond of Ari, anyway."

"You know, *he* is going to be quite cross when he finds out I was allowed to come into the forest and he wasn't," the Oracle stated dryly as I pulled myself to my feet to follow them.

"If he had waited perhaps an *hour* longer," I began with a snort, earning an odd look from the Oracle, "I would have offered to have Djialkan fly him down here as well.

"Now, if he had remembered to introduce himself *before* asking me questions and attempting to sway me with his power as a *god*—the process would have been much quicker."

"Arianna is quite particular about at least introducing oneself first before questioning or fighting," Djialkan cackled, weaving through the myriad of elemental crystals above our heads. *"Gari, carry Arianna."*

"What? Carry? Why?" I protested as the Rylthra women rounded on me and hoisted me onto the large fox's back. "I can walk, you know. You don't need to make Gari carry me."

"You're going to sleep," Corentine informed me, tapping my knee, "I want to make sure you're completely out before we start working on your back."

"You don't need to put me to sleep. I'll be fine awake!" I protested.

"You'll be *fine*? How could you possibly be *fine*?!" the Oracle snapped. "Even if that was somehow possible, *we* will work better if we're not fearing sudden flinches or jerks out of you! Now, be a good girl and cooperate, alright?"

'I'll never understand Oracles,' I thought to myself, looking between the angry Rylthra. *'I should've known Corentine was up to something the instant their reunion wasn't a tear-filled sobfest.'*

Finally, I nodded my begrudging acceptance and lowered my barriers just enough to allow them to cast their combined sleep magic on me. It took but a moment before I slumped and landed face-first in Gari's warm fur, and perhaps another second before my mind slipped off into darkness.

My only hope was that I didn't have to relive my "memories" over and over again while the sister-Oracles worked.

CHAPTER TWELVE
Endearing

My days since leaving X'shmir had been filled with nothing but research. The X'shmiran prince shouldn't have possessed such immense power, yet the equipment I had used to measure his abilities was not broken. I had run every test, every analysis that I could think of, and even disassembled the Magitech down to its most trivial components. Yet nothing appeared to be damaged or malfunctioning.

Darius' aura felt negligible at best to my senses, but his results were what I expected from an Upper God such as War, Chaos, or Justice.

However, the X'shmiran Umbral Mage still managed to puzzle me more than the prince did. I couldn't come up with an explanation for her power, scent, or the control she exhibited over her magics. Then there was her resistance to *my* power. It infuriated me. I didn't like not knowing, yet there wasn't anything I could do at the moment to find answers.

According to what I had been taught over the past twenty years by the Elder Gods, the Lyur'zi of X'shmir couldn't possibly be who I thought she was. Even so, Arianna's crystalline heart had grown cold once more upon leaving X'shmir. That bone-chilling cold ached within my chest, sending occasional lances of pain through my torso.

'This is not conducive to my research.' I shook my head and then strode along the shelves of my laboratory, searching for a tome that *might* shed some light on the prince's unusual power. *'Tch, I can still smell* her *all over me. Perhaps another bath is in order.'*

"Nali!" a female voice called. I bit back an angry hiss as my tail jerked to the side, then glared over my shoulder at the haughty-looking Oracle as she spoke again, "Wow, you've really made a mess of your laboratory, haven't you?"

"I see you managed to escape being devoured by a beast during your extended stay in X'shmir. Unfortunate," I observed with a huff, turning my attention to a quartet of soldiers behind her and the large wooden crate they struggled to carry. "What is *that?*"

"You didn't *actually* think Sihix's people would just accept your gifts without giving their thanks, did you?" the Oracle snorted and crossed her arms.

I frowned as I turned to examine the Rylthra Oracle. She looked wearier than I had ever seen her. Her eyes had dark circles under them and there was a slight tremor in her hands as she gripped her elbows.

The Oracle's grip on herself was tight enough to turn her knuckles white despite her shaky grip. Unlike some of the younger Oracles, it was unusual for this one to show a sign of something being "wrong" after a vision.

"You haven't been sleeping," I stated, watching as her twin tails jerked behind her and she laid her ears back, hissing at me. "A vision…or something else?"

"My sister, *Corentine*, needed my help in the Sihix Forest," the Oracle snapped, bristling. "Here. *These* should explain it all—I need you to examine them anyway."

She opened her shrizar and dumped a sealed bag of blue-silver chains on a nearby table. I spotted the glowing angelic runes on the mangled metal and released a deep growl.

"This suddenly became less about 'who' she might be, and more about what we're going to do about the X'shmirans," I muttered as I strode over to the desk, lifted the bag, and tested the weight in my palm. "Silver is not this heavy."

"One hundred eighty-six." The Oracle stated matter-of-factly, snorting when I twitched in response. "My sister and I couldn't figure out what they're made of. I haven't been able to find anything capable of melting the metal, let alone warm it. The girl said they were molten when her torturers laid the chains across her flesh.

"That's why we were so late to return, mind you. Even Corentine didn't realize that Arianna had *that* many chains encased in her back."

I clenched my jaw and looked at the heavy bag of chains. *'In her back? How did she move so fluidly in combat when there was this much to fetter her?'*

"Nothing has been able to melt them?" I asked for confirmation, watching the Oracle give me a nod and a displeased grimace. "What about where they came from? Angelic runes in *X'shmir,* of all places, doesn't make sense."

"The girl doesn't trust me." The Oracle shook her head and then released a heavy sigh before continuing, "I don't know what's wrong with Sihix, Nali, but that girl doesn't want to talk about anything that has to do with the forest or with X'shmir. She was quite blunt in stating that I haven't earned her trust or her interest."

"Even after you helped heal her?" I frowned, setting the bag down before turning my attention to the Oracle in full. "What of Darius then? Has he given us a response in regards to attending the academy?"

"I don't know when he talked to Arianna, but apparently he got her 'permission' to attend." The Oracle frowned. "I couldn't get much information out of any of them regarding X'shmiran ways, but Darius had to get the approval of his Lyur'zi in order to attend the academy. From what I did learn, it sounds like it's because she alone is responsible for his safety."

"They will both be coming?" I asked, causing the Rylthra to nod her head again.

"She was rather inquisitive when she wasn't acting like, well, one of us," the Oracle remarked with a sheepish grin. "After seeing her rip into a beast I was already inclined to agree that she isn't Human. That she was able to survive *those* in her flesh for so long only furthers my belief.

"I think it's time for a drink or fifty after that mess. How about you and I—"

"Not interested," I dismissed the ever-persistent Oracle's offer with a shake of my head, ignoring her irritated expression. "If that's all, I have research to attend to…and a mountain of fan mail, it seems."

The Oracle hissed at me again, turned on her heel, and then stalked out, bristling in response to my swift rejection as always. Perhaps one day she and the other Oracles would learn that, regardless of their role, I had no interest in any of them.

My soldiers, at least, looked amused by the exchange. They shot me knowing looks before saluting me and taking their leave, following the angry Rylthra.

'Tch, so many distinctly Devillian scents.' I thought as I strode over to the crate. Resting my palms on its edge, I looked over the absurd number of packages filling it. *'Are they simply that grateful, or is the Sihix Forest in worse shape than I thought?'*

I lifted one of the envelopes and sniffed, a small frown settling onto my face. Someone had the gall to scribble "read me first" in almost indecipherable Draemiran characters. Skimming the contents of the envelope, I grimaced when I discovered it was from our head Oracle's sister, Corentine.

"Just great. There really *is* two of them," I muttered in displeasure before turning to motion at the doors of my laboratory, slamming them shut and then snapping the lock into place. "Really, 'Vraelimir-y'ric?' She could have just told them my name. Why must Oracles complicate *everything*? Humph."

Discarding Corentine's curt but appreciative letter aside, I stared down into the crate once more and shook my head. The miasma of scents contained a mixture of Devillian, Human, Elven, and even a few more bestial races.

One scent stood out above the rest, and it was not one I expected to find. At least it made *her* letter easy to find.

'Her Draemiran appears to be much better than Corentine's at least.' I frowned and examined the outside of the envelope. My eyes ran over the neatly-written characters that spelled my surname and the honorific attached to it. *'Did Djialkan help her, perhaps?'*

Shaking my head once more, I pried the envelope open and strode over to a leather chair. Once comfortable, I pulled out several sheets of folded parchment from the envelope. My curiosity wouldn't let me put it off until later.

I was stunned to find Arianna had written the entirety of her letter in Draemiran. I even flipped through the pages a few times just to be sure. A quick sniff confirmed the absence of Djialkan's scent.

'Someone taught her our language?' I wondered, examining the first few lines and following the strokes of the pen she had used. *'Djialkan and some of the people in Sihix perhaps? I can't imagine that they or the X'shmirans actually believed it necessary for her to learn Draemiran.'*

A crooked grin stretched across my face, followed by a low chuckle when I read the first line. She seemed to share my displeasure with Corentine's chosen way of addressing me.

Really! As you can see from all of these letters and packages from your **adoring** *fans, Corentine enjoys making things more difficult or elaborate than they need to be. "Vraelimir-y'ric?" I hope you don't mind if I simply refer to you as Rely'ric instead. That damned fox and Djialkan don't appear willing to tell any of us your name.*

That aside, I would like to thank you for your gift. I thought I was being sneaky while Djialkan and I listened to you play your violin but, clearly, that wasn't the case. You earn points for noticing we were there. Perhaps the Mists don't interfere with your senses quite as much as I originally thought. I'll forgive you for forgetting to introduce yourself **properly**. *At least a little bit.*

As much as I adore music, I would like to also thank you for the medicinal supplies you gave to the people here in Auvry'e—that's the name of the city we've built within the Sihix Forest. There are many people that live here but they have limited access to healers and herbs. Very few of the mages in Sihix are capable of healing without the aid of a focus or other magical contraptions. Many of the people here have been bedridden for months or years due to illness or injury.

Thanks to your gifts, Corentine and the Guardians were able to heal everyone in Sihix while still having leftover supplies. Oracles, Seers, High Priestesses—whatever you want to call them—can be incredibly troublesome as I'm sure you're aware. But despite her flaws and terrible temper, Corentine has taken on a rather motherly role in the forest.

*I doubt she said much in her own letter, but know she's very grateful as well. It's been tearing her apart for **years** that she's been unable to help her people the way she'd like to.*

Lastly, I would like to offer an apology for my behavior when you pursued me across X'shmir. I have little time available right now to explain but suffice to say my freedom to speak is severely lacking. You will probably notice that I wrote "the Mists" not "the mists." That was intentional. There is something wrong with the sky in X'shmir and it is largely responsible for discovering those who break X'shmiran law.

Once again, thank you for your gifts. Music is something that has been regrettably missing from my life since I became an Umbral Mage. The moment I heard you playing I knew it couldn't possibly be someone from X'shmir. Humans here insist that music be played... Mechanically, I suppose, would be the word for it. To them music is not an art or expression; it is a series of sounds to be played in precisely the way their sheet music dictates.

It was refreshing to hear someone else that knows how to play an instrument with their heart and not with their mind, so to speak. Therefore, thank you for that as well even though I know it wasn't intentional.

*Perhaps when I come to Dauthrmir in a few months I will have enough time away from Darius to answer your questions about the beasts. Or really, **any** time away from that one would be a good start.*

Glancing at the end of the final page, I laughed in response to her "signature."

"I can know her name once I introduce myself *properly*, is it?" I grinned, shook my head, and then glanced through the pages once more. "She's interesting, I'll give her that much."

I tapped my claws absentmindedly on the arm of my chair as I read Arianna's letter a few times over, catching a few places where she had used magic to erase improperly written characters. It looked as though she had been rather meticulous in her endeavors to write Draemiran in a concise manner. She had gone as far to infuse the parchment with just enough of her darkness to keep the message from being altered or obscured by outside sources, and I found it strangely endearing.

Was she being careful for a reason, or was she naturally cautious?

'"The Mists" is it?' I skimmed over the way she had written it. *'A title, not a "thing." Something that watches for lawbreakers... I rather dislike the sound of it.'*

I pursed my lips and glanced toward the remainder of waiting letters and gifts. Rising to my feet, I dismissed the entire crate into my shrizar and then headed out of my laboratory and through the winding halls of the Dauthrmiran palace. I didn't like the idea of "the Mists" but my immediate concern was the wellbeing of the Sihix Forest and its people. *Including*, but not limited to, Arianna. I hoped that Lucifer and I would be able to concoct a way to sneak more supplies into the forest to aid them.

'For now I need to put aside who she might *be,'* I told myself with a

grimace, attempting to shove her scent from my mind. *'Regardless of who she may be, the X'shmirans have committed a heinous crime. Such treatment of anyone, of any rank, is unforgivable. If they follow the Old Ways to that extent... Ugh. I can only hope that they don't follow the method of "worshiping" Chrot'zi as well.'*

The mere thought made me shudder and my stomach turn. No matter how unbiased I tried to be, the thought of *my* Arianna being tortured with molten chains tore at my heart more than anything else could. I had hoped that no one had made her suffer, and that desire had already been shattered once when I saw the state Limbo had left her in. The concept that she had been subject to further torture upon leaving that damned place was almost too much to bear.

For the past twenty years I had told myself, over and over again, that I had *rescued* her from Limbo. No matter what the Elders claimed, regardless of the blame they tried to put on me, I truly believed that I had rescued Arianna from that place.

The idea that the *Elder Gods* had instead sent her somewhere to endure more torture was unforgivable. It made my heart ache. More torture was the *last* thing I wanted for Arianna, but it was beginning to look like that was exactly what she'd found beyond Limbo.

If the X'shmiran Lyur'zi turned out to be the same Arianna, and the Elder Gods were responsible for her arrival there, I wasn't certain what I would do. Turning against the Elders was an unforgivable offense among the gods—if I turned against the Elders before the rest of my plans were prepared, I would be Exiled and the Elder Gods would be even farther beyond my reach.

'Tch, if it is her, *Lucifer will have my head* and *the Elders' heads.'* I grimaced, approaching the Emperor's throne room. *'For now I will assume that the X'shmiran Lyur'zi is a* different *Arianna. It isn't an uncommon name.'*

After steeling my nerves, I approached the throne room door at a brisk pace and hoped that Lucifer wouldn't fly into a rage. If he demanded we destroy X'shmir for following the Old Ways I would find it very hard to disagree or argue with him.

It wasn't time for them to die. Not yet.

CHAPTER THIRTEEN
Nightmare

"Please, someone, just get me out of here!"

'How long has it been since I lost my will to scream and beg like that? The poor thing.' *I shook my head, listening to my blood splash into the ever-growing pool beneath me.* 'Still, it *does* hurt… I think.'

I couldn't say for certain if the 46 blades I hung suspended from still caused me pain. Although I was very aware of the cold weapons I dangled from, and the creaking of the chains attached to them, I'd grown numb to them. I had been there so long that the constant drip of my blood was comparable to the ticking of a clock.

Opening my eyes for a few moments, I was met with utter darkness. Darkness was my friend in this place—wherever it was. It soothed me, comforted me, and kept me warm. If it was dark, it meant that my captors weren't there to torture me.

While Darius was terrified of darkness, I had been in tune with it all my life...I thought. My memory was hazy but, at the very least, being in that situation gave me new insights into the power of darkness. I was forced to confront and accept my own dark desires the first time the bastards tortured me. Since then I had grown to accept that it was only natural to regret my decision to protect my brother.

'I wonder if they're even holding up their end of our bargain,' *I mused as I closed my eyes, satisfied that I was alone aside from the darkness and Djialkan, wherever he was hiding.* 'For some reason I doubt they will really leave Darius alone...but at least I tried. That has to count for something.'

Taking the torture meant for myself and for another had been a chore at first. I had grown accustomed to it, perhaps faster than I should have, but there didn't seem to be another option.

In that place, it was either learn to deal with the pain or go mad.

Of course, I could have let Darius take his portion of the punishment— I had even wished it upon him several times early on. However, by the time the third blade pierced my flesh, my desire shifted. I wanted to destroy the corrupt creatures that had captured us, and I wanted to destroy their brethren in the outside world.

The 47th sword pierced through my back unannounced. I coughed, tasting blood in my mouth as the blade blossomed from the right side of my chest.

'Did that hurt? I can't tell. Since I taste blood it must have pierced my other lung. That would hurt, right?' *I resisted the urge to shrug.*

"*Is your mind that far gone that you don't even scream anymore?*" *a male voice sneered, causing me to crack an eye open to look at the Angel standing before me.*

For some reason the light around him was dim this time. I had to strain to make out the rows of jagged shark-like teeth that lined his lipless mouth. He reeked of rotting flesh and mold. Many of the feathers in his once-white wings had sloughed off long ago, along with most of the down that accompanied them. It was almost a pitiful sight.

I might have actually felt sorry for him had the bastard not been responsible for 46 of the 47 blades that pierced my body.

The 48th blade pierced through the top of my foot this time, managing to rip a hoarse scream from my lungs. 'Fucking bastard!'

My attention shifted away from my pain and the Angel when I spotted the air and shadows rippling behind him. Power radiated from the spot but my torturer seemed oblivious to it. The magic felt and smelled familiar somehow yet I couldn't place it.

"*To think a filthy bitch like you would interfere with the gods' plans!*" *The Angel spat in disgust as he looked at me.* "*You know, if you hadn't been such a thorn in* Their *sides, you wouldn't be here. You would still be living out that lovely life of yours, carefree—*"

My torturer turned around and then froze as the rippling air before him warped and twisted, spewing forth a figure robed in black. An obsidian-scaled tail whipped back and forth behind the new figure, poking through a slit in the back of the figure's attire.

The black-robed figure looked toward the one in white with a condescending expression and summoned dozens of blue-white Magefire orbs into the air around both of them. Unlike the harsh light that accompanied the Angels, this light was soft and pleasant.

I watched in silence as the new man looked around the room with displeasure. He scented the air a few times while surveying the room. His hood obscured most of his face from view, but not enough to hide the turn of his mouth when he looked down at the pool of blood beneath him. Even though he towered over the Angel, the blood filling this room reached the new man's knees.

"So, this is where you've been hiding," *the man's voice was frigid and smooth as he spoke. He reached up to lower his hood, revealing twisting platinum horns, frosty blue eyes set in black sclerae, and long layers of pure white hair.* "To think they would send *me* to clean up an Angel's *mess...*"

"What is a false god like you *doing here?!*" *the Angel yapped like a small dog, though the Devillian man seemed to ignore him and examined me instead.*

'A false god?' *I bit back a bitter laugh.* 'He must have lived in this place longer than me if he thinks this man isn't an actual deity.'

The glowing bi-colored Brands of Divinity on the new figure's skin made his position as a deity obvious. I got the feeling he was probably a very important one as well. I couldn't think of any deities I knew of that had black Brands on their right, and white on their left.

"You think that being an Angel means you're above me?" *The white-haired Devillian leveled a platinum spear at the terrified Angel's throat.*

"A prime example of your guilt hangs in this very room. Why don't you try your excuses again if you wish for mercy?"

"My guilt?!*" The Angel scrambled backwards and tripped over his own feet in his desperation to flee the wrathful god. "I'm keeping Avrirsa safe by keeping this monster from leaving this place! What would an Adinvyr bastard like you know of guilt?!"*

"Ahhhnnn… But it's so wonderful to be like a monster, isn't it?" I teased with a purr, watching as the Devillian's tail adopted a playful swing.

"Reiz'tar, do you have any objections if I take the pleasure of ending this miserable fool's existence?" The white-haired man bowed to me in a flamboyant manner. A mischievous smile spread across his lips as his frosty eyes ran along the curves of my body.

'It's been a long time since someone referred to me with such a high honorific…' *I parted my lips to speak but changed my mind and shook my head instead with a small smile. My throat was far too dry to speak further.*

I closed my eyes when they both disappeared from view and simply listened to the sound of their battle. It sounded like the Angel wasn't putting up much of a fight, and it wasn't long before I heard him flapping his decayed, useless wings in an attempt to flee. By the sound of things, the Devillian deity had his own set of wings to utilize and I soon heard the Angel's corpse splash into the pool of blood somewhere behind me—in chunks.

"You really are in a sorry state, aren't you?" the white-haired deity

purred, trailing his fingers along my jaw. "I can hear your breathing, you know. I'm aware you're still awake."

Reluctant, I opened my eyes and watched the Devillian grin at me, revealing his long upper and lower fangs. From so close I could see for certain that his sclerae were indeed black and that it wasn't just some trick of the light. The contrast with his pale eyes was quite nice, I thought, even though everything about him looked…foreign. As a Devillian, he was just so different from a Human or Angel—I wasn't sure what to think.

'He looks vaguely familiar,' *I considered.* 'Handsome too.'

"Do you know how long you've been here, my dear?" he questioned as he tilted my head from side to side, his eyes running down my throat. "Ah, and no need to speak. I can hear your thoughts just fine—and I assure you that I'm flattered by the attention."

'No,' *I responded, suppressing the urge to shrug when his eyes flicked back up to my face.*

After a moment he leaned forward and flicked his tongue across my lower lip. He savored the taste of my blood with a contemplative expression on his face. I wasn't sure why, but I got the distinct feeling that he was disappointed by my lack of reaction.

"Mmm…you look Human, but you certainly don't taste like one," the deity remarked, running his clawed fingertips down the front of my throat.

He fell silent and examined me again. He seemed genuinely intrigued as he took in my nude, bloodstained body and the dozens of blades I hung from. However, it seemed like he was inspecting my feminine form instead of judging the swords or gauging a way to remove them. Despite that, I didn't sense any ill intent from him, so I remained silent. His eyes often wandered to my lips, eyes, and my long curls. If I didn't know any better I might have assumed that he was fond of my eyes.

'You look like...' I trailed off with a slight frown as he brought his gaze back up to my face in response, an inquisitive expression settling onto his masculine features once more. 'No, no. That can't be right. He was a child when—'

"Tell me, where would you like to go?" He purred the question and brought his hand up to my chin, his grip gentle yet firm.

'Where would I...?' I blinked at him in disbelief as he smiled playfully once more, his scaled tail swaying behind him in a catlike manner. 'What does that matter? You've almost finished rejoining the worlds that were separated from Avrirsa, haven't you?'

"Ohhh? You're an interesting one." He leaned closer as he continued, a warm smile replacing the playful one. "You're all chained up in Limbo and yet you were able to discern not only that some of the worlds were split, but also that I am the one bringing them back together?"

"Mmm...well, is that your final answer, my dear? Isn't there anyone you would like to see?"

'Ah, I do have a twin brother... I think?' *I trailed off with a slight frown and averted my gaze from the playful deity.*

"A twin brother you say? Now that is interesting," he remarked, running his thumb along the length of my lower lip and then chuckling when my face flushed. "How I wish I could stay with you longer. It's a rare treat to find such an exceptional woman that isn't terrified by the gods."

'There is also…' *I hesitated, flicking my gaze toward him again.* "What is it?"

I averted my eyes again as my pulse quickened and my lips parted in thought. The tangle of memories inside my head was next to impossible to sort through but I tried anyway.

'How am I supposed to know which lives were real and which ones weren't?' *I muttered, absentminded, forgetting the deity could hear me. My eyes ticked back and forth as I tried to find a clue as to what I was searching for. It was on the tip of my tongue but I'd lost it.*

"May I have a look?" *His voice was filled with interest. I looked toward him again and then nodded my acceptance; he could probably make more sense out of my memories than I could anyway.*

He brought both of his hands up to cup my face and closed his eyes. With startling ease he willed his consciousness into my mind and explored my memories at a speed I couldn't follow. The intrusion brought a brief spike of pain through my temples, making me wince, but it was gone as fast as it came.

Through door after door he flew through my mind uninhibited. There was something incredibly familiar and comforting about his presence in my mind but, for the life of me, I couldn't place it.

I closed my eyes once more and let myself relax even though I sensed his displeasure growing. I'd known that many of the memories in my head were false lives that the Angels and their masters had conjured as another way to torture me. In all honesty, I didn't know how many of them there were anymore. Time flowed in a strange way in that place, making it impossible for me to tell how long I'd been there or just how many lives I experienced.

"What's this…?" his voice wavered and his hands twitched once.

After what may have been several minutes or several hours, he withdrew his hands from my face. In the next moment, I felt his fingers touch the decorative-looking sword that pierced my heart.

The gaudy silver sword was covered in golden filigree. Its hilt, pommel, and crossguard were just as lavish. Several large sapphires rested in the hilt and pommel alike, with several more at the thickest sections of the blade.

"The bastards never removed this?!" the Devillian deity exclaimed, his growing rage tinging his aura even as he tried to wrestle it into submission. "You…really don't know how long you've been here?"

'Since I was a child, I think,' *I replied as his hand came up to my face once more, but I kept my eyes shut.* 'I'm not supposed to look like this you know…

'You still have important matters to take care of, don't you? You…you should leave. Before They come back to see why that wretch hasn't submitted his report.'

"But you're what I—" He flinched and took a sudden step back from me. I cracked an eye open for a moment to look at him, but his hurt expression was too much for me to bear, so I closed my eyes again.

With an expression like that *on his face there was no longer any doubt in my mind who he was. It gave me a confirmation of one real memory at least.*

"Then… 'this you' is just your bound powers? Or your soul?" There was

something strange about his voice. I opened my eyes again to find he was holding up a floating crystal in the shape of a lotus. "Very well... I will release you. But first..."

My eyes widened when he suddenly leaned forward and gave me a deep, passionate kiss. His tongue explored my mouth as he cradled my head in one hand. The power and emotion radiating from him almost overwhelmed me.

I was certain that my face must have turned a brilliant shade of cherry, and I began to think my heart might beat out of my chest if it pumped any faster.

"Mmm, you really do taste incredible." He mused with a wistful smile as he turned away, raising a few clawed fingers to his parted lips before pausing and casting me a sultry sideways glance. "Good night, Reiz'tar."

With a snap of his fingers, my consciousness slipped and I fell into complete darkness.

"I hope that you will remember me. Limbo seems to have this terrible knack of making people forget.

"Still, I will find you. If...if you are truly alive after all this time, I will find you. I have to.

"Please...try to survive until then, at least?"

He sounded like he was on the verge of tears. I hated it. That was the worst thing about that nightmare—those memories. Whichever it was.

The pain in his voice and on his face, the disbelief. The hurt when

I said he should leave. It was one of the rare times when I regretted saying what my instincts told me.

"Damn it," I mumbled, groping around for the blankets that had slipped off of me in my sleep.

I shifted onto my stomach in bed and then yanked the bedsheets and comforter up over my shoulders. Wood still crackled in the fireplace at the other end of the room, but I didn't dare open my eyes yet—it always seemed more difficult to go back to sleep once I opened my eyes.

'He seemed so shocked to find me alive back then.' I nuzzled into my pillow then sighed. *'I guess he really did believe those bastards actually killed me.'*

Dwelling on a mostly-forgotten past served little purpose aside from frustrating me further but it was difficult for me to shove the thoughts aside. It was probably better to pretend that none of it ever happened.

He was a deity now, and most likely had his own goddess to take care of. Or perhaps a god? He didn't quite strike me as someone that would be interested in men but neither did most of the men my brother brought back to the castle.

For years, I had dismissed my nightmares and dreams as just that— nightmares and dreams. Now, after seeing *him* in person, I wasn't so sure. His scent, his height, his presence, and even his subdued power were too close a match for me to ignore. But…I knew it was pointless to ask Djialkan or Corentine for information.

My life belonged to X'shmir now. Whatever my past may have once been didn't matter.

'*Doesn't matter…*' I clenched one hand into a fist and turned my face into the pillow, swallowing the lump in my throat. '*Ugh. Maybe…maybe I'll feel better once I've slept more.*'

I wasn't sure how long I'd been asleep before the sensation of hands running down my inner thighs jolted me awake. I tumbled out of bed, onto the floor, and summoned a blade of ice to my hand. A quick survey of the room revealed it was empty. I inhaled, preparing to sigh, and instead paused as the scent of sweet spices filled my head for a split second before disappearing again.

Bewildered, I brandished my blade and turned to look behind me. Again, there was no one there. There was no sign of anyone having come into my room and Djialkan was still fast asleep by the fireplace. The only sounds I heard were the crackling flames, Djialkan's steady but deep breathing, and my own rapid heartbeat.

'*What in the hells was that? Why do I smell* him *here?*' I pulled myself to my feet and then shivered in the cool air. '*Ugh, perhaps I should have worn pajamas to bed. It's colder than I expected it to be… Need more logs on the fire.*'

The wooden floor of my cabin groaned beneath my feet as I tiptoed to the fireplace. A log cracked and spat sparks, but even that wasn't enough to wake the nearby fae-dragon. I fetched more wood from the nearby room, stoked the fire, and then glanced at my bed in thought. There was no way I could return to sleep.

'Just where was my mind wandering off to?' I pawed at my thighs, attempting to rid myself of the lingering sensation of clawed fingers. Nothing like that had ever happened before. It felt so *real* that I found myself striding through the cottage and double-checking to make sure Djialkan and I were the only people in it.

Nothing. Aside from Djialkan, I was alone. The word sent a chill down my spine. Alone. It was something I never wanted to be again. Something that almost broke me during my time in Limbo. If the X'shmirans had their way, I would be alone once again. Left somewhere to rot away, or die trying to fend for myself.

The Sihix Forest would welcome me if it ever came to that—if the X'shmirans couldn't find a way to isolate me.

I shivered and shook my head hard. This wasn't the time to think about such things. There were so many more pertinent issues for me to focus on. Some of which I even found pleasant.

I was cautiously optimistic about traveling Below. So many places to see, so many new people—new races!—that I'd never met before. More beasts to hunt, and of course there would be interesting foods to try! I wanted to be excited, I really did, but I couldn't bring myself to feel that way. My role during the trip was as it always had been—to protect Darius. I knew better than to hope for anything more than that.

'At least I'll have some respite from his company.' I padded over to a dresser and pulled a set of warm clothing from it. *'Darius won't want to be there for discussions about fighting beasts. Not political enough for*

him. Perhaps if I'm lucky the Devillians will call on me more than once.

'Or…should I withhold information so that they have *to call on me again?'*

Although the prospect tempted me, I shook my head and decided against it. I knew from my interactions with Devillians in Auvry'e that withholding information wouldn't go unnoticed. Causing conflict between me and X'shmir's potential allies wasn't in my best interests. I would have to find some other way to distance myself from my brother while in Dauthrmir.

I stopped in my tracks the moment I moved to put on my bra and my fingers came into contact with smooth skin. No scars, no chains. Not even the sting of wounds or the tautness of damaged flesh.

'They…healed me completely?' I dropped my clothes to the floor and darted into the bathroom. After turning my back to the mirror I craned my head over the shoulder.

No sign of the years of torture remained. Gone—all of it. Not even the slightest discoloration of burned or scarred skin remained.

Stunned, I pulled my hair over my shoulder and exposed all of my back just to make sure. Just how much power had they wasted healing me? Eighteen years of damage was just *gone* without a trace. If Corentine and Djialkan had had the opportunity to heal me after every "session," reverting my skin to this state would have been easy.

Years of damage took immense amounts of magic to heal and, even then, it should have left scars. Corentine, the Oracle, and Djialkan combined shouldn't have been capable of mending me to that extent.

No wonder the fae-dragon was out cold—he would probably be out for several hours more while his energy replenished.

'*Unbelievable…*' I glanced at my back again before moving out of the bathroom to reclaim my discarded clothing. '*I hope they didn't overdo it. If they damaged themselves while healing me…*'

"Who in the hells?!" I whirled into a roundhouse kick but my leg met nothing. With a muttered curse I followed through with the motion and then adopted a defensive stance. *That* was unmistakable. Someone had dragged their fingers, claws and all, down my spine.

Yet, again, there was no one in my cottage.

'*Am I finally losing it?*'

CHAPTER FOURTEEN
To Dauthrmir

Two months later...

"Ari!" Corentine called as she strode into my cottage with a cheerful grin nestled on her face.

As usual, Shir and Gari trailed behind the High Priestess by a few paces. Somehow they managed to squeeze through my door and into the kitchen. Today, a third and much smaller fox accompanied the two larger ones—carried by her scruff in Gari's mouth.

"How are you this morn— What is that *scent?*" Corentine shoved past me and proceeded to search the rooms with a bewildered look on her face.

I shrugged to myself and then turned my attention to Shir, Gari, and the small little fox that accompanied them. Gari set the young fluffball down on the floor, huffed in Corentine's direction, and then laid down beside the kitchen table. Shir joined her mate and rested her head on his paws, ignoring her rambunctious daughter.

The fluffball, Alala, was close to the size of a normal, full-grown fox. However, she was still only a kit. In perhaps a few years—or a few centuries—she would reach the horse-like size of her parents.

Alala was one of several kits from Shir and Gari's first litter. Normally, she was always underfoot when I was in Sihix, but over the past two months she had kept her distance from me while I trained with my new repertoire of weapons. She would often sit alongside Djialkan, silent, which was something she almost never was.

"Shir, Gari, Alala," I pivoted away from my stove to get a better look at them. "Would you like breakfast too?"

The trio warbled and Alala scampered over to me, running a few circles around my feet before pouncing on my right one. Before I could react, she darted off through the house to chase after Corentine. Shir and Gari exchanged a few varied noises before settling into comfortable positions once again. They always sounded like they were talking but, for the life of me, I had no idea what they were saying. What I did know was that they looked amused despite the way they kept scenting the air.

'I guess I wasn't just imagining his *scent again this morning...'* I shrugged to myself and then resumed cooking breakfast. *'That begs the question... Have I not been imagining his "touch" either? Hmm, that*

could be extremely awkward.

"Eek!" I jumped, almost dropping my spatula when I felt a pair of large, masculine hands smooth down my sides and to my waist.

I turned to brandish one of my blades, only to find no one there. *As usual.* Shir and Gari sniffed at the air again before making an absolute *ruckus.* They sounded like they were laughing at me.

Corentine, at least, looked concerned when she rushed into the kitchen with Djialkan and Alala perched on her shoulders. The big grin that split her face in the next moment—combined with Djialkan's laughter—told me that Shir and Gari must have said something to them.

"Something to tell us, Ari?" Corentine asked with a wolfish grin which widened when I shot her a disgruntled glare. "What do you think, Djialkan? The Mists must have weakened considerably if she's feeling *him* reach out in his sleep."

"It is unusual." Djialkan chortled. *"How long has this been going on, Arianna? I would imagine that I would have noticed similar* shrieks *before."*

"Since you lot healed me," I grumbled while pouring pancake batter into one of my pans. "Reaching out to me in his *sleep?* Isn't that a little farfetch—?"

"Well, he is an *Adinvyr* isn't he?" Corentine remarked, making me twitch. "The real question here is: Was he reaching out to child-you or you-you? We don't know if he's realized who you are, but he's certainly been showering Sihix with gifts hasn't he?"

"And we've needed all of it," I pointed out with a half-shrug. "You can't realistically deny that both X'shmir and Sihix have been doing poorly as of late, and the harsh winter hasn't helped.

"More than anything I'm surprised that the Vorpmasians were able to convince my brother to allow them close enough to leave their 'offerings' by Sihix's borders."

"Waaah, I'm going to miss your cooking while you're gone, Ari!" Corentine whined as I carried a few platters of food to the table, stepping carefully over Shir and Gari's paws as I walked. "Make sure you get us lots of presents, okay? It's been so long since any of us have been to Vorpmasia after all!"

"I'll do what I can," I assured her, placing the platters of food on the table as I continued, "I can't say I'm thrilled about those flying deathtraps though. If their calculations are correct, it could take two days for us to reach Dauthrmir. That's far too long to be in the sky on one of those…things."

After retrieving a pot of tea and three cups, I strode over to the table and sat down across from Corentine. Djialkan shifted into the form of a Devillian boy and reached out a hand expectantly while batting his silver hair out of his eyes with the other. He looked grumpier than usual, so I decided to just hand him his cup in silence before giving Corentine hers.

"Oh by the way, Ari, Alala is going with you," Corentine stated, causing me to choke on my tea. "Shir and Gari had Sihix withdraw his power from her so that she can accompany you. You're going to need more than one Guardian while Below, so—"

"You can't just spring something like that on me, Corentine!" I exclaimed between coughs, while Alala jumped off Corentine's shoulder and began pouncing between my thighs as if she was chasing something. "You know I love Alala, and I know she's still technically a Guardian fox, but isn't she still far too young to— Ouch!"

"She's ready," Corentine tilted her head as I tried to pry Alala's teeth from my forearm. "Guardians grow with their ward and their combined power. Once you two have bonded sufficiently, she will be able to shift the way Djialkan can.

"She's been threatening to accompany you with or without our permission for *weeks*."

"Alala, you're sure?" I questioned, checking my forearm for signs of tearing as the fox yipped at me. "Djialkan, you're alright with this?"

"I am more than 'alright' with Alala's presence." Djialkan gave me a sharp look. *"I do not know what Corentine has Seen, but I am aware of other dangers we could face Below. Along with my duty to protect you, there are also other matters I must look into. Alala's presence will help put my mind at ease when I am separated from you."*

"Then it's settled." I nodded while scratching Alala's chin. "Welcome to the team, Alala! Will you take your fee in pancakes, meat, or belly rubs?"

Corentine just laughed at me and shook her head. Alala, however, was quick to roll onto her back and then wagged her tail like crazy. After a few rubs, Alala stole a pancake off my plate and hightailed it out of the kitchen. I arched an eyebrow at the sound of her warbling coming from my bedroom and then shrugged.

"What else, Corentine?" I questioned as I filled plates with more food and then set them on the floor for Shir and Gari. "You look apprehensive."

"I'm nervous about a lot of things." Corentine sighed, nudging a strip of bacon. "Most importantly… Shir and Gari have created new attire for you that is suitable to the warmer weather Below. I can't have you walking around naked down there—not with the number of Adinvyr around—but we can't have you boiling in your X'shmiran robes either.

"Your brother isn't going to be of much help. Even *if* he wants to, he can't."

"Your Brands and your jewelry are also problems," Djialkan pointed out when Corentine hesitated. *"As I have told you before, Devillians are a warlike species as a whole. Some more than others. Trust is earned, not given.*

"Your mask and hood will already be a point of contention, but it is nothing compared to the problems you will face if you attempt to hide your jewelry or your Brands. Any mage will be able to sense your jewelry and know who it is from."

"Define 'problem,'" I pouted around my mouthful of pancake.

"Instead of seeking you out so that they may test their own power against you, they will be looking for ways to cause you harm or force you to reveal what is hidden—or what they perceive is 'hidden.'" Djialkan

huffed, an irritated scowl settling on his face. *"You wanted to avoid conflict and confrontation outside of sparring and training, yes? Releasing your Brands and having your jewelry in plain sight is a step towards that goal.*

"Aurelian's gifts have unmistakable energy. Every god and demigod in Avrirsa has similar jewelry or equipment that he and his wife forged. They are things that people display with honor. If you try to hide them, not only will they be suspicious of you, but they will also—"

"I get it, Djialkan, I do. However, they're not going to be able *see* my Brands beneath all my clothing. You know as well as I do that I'm going to have to conform to X'shmiran customs." I sighed. "Mask, hood, gloves, and shirts, dresses, or robes that reach the underside of my chin—my Brands will be covered completely. At least some of my jewelry can hang over my robes, but most of that will be hidden as well."

"Once Darius sees for himself how warm it is Below I doubt he'll make you adhere to X'shmiran traditions for clothing." Corentine shook her head. "I may not like the boy, but I know he wouldn't try to kill his own sister. *Especially* not by roasting you to death. However, much of what Shir and Gari have made for you is in lightweight materials that still fall in line with X'shmiran clothing. You should be fine either way.

"Ah…but it's about time you got going, isn't it?"

"Darius is trying to make them leave early?" I asked, watching the rapid nodding of Corentine's head. "Djialkan, let's hurry and fill my shrizars. I can sense beasts stirring near the plateau."

"The Mists really have weakened quite a bit," Corentine murmured with a faint frown. "Shir, let's find something for her to wear during her trip. Afterward, Ari can shove the trunks into her shrizar herself."

I downed the rest of my food in a hurry before rising to my feet and briskly moving throughout my cottage, tossing things into my shrizars as I went. Djialkan and I were used to hurried packing and were finished in a matter of minutes.

Alala leapt up onto the kitchen table and warbled at me as I approached in my bra and underwear. I arched an eyebrow at her before shifting my attention to the massive pile of trunks Shir and Gari had summoned in my kitchen.

"Put this on." Corentine shoved a set of mages' robes, black breeches, and a sapphire blouse at me. "After that, one of your leather overrobes should suffice against the chill outside."

"Isn't this…a lot?" I motioned at the pile of trunks before tugging on the breeches, my shirt, and then stretching in different directions to test the fit.

"You'll need it," Corentine answered. "Some of the citizens made you things as well; they didn't want to be left out."

"You all spoil me." I pulled on the mage robes and then fastened them in place with an underbust corset. "Any more messages I need to deliver for you?"

"None." Corentine grinned and shook her head. "You've done a lot for us, Ari. Providing you with necessities is the *least* we can do to repay you for everything you've done, and everything you *will* do. Don't worry yourself over it.

"We'll see you in a few months probably, alright? Try not to kill anyone important—including yourself!"

Corentine gave me a quick hug before stepping back and giving Shir and Gari enough room to nuzzle their daughter and then me in turn. After a few more warbles from the foxes, the trio left, leaving me looking between Alala and Djialkan for a moment. Djialkan had already shifted back to the form of a dragon but I could still make out the expectant look on his scaly features.

"That's her way of trying to rush us to leave, huh?" I sighed and then dismissed the trunks into my shrizar. "Alright then, you two. Let's go."

"I almost forgot something really important!" Corentine yelled and ran back over to me with a small lacquered box. "This! Important."

"How very descriptive of you," I commented sarcastically as I took the box from her. Tilting my head, I opened the lid and examined the contents. "Isn't this the crystal that I...?"

Within the lacquered box rested a crystal about the size of my palm. When I was a child, I had found it while wandering through the caves beneath X'shmir. It had been clear and pure when I found it, lacking any elemental affinity. That made it the perfect medium for practicing and exercising my control over darkness. I had infused it with my darkness many, many times until it eventually became a pure dark crystal. Black energy with wisps of cobalt and violet swirled beneath the faceted surface now.

Platinum filigree encircled the crystal. Attached to the top were a series of delicate-looking chains. Small charms and bells ran along the length of the chains and up to what looked like a series of clasps. Stripes of sapphire, white, and black brocade were woven through the chains, with a few tassels of sapphire and black hanging from the base of the crystal. By the size of the ensemble, and the clasps at the beginning, I doubted it was meant to be used as jewelry.

"Im-por-tant," Corentine reiterated, pointing at the dark crystal. "Djialkan, you remember right? Don't let her give it to anyone, don't let her use it for herself."

"Looks like it'd go on a weapon," I murmured as I tugged at the chains, listening to the jingle of bells. "Let me guess; I can't use it or gift it because of 'Devillian reasons?'"

"Draemiran reasons." Corentine corrected me with a grin. "Keep it in your shrizar. Once you've read about it or otherwise discovered the significance of decorations like this one, *then* you can contemplate gifting it to someone."

"I will see to it that she does not give it away on a whim." Djialkan nodded his head at Corentine. *"Let us be off, Arianna."*

"Don't worry, Corentine," I said with a small smile, dismissing the lacquered box into my shrizar. "If you say it's important, and Djialkan agrees with you, it must be *extremely* important right? I'll be careful."

"You better be!" Corentine pouted. "Off with you, else you'll be late! Don't forget those Brands of yours either!"

I took off at a run through the forest and released the seals on my Brands. For as long as I could remember, I always had white Brands of Divinity running along the right side of my body, and black on the left side.

Perhaps that wasn't saying much but, to me, it had been a big deal as a child. I knew no one else in X'shmir that had such markings and Darius was quick to grow jealous of that fact. Shaking the thought from my head, I chose to keep my power behind my seals. *If they're really attempting to leave early… I don't need beasts appearing to slow me down.'*

I dashed between the translucent trees and up their branches, heading for the plateau. Djialkan and Alala seemed content to remain on my shoulders as I twisted my way through Sihix, and a few times I reached up to scratch their chins. When I wasn't lavishing them with attention, I couldn't stop fidgeting with my mask and hood. I didn't want to admit it to my Guardians or to Corentine but I was nervous.

The moment I stepped out of the Sihix Forest and onto the snowy plateau I staggered as Darius' panicked voice burst into my mind without warning.

'Ari, please!' Darius' begging bordered on a scream. I felt my blood freeze as my mind raced through possibilities of what could be wrong. *'There are so many fucking beasts blocking us from accessing the airships! Please, help us! There's too many even for the Vorpmasians to—'*

'By the gods, Darius, lower your voice!' I winced, holding a hand up

to my head. *'Where are they?'*

'Between the forest and the ship,' Darius replied, quieter now, but his voice still shook with fear. *'Ari, there's too many for my escort to handle!'*

I grew still when the scent of the Chaos Beasts finally reached me. A twisted grin sprawled across my face and my bloodlust skyrocketed. Djialkan and Alala both tensed in response before leaping off my shoulder and retreating toward wherever Darius and his "escort" were.

My senses honed in on the nearest beast and ignored everything else. I practically salivated at the chance to rip the damned creature apart. A group of Vorpmasian soldiers attempted to fend off the beasts with magic off in the distance, but Darius was right—there were too many.

'His escort to the airships?' I considered. *'He really was trying to leave without me.*

'Ahhhnnn... But there's beasts to kill! I can kick his ass later.'

Snow flew into the air around me when I burst into a full run across the plateau. A wild grin split my face and a delighted laugh tickled the back of my throat.

I summoned armor from my jewelry as I ran. Black plate armor flowed from the gems like liquid and wrapped around my curvaceous body before solidifying. Although it was full plate armor, it was skintight and moved like cloth along my skin. Tufts of white fur stuck out from between the pointed plates. The telltale engravings of moons and stars swirled outward from the electric blue sapphires that dotted sections of the armor.

Over the past two months, this particular set had become one of my favorites among Aurelian and Elise's gifts to me. Not only did it provide me with the protection against beasts, but also warmth and shielding from X'shmir's harsh climate. And best of all, no one would mistake me for anything other than an Umbral Mage in armor like this.

"You should all *duck*!" I roared as I charged toward the Vorpmasian soldiers, leaving a trail of shadow and disturbed snow in my wake. "Ahhh, you really found some fun toys for me to play with didn't you, boys?!"

With a glee-filled cackle I leapt over the soldiers' heads. In one motion I summoned my scythe and tore the long blade through the throat of the nearest beast. I released a contented sigh when I felt the blade slice through muscle and bone with ease. It had truly been too long since my last hunt.

'This is going to be enjoyable.'

The soldier's eyes bore holes into my back, tracking my movements as I dashed across the snow. I had a feeling that the crest on my cloak had drawn their attention but I didn't care. They could question me about it later if it bothered them.

For now, I had blood to spill!

I heard the beast's head topple into the snow somewhere behind me as I searched for my next victim. A house-sized beast bore down on a group of Vorpmasian soldiers, backing them toward the tree line that separated the plateau from X'shmir. I launched myself at the beast as it reached for one of the injured soldiers. Grabbing the creature's arm, I tore it clean from its socket and then grinned when it wailed in agony.

"Ari, calm down!" Darius yelped from the edge of the forest as I began hacking the limbs off the nearest beast to me. "I wanted you to *kill* the damn things, not *play* with them!"

"Same thing!" I laughed, slicing the beast's head in half with a blade of wind. "After I'm done you have some explaining to do, *Your Highness.*"

A malicious grin sprawled across my face when I rushed the final beast. I leapt into the air, my scythe's blade trailing behind me, and then severed one of the creature's arms from its torso before it could finish turning around. Leaping out of reach, I summoned darkness around my scythe's blade and then licked my lips.

"No harm in having some fun, right?" I giggled, striding along the surface of the snow and examining the beast's movements as it wailed in pain. "Aw, I'm sorry. Did that hurt? Here, let's make things *'even.'*"

I darted forward and ripped the beast's other arm from its body with my left hand. With my right, I dragged the length of my blade through the beast's hide. The crystals inlaid in my armor and jewelry formed a dim barrier between me and the beast, deflecting the splash of its oil-like blood. I laughed openly as the Chaos Beast howled in pain again and attempted to squash me underfoot.

A light leap upwards allowed me to land on the beast's back while it was hunched over in pain. I ran along its spine and up to its neck, and then decapitated it with a single blow to its thick throat. It continued to scream in agony and fumbled around from side-to-side in a pitiful attempt to reach me with its second set of arms.

'Oh? Is its brain not in its head?' I wondered as I removed the beast's remaining arms, sending them skidding unceremoniously through the snow.

Intrigued, I carved chunk after chunk out of the beast with my scythe. I coated my blade with darkness and fire, extending the reach of my blade in search of vital organs so that I could stop the beast's pathetic gurgling. Pursing my lips in displeasure, I conjured blades of ice and pierced the beast's open hide. Blood poured from the beast even quicker than before, pooling and melting through the snow beneath us. Yet even my blades of ice couldn't find the damn thing's heart or brain.

"Mind slinging me *up*?" I called to the Devillian soldier I sensed approaching me and then motioned up to where the beast's head once was. "You're strong enough to do that while I'm wearing armor, right?"

"*Up?*" The armored Devillian sounded skeptical as he approached me with a cautious gait, looking from me to the beast and back, "If you insist…"

I grinned broadly and reached a hand out to the Devillian soldier, not caring if I showed my fangs. His hand was much larger than mine and dwarfed my wrist when he grasped it. A slight nod was all I gave him to show that I was ready. With ease he turned and slung me upwards through the air as requested. Laughing in delight, I flipped my grip on my scythe as I neared my target location. Using shadows, I stopped my path and floated above the gaping wound that used to be the beast's head.

"You might want to back up a bit," Darius called in a dry tone from somewhere below while I perched on the shaft of my scythe, crossed my legs, and then lifted both of my hands into the air beside me. "She enjoys killing these things a little *too* much."

He was probably right about that but I didn't quite care. I enjoyed it, and that was what mattered to me. A whirlwind grew between my hands with wisps of shadow intertwined within it. I hummed to myself and tilted my head in consideration, watching the beast stumble around below me. It seemed determined to do *something* even though I'd taken its arms and head. Cobalt flames and large shards of ice joined my growing whirlwind. I grinned, watching with satisfaction as the whirlwind expanded in all directions.

With a dismissive motion, I sent the discordant maelstrom of elements spiraling downward. I watched my creation collide with the wound between the beast's shoulders. Blood, skin, and shards of bone flew in every direction as the whirlwind tore through the creature, leaving no recognizable organs or other components behind.

"Wasn't that a bit overkill?" the large Devillian inquired of me as I landed on the snow near him. I just smiled in response.

"Any others, Ari?" Darius asked, approaching at a brisk pace and watching me as I sniffed the air before shaking my head at him.

"I don't know how she smells *anything* with how strong *her* scent is," a soldier muttered dryly, earning a sharp jab in the ribs from one of his comrades.

"Well, as long as I don't smell a quarter as bad as the beasts do— we're on the right track!" I retorted before turning to motion at the Devillian that had tossed me. "Thank you for complying with my sudden and unusual request. I'm afraid I didn't catch your name."

"General Eyrian Il'thar, the first son of Ve'r and Aelia Il'thar—the God and Goddess of Draekin, respectively," the Devillian replied with a bow as he removed his helmet. He then offered me a hand, a broad and boyish grin stretched across his otherwise rugged features. "That was an impressive display, Lyur'zi. I had no idea there was someone in X'shmir who fought with such deadly grace."

Eyrian's skin was tan as if he spent much of his time outdoors, and was a stark contrast to his pale green eyes and black sclerae. His horns and claws were white like bone. A shaggy mane of aqua hair with darker blue streaks hung loose around his shoulders. He kept tucking stray strands behind his pointed ears now and then as he looked around—I wasn't sure if it was a nervous tic, or if his hair was just that unruly.

Patches of variegated blue and aqua scales covered portions of his skin. If there were more, it was hidden by the rather formal set of armor he wore. A thick draconic tail with similar scales swished behind him and, upon further inspection, I realized his horns were quite draconic as well. He too had a slight accent as he spoke, but it was much different from the deity that chased me two months prior.

'They must be from different regions of Vorpmasia. Just how big is *the Empire?'* I shifted my attention back to Eyrian's face.

"I'm Arianna Jade Black," I offered, accepting the Devillian's hand and watching as a brief expression of surprise crossed his face. He promptly bowed a little deeper and then kissed the back of my armored hand. "By your surprise, I'm assuming my twin and our *parents* left out some important information."

"*Twin?*" Eyrian inquired in disbelief as he straightened and then looked from me to Darius and back. "I was under the impression that you were his younger sister, Arianna-jiss."

"She's half an hour older than me!" Darius grinned as he circled me and examined my armor. "Ari, when did you get all *this*? New armor? New weapon?"

"It appears Aurelian favors you." Eyrian frowned slightly as he too examined my armor and scythe. "Else you are more powerful than your sibling led us to believe."

"Arianna, are you quite finished with bathing the plateau in the blood of beasts?" Djialkan snorted from somewhere behind me. *"Return to your robes at once! Alala and I refuse to settle on such uncomfortable pauldrons."*

"Oops. Right," I mumbled, turning to look at Djialkan and Alala. My scythe and armor disappeared back into my jingling jewelry as I crouched down to pick up the white fox and the black fae-dragon. "I'm sorry, you two!

"Now then, *Your Highness*. You told me we weren't leaving for another hour. Care to explain?"

"Darius-zir?" Eyrian frowned at my brother before shifting his gaze to me. "It's a good thing you arrived when you did it seems."

Darius looked nervous as he glanced between us, a little color draining from his face. He even shot me a begging expression, though it was brief. Fraelfnir, who was draped around my twin's shoulders, did not seem impressed with Darius' reaction in the slightest. Even though I was the one who confronted him, Darius still looked to me for rescue out of sheer habit. What a pain.

Instead of coming to his rescue, I turned my attention to my own fae-dragon companion and waited for Darius to think of a response.

'Djialkan, -zir means "prince," right?' I questioned while Alala nipped and tugged at the edge of my hood. *'I'm still a little rusty with Draemiran honorifics. They have so many!'*

'-zir is for males and -jiss is for females,' Djialkan offered. *'Their language is more complex than the common tongue, especially when it comes to honorifics, but you are essentially correct.'*

"I just want to get going already!" Darius finally sighed in exasperation, his shoulders slumping when he realized I wasn't going to make excuses for him. "Mother and Father still refuse to allow foreign publications into X'shmir, so I've been bored out of my mind when I'm not working! Finally, we can go Below and—"

"You do realize that Fraelfnir and Djialkan already taught us much of what we need to know about Vorpmasia, right?" I pointed out with a heavy sigh, shaking my head at my twin. Eyrian shot me a questioning look, so I turned to him to elaborate. "Our companions always felt that we should know about the world Below, and not just what the X'shmirans would like to pound into our heads. Unfortunately, up until the Empire stumbled across us, the majority of our people didn't believe that sentient, non-Human beings existed.

"Djialkan and Fraelfnir have given Darius and me both a proper education over the years...but I am the only one who actually listened."

"Arianna has been exposed to Elves, Centaurs, Devillians, and a handful of other beings during her stays in the Sihix Forest," Fraelfnir added, puffing golden-white mist from his nostrils as he spoke. *"Darius has not shared the same form of exposure."*

"The 'good son' believing wholeheartedly in his parents' ways, is it?" Eyrian arched an eyebrow at Darius, who flushed furiously. "In that case, Darius-zir, I recommend you study hard upon arriving in Dauthrmir. You will need a thorough understanding of our varied culture.

"Arianna-jiss, is there anything special you require during your stay?"

'Respond to him in Draemiran so that Darius does not understand,' Djialkan interrupted my thoughts. *'We can't have your brother knowing about our plans. Not yet.'*

"I seek access to Dauthrmiran libraries and information on the Aledacian Forests," I stated in formal Draemiran, crossing my arms and watching the startled expressions that crossed not only Eyrian's features but many of the soldier's as well.

"Arianna-jiss," Eyrian began slowly with a frown tugging at the corners of his mouth, before continuing in Draemiran himself, "this is sensitive information? Your brother looks confused."

"You have seen for yourself that the people of this country hold a special fear in their hearts when it comes to both Umbral Mages and the Aledacian Forests," I pointed out with a slight tilt of my head, examining Eyrian's strangely flushed complexion. "I admit my Draemiran may not be up to par. Did I say something offensive, General?"

"It isn't that." Eyrian's face flushed darker as he shook his head. "Draemiran just… It suits your voice better than the common tongue. It is a little strange to find someone outside of Vorpmasia that can speak it. Is this Djialkan's doing as well?"

"The Adinvyr women within Sihix insisted on teaching her." Djialkan huffed as Alala darted into the back of my hood. I frowned slightly as her tail thwacked me across the face before disappearing entirely. *"This conversation can wait, I suppose. Alala is rather insistent that we leave. **Now.**"*

"Anyone going to clue me in?" Darius demanded, crossing his arms and stomping one foot in his impatience.

"Umbral Mage business," I stated sweetly, smirking a little when I heard several soldiers start snickering. Turning to Eyrian, I continued, "Far be it from me to argue with the fluffball or the scaly one. I suppose it is a little too chilly out here for this conversation anyway."

Eyrian grinned at me and then broke into a laugh when Alala poked her head out from around my neck. Alala warbled by my ear, making me wince. I reached up to scratch her chin which only served to make her warble and chirp even louder. Djialkan let out an irritated huff from my other shoulder, so I reached up and gave him attention with my other hand.

"Once we board the ship, I will call ahead and let my superiors know that we finally found you," Eyrian informed me before glancing off in the direction of the city. "Do you need time to return to the castle and fetch your belongings?"

"I have everything I own in my shrizar." I shook my head. "If we need to leave immediately you can consider me prepared, General Il'thar.

"Though, I would be lying if I claimed to be happy about these flying deathtraps that you lot call 'airships.'"

'Ari, you have permission to speak with the people on the ship until we get to Dauthrmir,' Darius informed me in a matter-of-fact tone, causing me to beat down my urge to slug him. *'Once we arrive you may only speak to me, Djialkan, Alala, and anyone you must fight with or against.'*

A quick glance toward my brother showed me that he was *extremely* displeased that I'd be accompanying him to the surface, but this wasn't an unusual order from him. I wasn't thrilled that I had to babysit him either, but it was still better than the alternative. Instead of telling him as much, I decided to just follow him and the Vorpmasian soldiers in silence. Darius seemed in a rush to get away from me, and was soon out of both sight and earshot alike. However, the soldiers all still appeared distressed by something.

'Finally "found" me?' I thought distractedly. *I'm not sure how I feel about the concept that they were looking for me. I've been delivering the letters and gifts to their ships after all. I wasn't exactly unapproachable.'*

"General Il'thar," I began under my breath as he fell into step with me, "why do your men keep giving me such strange looks? Did I injure someone during the battle?"

"Not at all!" Eyrian exclaimed, shaking his head so hard that he sent strands of hair flying into his eyes. "They are confused by the crest on your cloak. The design is eerily similar to General Vraelimir's personal crest.

"Your armor and weapon are also questionable. The God of War has never given gifts to a mortal before—so we are curious about that as well."

'"General" Vraelimir, huh?' I arched an eyebrow. *'A general is he? The Vraelimirs are the patriarch and matriarch of Adinvyr, if I remember right.*

'So, General Vraelimir is a demigod-turned-god? That's interesting. I wonder why he still holds the title of "General?" That seems a little strange. Wouldn't deities consider themselves above such ranks or affiliations?'

"*The crest is Aurelian's doing,*" Djialkan snorted. "*I can assure you that her crest is fitting. Hopefully* that one *will be able to put aside his pride and accept it.*"

"Djialkan, Nalithor is much less prideful than when you knew him," Eyrian spoke dryly. I felt as if my blood had stopped pumping for a moment in response to hearing the Adinvyr's name. "As long as she can prove to him that she's an incredible fighter—such as she just displayed on the plateau—there shouldn't be a problem. Looks like the symbol of a fox suits her, too.

"What's the cutie's name?"

"Alala," I answered as the fox warbled at Eyrian from the back of my hood. "She and Djialkan are both my Guardians. Though, it's apparent you know Djialkan well, so I suppose you already knew that."

'Nalithor... So that's his name then, is it?' I wondered. 'Nali... Nalithor. I feel as if I shouldn't have been able to forget something like that.'

"I was good friends with Djialkan's former ward," Eyrian offered. I had to bite back a depressed expression as I listened to him continue, "At least, I would like to say I was. I was such a young child back then that most people seem to forget I was even there."

"Well, you were *a decade or two younger than the both of them."* Djialkan grunted in laughter. *"You were always chasing after them regardless. I trust you can at least keep up with Nalithor now?"*

"I see Djialkan's personality hasn't improved any." Eyrian's voice dripped with sarcasm, earning a laugh from me. "In all seriousness, I must apologize to you, Arianna-jiss. Not only did your brother fail to mention to us that you are both the princess *and* the Lyur'zi, but we failed to convince the Royal Family to allow you to abide by Vorpmasian laws regarding Umbral Mages.

"You will need to wear your mask and hood still while in Vorpmasia. I will see if we can find a way to convince your parents to change their minds. Until then, I recommend you tread carefully. We are a warrior-like species as a whole—Draekin and Adinvyr even more so."

"I understand." I nodded to Eyrian, "Regardless of whether or not I hide my face I expect that I will have to earn the trust of others, General Il'thar. It shouldn't be a problem."

"Very well." Eyrian bowed to me. "Follow the signs to the bridge. Your brother should have been brought there. I will be along after I've made my report. Rooms have been prepared for both of you as well, if you would prefer to rest or change. Any of my men can direct you there."

I thanked him in Draemiran before moving away and following the signs he'd pointed out. As uneasy as our situation made me, I couldn't deny that I wanted to watch our descent to the Below. Darius and I had only ever read stories about what the real sky looked like. Now we finally had the opportunity to see it for ourselves. I'd be crazy to miss it.

The faint hum of magical energy from the ship's engines made my skin prickle as I strode through the winding hallways of the airship. I opted to take a more leisurely pace so that I could examine the myriad of paintings and artifacts on display along the passages.

Looking around, it became clear that this ship was one meant for delegates—not for military use. It felt far too posh for a tool of war.

Chandeliers, intricate paintings depicting important parts of Vorpmasian history, and replicas of historical items were scattered everywhere I looked.

It fell in line with my brother's tastes for sure. Mine? Not so much.

'I will regale you with the important details of Vorpmasian culture on our way to the capital,' Djialkan informed me with a nuzzle as I padded closer to our destination. *'As a society based around sorcery, Magitech, knowledge, and* war *there is much you need to know of them.*

'It has been some time since I initially taught you about Devillians. While much has likely changed in the past two hundred years, I believe a refresher course is still in order.'

'Start off with what should keep me out of trouble then.' I shrugged. *'And… Suggestions on how to avoid* Nalithor *would be helpful as well.'*

'That will be difficult!' Djialkan laughed. *'No one is allowed to seal or otherwise hide their power in Vorpmasia. He will sense you straight away, and he will find it strange that a Human radiates so much power. I doubt you will be able to keep him off your tail.'*

'I don't have *a tail.'* I sniffed in irritation as I strode onto the ship's bridge and over to a row of large windows.

'Not anymore,' Djialkan countered. *'If we can figure out how to undo whatever made you Human in the first place…then you will have one again.'*

'Let's focus on reeducating me about Vorpmasia.' I grimaced at my hooded reflection and then reached up to pet both Djialkan and Alala.

'You know,' Djialkan began thoughtfully, *'he got quite the taste of*

your power while you were running away from him. Isn't it a little arrogant of you to think that you could avoid him—a god—*after he chased you so far?'*

'...*I see your point,*'I muttered, glancing down at the snowy ground beneath the ship as it grew distant.

Being stuck on this flying contraption for two days was going to suck. I just wanted to find someone or *something* interesting to fight.

೮Q೨
CHAPTER FIFTEEN
What IS She?

The sound of the academy's clock tower bell rattled the window panes of my laboratory. I paused, glancing up from the pages of a leather-bound book, and then frowned. *'Afternoon already?'*

Over the course of the past two months I had studied and examined samples taken from X'shmiran beasts. Although our men weren't keen on remaining in the flying country, the beasts they slew proved to be excellent practice for them, and the beasts' remains proved interesting. Frustrating but interesting.

I determined that the X'shmiran beasts were physically similar to their terrestrial brethren in construction. This close similarity is what baffled me. Aside from their construction, Rilzaan and X'shmiran beasts were just so *different*.

While both "breeds" of Chaos Beast appeared to share the same forms of blood and venom, the X'shmiran beasts were many times stronger than ones that originated in Rilzaan, and far more grotesque in appearance. The nonvenomous ones had oily black blood, whilst the venomous ones carried putrid yellow blood; that, at least, was akin to beasts native to the Rilzaan Continent.

However, the X'shmiran beasts' outward appearance was like some horrific chimera. A poorly-executed fusion of mismatched body parts. In some cases the beasts were little more than a pile of rotting flesh. How they moved, let alone attacked, was beyond me.

'Our soldiers and battlemages alike are struggling with the damned things, demigod or otherwise.' I grimaced and flicked stray hair out of my face. *'The moment someone releases their power to fight, even more beasts appear! How in the hells did that woman slay them so quickly?'*

I clicked my tongue in displeasure, snapped the tome before me shut, and then stalked over to a nearby bookshelf to replace the tome. Getting *her* off my mind proved to be…difficult at best. Sometimes it seemed as though her scent had permeated me to my core. Every time I thought I'd convinced myself that she wasn't the same Arianna, that musky jasmine-vanilla scent of hers arose and threatened to overwhelm my senses.

'Even in my dreams she still hides her face from me.' I sighed and shook my head at the unbidden thought. *'I'm not going to get any work done if I do nothing but contemplate her.'*

I pulled down several tomes and tucked them beneath my arm. Scanning my collection, I searched for anything else that could be of use to my research. However, a series of beeps blared from the direction of my desk, interrupting me. I flinched, causing my tail to smack into the floor.

Muttering curses, I shook the pain from my tail and stalked to my desk. I dropped my pile of books haphazardly on the right side before sitting down and smashing a glowing teal button with one clawed finger. The shimmering crystal screen refused to rise, and the infernal beeping refused to stop, so I mashed the button several more times. Finally, I slammed my entire first into the button out of frustration and the damned thing cooperated. The screen flickered to life, revealing a solemn-looking Eyrian for me to glare at.

"I'm busy," I stated.

"Nali, it's important," Eyrian countered when I turned to sever the connection. *"You didn't tell me that their Lyur'zi can fight like that."*

'Their Lyur'zi...' I bit back a scowl and shifted my attention back to Eyrian's defiant expression. *'Ah, that's right. With X'shmir's current location, they must have picked up our "guests" today, not tomorrow.'*

With a heavy sigh I settled into my oversized leather chair and shot Eyrian a look to let him know I'd tolerate the interruption—for now. I, for one, did not want to dwell on a woman that was most likely a copy of Lucifer's heiress. However, Eyrian's expression told me that my friend had something important to say.

"I *did* say she felled two beasts," I responded. Before continuing, I shifted my tail away from the legs of my chair so I could scoot it closer to the desk without inflicting harm. "Unfortunately, 'the Mists' interfered with my ability to determine if Djialkan was helping her. However, seeing as she is a *Human*, I would assume he was."

Even when Human mages existed a little over two hundred years ago, trios of them had been incapable of handling even the lowest ranking Chaos Beasts. Umbral, Astral, Sandstorm, Maelstrom, Fire, or Water Mages…it didn't matter what their affinity or affinities were. Humans stood as little chance against the beasts as an ant beneath my boot. Either Djialkan was helping her, or she wasn't Human. Those were the only options.

"There's no way Djialkan was interfering to this extent," Eyrian said with a firm shake of his head before taking a deep breath and covering half his face with one hand as if trying to calm himself. *"Nalithor… Darius and almost all of my men would be lying dead in the X'shmiran snow if Arianna-jiss hadn't appeared and taken action."*

I grew still and just stared at Eyrian in disbelief. The Draekin general had taken many men with him because we *knew* how great a problem Chaos Beasts in X'shmir could be, and because we hadn't yet perfected the art of fighting them. Although he exaggerated at times, matters like this were not something I expected him to twist. He looked almost ill.

"'Appeared?'" I frowned, tapping my claws against the arm of my chair. "I was under the impression that she agreed to accompany her Astral Mage to Dauthrmir?"

"Darius-zir lied to his sister about the time we were leaving." Eyrian scowled, baring his fangs in a growl before continuing. *"I redirected their attention and had a brief conversation with her...in* Draemiran.*"*

"So, she can speak it as well as write it?" My frown deepened and I flicked my gaze away in thought for a moment. "I assume you bring this up because she had something important to discuss."

"I had asked her, in the common tongue, if she required anything 'special' for her stay in Dauthrmir," Eyrian began with a small grimace, his face growing flushed. *"My intention was to probe and find out if the X'shmirans had wounded her once more—as per the agreement you, the Oracle, and I came to.*

"Instead, she stated that she desires access to our libraries and information on the Aledacian Forests. Apparently, she spoke in Draemiran because her brother does not understand it. For some reason she feels the need to keep her interests hidden from Darius-zir."

"You're *blushing*," I spoke in disbelief before breaking into a grin. "Should I be concerned about something else she said?"

*"**I am not blushing***!*"* Eyrian snapped, his face growing redder. *"Djialkan and the Adinvyr women of Sihix have taught her Draemiran well. It...suits her in a strange way. That's all."*

Eyrian's face turned several shades darker as he fidgeted in his seat. I arched an eyebrow at him. He seemed genuinely flustered by the X'shmiran princess. If I knew Eyrian as well as I thought I did, the fact she saved him and his men only served to fluster him further. She must have put on quite the spectacle to have made Eyrian act so...boyish.

"It will take two days for you to reach Dauthrmir, correct?" I considered for a moment, watching as the Draekin simply nodded his reply. "Were you able to acquire X'shmiran texts this time?"

"Darius-zir still insists that Arianna-jiss owns the only copies." Eyrian's face twisted into a sour expression. *"There's a strange tension between those two, but I don't sense anything terribly off. However, he's* absolutely livid *that Arianna-jiss hasn't returned to the city in the past several months.*

"I want to show you what Arianna-jiss did to the beasts, Nali. That woman is—"

"I refuse." I crossed my arms. "I won't have my opinion of her abilities skewed prematurely."

"Stubborn Adinvyr." Eyrian shot me a pointed look. *"You're still insisting that she must be a 'fake?' Do you really think you'll be able to determine that just from fighting her?"*

"It will be a good start." I huffed. "Anything else, Eyrian? I have work to do."

"Fake or not, this woman isn't Human." Eyrian's tone was flat as he rummaged around in his desk. *"She has gifts from Aurelian and wields them with… Let's say 'chaotic grace.' I won't show you the recording of her fight; I'll respect your decision on that matter.*

"This is the aftermath of what she did to the beasts."

Eyrian lifted a small crystal orb and slotted it into place on his end. The Magitech device on his desk chirped several times before rendering a still image of the X'shmiran plateau. The corpses of the Chaos Beasts were almost unrecognizable and the once-white snow was stained a solid brownish-black. Particles of flesh, bone, and other questionable matter were strewn across the snow. The drifts looked as if something violent had disturbed them and tossed them out of place.

As startling as the scene was, it was Eyrian's statement about gifts from *Aurelian* that struck me. Aurelian and his wife rarely presented equipment to anyone that wasn't a deity or demigod. Furthermore, the other deities had not been permitted access to X'shmir as of yet. They were waiting for me to establish ties with the Sihix Forest first, and for Vorpmasia to help the Humans restore their city and ruined temples.

"She didn't have such items two months ago," I murmured, watching Eyrian nod his head as he mumbled something about Darius being surprised as well. "Eyrian, how many beasts were there? I see some corpses that don't appear to be...*exploded*, shall we say."

"It was a full pack." Eyrian slumped in his chair. *"She came barreling out of the Sihix Forest with a storm of darkness around her. I haven't seen a woman that pissed off in a* while! *For a moment I thought she was going to wipe everyone out in her rampage!*

"Instead, she relieved the pressured soldiers of their individual beasts and then moved on to the remaining ones. In all, there must have been a dozen beasts, at least, *and all of them were Dux-class."*

"That many? If they weren't Duxes it wouldn't be surprising, but..." I shook my head. "It will be interesting to hear what *she* has to say at our meeting.

"You made it sound as if Darius-zir wanted to leave her behind.

Hmmm, Eyrian, you should take her aside as soon as possible and fill her in regarding the academy and the meetings she's assigned to attend. I get the feeling that the prince hasn't informed her.

"Now, as for the beasts she slew—"

"I already spoke to Lucifer about it; he had me relay orders to the scholars stationed in X'shmir. They should be preserving some samples and sending them to you in the next shipment." Eyrian made a vague motion with his hand. *"Lucifer is also sending several more groups of battle-ready Archmagi and researchers to X'shmir. We secured permission to use a remote section of the island so that we can test just how strongly X'shmiran beasts are attracted to magic."*

After a few minutes of idle chatter, Eyrian finally left me to my research. However, it was far too late for me to continue studying the beasts. My mind was already spinning with the information Eyrian provided me. At this rate I would have to rethink my definition of "impossible" entirely! It was already difficult enough for me to be unbiased when it came to *her*, and now I'd seen the aftermath of her hunt.

I loathed admitting it but Eyrian was right. The princess was no normal Human.

'Princess.' I crossed my arms and leaned back in my chair. *'We suspected it, certainly, but Eyrian spoke as if he'd acquired confirmation. He isn't that careless.'*

The damage that woman inflicted to the beasts was difficult for me to grasp. Soon enough, I found myself rising from my seat and pacing along the shelves of tomes and scrolls as if I'd find something to explain the situation we'd found ourselves in. A Human, with that much power, was unheard of as far as I knew. Most Elves and Devillians wouldn't have been capable of doing that to their prey either.

Rilzaan Dux-class beasts required a deity, or a group of demigods, to slay them. It was possible for a lone demigod to kill a Dux on his or her own, but such instances were few and far between, and required high levels of both skill and intellect. X'shmiran beasts seemed like they were on a whole other level above Rilzaan beasts entirely.

'Are they truly that much stronger, or are the Mists to blame?' I stopped by a window and leaned against the sill, looking up at the moons and stars above. *'That woman—Arianna. She seemed convinced that the Mists were keeping me from sensing things. Do they dampen our power as well?'*

Either option made me uneasy. I dug my claws into the stone sill and narrowed my eyes at the sky before turning away and stalking across the laboratory and to the door. All the samples from both Rilzaan and X'shmiran beasts were stored beneath the academy for easy access by the school's researchers. Although it was growing late, I knew I wouldn't be able to sleep any time soon.

'I will compare the samples again.' I shrugged on an overrobe as I walked through the palace. *'If there is a difference in strength between the beasts it should show in the lingering aether.'*

"Need a hand, boy?" A familiar voice broke me from my thoughts, drawing my attention to Lucifer. "I know that look. You're heading to the academy for more research, right? Eyrian's report shook you."

"It didn't *shake* me." I twitched, before sighing and nodding. "I want to compare the aether lingering in the beasts, see if I can narrow down the differences in their strength. Eyrian's men shouldn't have struggled with the beasts that much, even if it was a pack."

"Aye, and the *'princess'* shouldn't have been able to do *that* to them." Lucifer shot me a knowing look. "I'm free from my duties for the rest of the night. Let's see if a second set of eyes helps with your research. You've been staring at them so much you've probably gone blind to the differences.

"Let's go. I've wanted to take a better look at these samples we've been shipping in anyway."

CHAPTER SIXTEEN
Beneath the Mists

'*We should break through the Mists soon...*' I observed from beneath a pile of blankets, my eyes trained on the seamless windows in front of me. *I'm surprised the Vorpmasians are letting me do as I please while on their ship. Do they not see me as a threat? Or... Ah, is it because I saved their men from the beasts?*'

Much to my surprise, I had not needed to convince anyone to direct me to a private deck, or to leave me to watch our descent through the clouds in solitude. Quite the opposite, really. They were more than happy to direct me here, and even took a detour so that I could acquire food and drink to share with Djialkan and Alala.

On our way here, they had informed me that the cameras in this section would be shut off so that I could remove my mask safely. *That* had taken quite a bit of explaining. I still didn't quite understand what a "camera" was, but Djialkan assured me I had nothing to worry about.

I was rather disappointed to find that we were aboard was a luxury ship and, as such, there was nowhere suitable for me to work on my training. Despite my battle against the beasts a day prior I still felt a strong urge to massacre something. I had too much pent up frustration after training almost exclusively inside the Sihix Forest for two months, and I still wouldn't be able to start training again for *at least* another day.

'That the Mists have spread this far seems strange.' I scanned the seemingly endless expanse of violet that surrounded our ship. *'No wonder the scouting ship found their interests piqued. They're lucky they didn't get lost within it... Or did something guide them?*

'Perhaps the Mists are weakening because it's spreading itself too thin? That one's presence has been getting stronger the farther we get from X'shmir after all, so the Mists are certainly thinning.'

"*You are surprisingly calm,*" Djialkan commented from where he had curled up on my hip. "*I doubt this is because you are leaving X'shmir.*"

"Of course not. I know it's only temporary." I curled my right hand into a fist and rested my cheek against it. "I won't deny that it *is* a relief, seeing as I will likely get to fight quite a bit in Vorpmasia. The beasts in X'shmir have grown too skittish.

"That said... I'm just glad that Darius will finally receive the training he needs. Shielding his power and thoughts constantly is tiring."

Djialkan laughed in amusement and then shifted to get more comfortable. I simply returned my gaze to the violet skies beyond the window. I had slept for the entire first day of our flight but still felt somewhat drained. I wasn't sure if I'd overdone it against the beasts. Perhaps I was still catching up on a lack of sleep.

For now, my curiosity overruled my sleepiness. I wanted to see for myself what the world Below looked like, and there was no way in the infernal hells that I was going to sleep through such an opportunity.

Briefly, I had been curious about the Draekin that appeared to be in charge of the men and women working on this ship. Eyrian was surprisingly handsome, and rather well-built, beneath all those layers of imperial armor. He was rugged and masculine, but still had a boyish charm in the way he grinned and interacted with his soldiers.

Alas, I couldn't spar with him here, so I lost interest.

Instead, I poked around the ship and examined all the strange Magitech devices they had there. They seemed to have a machine or gadget for everything, and each of them seemed to run off of crystallized aether of different elemental affinities. Several members of the crew noticed my interest and took it upon themselves to explain what some of the items did. I quickly discovered that the remnants of Magitech we had in X'shmir were outdated by centuries and were of Elven design.

One of the bubblier crew members had informed me that X'shmir once had close ties to several Elven countries before we essentially disappeared from existence. Apparently, we once had a rich trade agreement with the Elves because X'shmir's soil was rich with rare resources not found commonly Below. The Vorpmasians theorized that some of those resources could have been responsible for X'shmir's now-airborne status.

'It's strange to think that I'll be going from an essentially barbaric civilization to one that is practically run by magic,' I mused, sipping my tea. *'I wonder how terrible of an impression the two idiots have made so far. Perhaps if they overstep too much the Vorpmasians will slay them for me.'*

I smiled and giggled at the thought. There were few things I wanted more than the death of the X'shmiran king and queen. It was unfortunate that I had missed my chance to slaughter them. Now I would have to wait for someone else to do it.

My thoughts were interrupted when we abruptly pierced through the Mists and into open sky. The sight of the cloudless, brilliant blue sky stretching before me stunned me even more than the turbulent waters below us. It was a mere moment before the change in scents hit me. I sent Djialkan tumbling from his perch when I shifted to lean against the windows.

"Ahhh, the Gal'edean Ocean," Djialkan commented as he regained his balance and perched on the arm of the sofa beside me. *"We appear to be flying quite fast… I am surprised it took us this long to reach it."*

"Ocean?" I questioned, pointing down at the water. "So, Eyrian smells like the ocean…kind of?"

"Except much less fishy." Djialkan chortled as I tilted my head in thought for a moment before nodding my agreement.

"Is it always so turbulent?" I asked, motioning at the waves beneath us and then motioning at the sky above. "And is *that* always so clear?"

"The Gal'edean Ocean is notorious for its violence," Djialkan informed me with another amused chuckle. *"The only way to cross it is by flight if you are not one of the ocean's inhabitants. I have never known the waves to calm for anyone other than Sea Elves, Merfolk, or other aquatic species. As for the sky, you will get your fill of clouds soon enough. Worry not.*

"You should enjoy the daylight whilst you can. It is always night in the part of Vorpmasia we are heading to. Although, unless something about you has drastically changed since you were last there, I doubt you will mind in the slightest."

"Always night? How is that possible?" I turned to drag the sofa closer to the windows so that I could sit again.

"Vorpmasia is an unusual place." Djialkan shrugged his wings. *"You recall Human legends of Devillians being the 'Creatures of Darkness,' yes? It is not entirely untrue.*

"Dauthrmir is, essentially, the birthplace of Devillians. Early on, when the Elders were still creating the races, a sizable chunk of pure dark crystal fell from space and collided with Avrirsa. The impact site is now known as the Dauthrmir Crater—and that is where Lucifer chose to build his city."

"Dark crystal?" I remarked. "Pure elemental power tends to corrupt, doesn't it? I assume something must be different about this crystal when compared to the Aledacian Forests."

"You could say that the crystal corrupted the land instead of the people," Djialkan offered in a contemplative tone. *"There is no place like the Vorpmasian Empire anywhere else in the known world. The people, the flora, the fauna—it is all vastly different compared to other regions.*

"My theory has always been that it is night there due to the crystal's influence. I think, when we are within range to see it, you will understand why."

"Ahhh, this is so exciting! It's a shame I'm going to have to play nanny to Darius for a while when we arrive." I pouted down at the waves beneath us. "Are there beasts in the Gal'edean Ocean as well?"

"Aye, but the natives have their own ways of taking care of the monsters." Djialkan nodded before tilting his head at me. *"What is it, Arianna?"*

"There's just…so much magic down here!" I replied, stunned, as I shifted my vision back to normal and rubbed at my eyes. "Way too bright. This could be a problem if I'm to continue wearing masks."

"X'shmiran masks will be of no help to you here." Djialkan nodded his head. *"You will have to wear the ones from Aurelian or from the people of Sihix."*

I nodded, despite my displeasure. The gifts from Aurelian, as well as the gifts from Sihix, were all heavily embellished. They were beautiful…but it seemed strange to wear them. I wasn't treated like a princess by most people in X'shmir, so wearing fancy things seemed inappropriate, in a way.

'Although, I suppose this jewelry is rather regal as well,' I contemplated, glancing down at the mixture of bangles and delicate chain bracelets around my wrists. 'Honestly, did Aurelian have to make my jewelry and crest look so similar to Nalitho...?'

My thoughts went silent when I spotted land rapidly coming into view. I found myself staring at the massive wall of granite, snow-covered mountains that lined the Rilzaan coastline. We didn't have mountains in X'shmir at all. All I could do was stare at the massive peaks in disbelief. It took me longer than it should have to realize there was a *city* nestled on the coast between the ocean and the mountains themselves. The sheer scale of the city, and the many-colored lights that dotted it, amazed me.

"*The Kingdom of Draekin, Gron'kial,*" Djialkan spoke as I pressed myself against the windows to get a better look at the buildings carved into the mountainside. "*It is the eastern-most portion of the Vorpmasian Empire, and one of three territories that still has a daytime sky.*"

"Avrirsa is *this* large and the X'shmirans expect my brother to conquer *all* of it?" I sighed, skeptical, before shifting back on the sofa. "They're even more delusional than I—"

A wall of power hit me, making my words catch in my throat. The sudden onslaught of unfamiliar auras startled me, but I was quick to recover and promptly began sorting through the myriad of presences. There were very few that I would have genuinely called powerful, but the sheer number of them astonished me. Most of them seemed oblivious to my presence. However, a select few took interest and prodded around the edges of my barriers.

Strongest of all was *his* power as it ran over my barriers like liquid, searching for even the tiniest crack to spill through.

Something about the feel and scent of his power sent shivers down my spine. I felt my face growing hot in response. It made it difficult for me to concentrate but I managed to recover enough to strengthen my barriers in response. *That one* was going to be difficult for me to deal with. I was able to counter him with ease but there was something about his presence that almost made me not want to.

"*All* Devillians are mages?" I questioned, looking toward the laughing fae-dragon.

"*Aye, they are.*" Djialkan cackled. "*I would wager that is part of why the Humans of X'shmir desired to strike at the Vorpmasians when they learned their own species would have their access to magic taken from them.*

"*Although Vorpmasia and X'shmir have never been on friendly terms by any stretch. They tolerated each other in the past, certainly, but...their exchanges were never pleasant.*"

"Which is why this entire situation is so strange?" I offered with a loose motion of my hand, watching the fae-dragon nod. "Still, with this many powerful people in once place, I may need to withdraw my shields from Darius' mind and focus solely on my own."

I fell silent and watched the snowy mountains of Gron'kial rush by beneath us, then turned my eyes upwards to the sky. After a few moments, I realized that the sky was quickly growing dark, and I could make out faint dots of light beginning to show themselves. Within a matter of minutes I was plunged into a world so incredibly foreign and beautiful that all I could do was stare out the window in shock.

Brilliant sparkling stars dotted the sky above me, dancing around Avrirsa's three moons, which were all in varying stages of their cycle. Beyond the moons hung the visage of two neighboring planets, both encircled by colorful rings. The larger of the two was a swirling cacophony of red and golden hues, whilst the smaller planet was a dance of smooth, rich blues.

I tore my gaze from the sky and looked down at the ground hundreds of feet below us, watching as the mountains gave way to miles and miles of plains. The strange sight entranced me, making the growing lump in my throat and the tremble of nerves in my hands shift to the back of my mind.

Massive trees dotted the plains, often in clusters, and rose hundreds of feet into the air. Almost every piece of flora I spotted had black trunks or stems and carried variegated blue, teal, or obsidian foliage. The grass itself was an incredible color somewhere between blue and teal, with blades of glossy black sprinkled in. Everything was blooming in softly glowing shades of pale blue, pink, purple, green, and white. Along the bank of the massive river that swept through the western portion of the valley, I spotted aquatic plants blooming in brilliant jewel-tone shades of blue and red.

"Where *is* this?" I finally asked of my companion.

"The Abrantia Valley." Djialkan chuckled, this time loudly enough to cause Alala to stir and lift her head up from where she'd been

sleeping. *"You see the pale forest to the northeast? That is the Ceilail Forest—the Forest of Ice. Abrantia shares its southernmost border with Draemir, the Suthsul Desert, and another of the cursed forests.*

"Visitors to Vorpmasia must cross either the Gron'kial Mountains or cross Draemiran borders to reach Dauthrmir. No one in their right mind would intrude upon the Abrantia Valley uninvited."

"How come?" I shifted my gaze to the sky once more, deciding to ignore the sensation of hands smoothing down my back for now— maybe I would kick *that one's* ass later.

"It is a refuge for the Varjior race," Djialkan answered. *"While they are not officially part of Vorpmasia, they do have close ties with the empire. They are not Devillians, but they are similar to Rylthra and Sundreht in the way that they are able to shapeshift into animal forms."*

"Is *that* the crystal you were talking about?" I pointed out the window, stunned as I examined the massive, spindly and twisted spires of obsidian that rose into the air on the far side of the valley. "Is that a *barrier* I see beyond them?!"

"Each of the Vorpmasian territories is surrounded by a barrier that beasts cannot cross." Djialkan leaned forward to peer at the spires as well. *"As you can see, the crystal that collided with Avrirsa was super-heated and essentially* splashed *into the form you see now.*

"The Guardians of the Lake used their combined powers to freeze and resolidify the crystal before it could transform their domain into a volcanic landscape. They now serve as the Guardians of Dauthrmir, and are the twin dragons you see on the Vorpmasian Imperial Crest."

"Bah, there's too much to absorb!" I exclaimed, slumping back against the sofa as I glanced at Djialkan. "And it's *spring* here? And *warm*? It's still winter in X'shmir!"

"Yes, you will not be able to hide your Brands and dress for the climate both." Djialkan shot me a smug look. *"X'shmiran clothing is far too warm for Vorpmasia. I do not mind if Darius melts, but I cannot have you melting as well."*

"That could be difficult if I'm expected to dress like a princess while—" I trailed off, tensing as we shot through the Dauthrmiran Barrier. Its magic made my skin prickle into goosebumps in an instant and I bristled in discomfort.

I forgot the sensation the moment I laid eyes on the terrain within the crater. It was similar to the Abrantia Valley, except many times more massive. The sharp obsidian spires we passed through spread so far to the north and south that I couldn't even make out the curve of the crater's rim even from so high in the air.

An enormous lake covered much of the crater's interior and was surrounded by a rim of lush farmland and then dense forest that led to the crater's walls. I spotted people working on some of the farms, while others were scattered across both boats and minuscule islands alike while they fished from the lake.

It took several minutes, even at our speed, before I got my first glimpse of Dauthrmir itself. The Devillian capital rose from the central point of the lake and sprawled across impossibly large floating stones. It appeared as though the city was structured in tiers, with the sprawling palace grounds at the highest point. Much of the city shone with polished obsidian or granite and, even from afar, I could tell that many buildings were adorned or plated with silvery metals.

Dauthrmir's buildings appeared to be spread out a surprising distance from each other, allowing for lush trees and other plants to grow amongst the buildings. From what I could see, the massive stones the city rested upon were rich with deposits of elemental crystals—some of which continuously poured water into the lake below, creating airborne waterfalls.

"What are those glowing strips?" I asked with a small frown, tracking the gentle curve of the strip-like lights that seemed to connect many parts of the city together. "Really, what are *all* of the lights…"

"The 'strips,' as you called them, are roads." Djialkan snickered at me. *"All of the roads and other lights you see are made of bioluminescent materials found only in Vorpmasia. Some of what you see is magelights, of course, but most are organic—even if treated or tempered with Magitech.*

"Many of the flora and fauna adapted to the endless night by producing light of their own. It occurs naturally in Devillians and Kelsviir as well."

Alala let out a loud warble from where she lay a few feet away and then took several bounding leaps before landing on the sofa. She used it to climb up and then began pawing at the glass window before us, tilting her head curiously as she looked somewhere below us and continued to warble. Djialkan released an amused snort and followed the fluffball's gaze, so I couldn't help but look as well.

Glancing down, it took almost all of my willpower to keep from running to hide behind the couch. Dauthrmir's massive, twisting Guardian Dragons themselves swam through the waters below us. I couldn't even *begin* to think of something I could compare the black and white serpentine pair to. They were so large! All I could do was watch as the white one arced out of the water and through the air, leaping clean over the airship before diving back into the lake. His head was many, *many* times larger than the ship. Even his *eye* might have been larger.

"You should get dressed and don your mask." Djialkan nudged me when I managed to rip my gaze away from the gargantuan dragons. *"We will arrive soon and I doubt you wish to be caught unaware by the crew coming to fetch you."*

I nodded and pulled myself off the sofa. After a moment of hesitation, I summoned lightweight clothing around myself, followed by one of my more elaborate leather overrobes. The floor-length robe was black leather and heavily embellished with platinum-brushed carvings of moons, stars, foxes, flames, and wisps of wind. Platinum clasps ran along the front of the high collar and then down the left side of the double-breasted chest.

Despite the warmer climate here, I wasn't quite ready to display my Brands yet.

"It smells surprisingly good here…" I murmured, pinning my curls into a loose bun as I scented the air a few more times.

"Arianna-jiss," a voice called, followed by a soft knock on the door, "General Il'thar sent me to escort you to the ship's bridge. We are soon to land."

"One moment," I called, summoning one of the decorative-looking masks from Sihix and settling it across the top half of my face. Once it was comfortably in place, I flipped up my hood and motioned for Djialkan and Alala to join me.

"My name is Aylaena," the woman who greeted me at the door offered with a bright smile, brushing her deep burgundy hair over her shoulder as she examined me with lime green eyes. "I'm a Sandstorm Mage in the service of Lord Xander Leukos—one of the Vorpmasian Archmagi."

"Sandstorm? Hmmm, wind and earth I assume?" I tilted my head, curious as I followed the taller woman through the ship. She had pointed ears like an Elf and tanned skin, but had a set of upper fangs. No lower fangs, though. "Ah... sorry. Call me Arianna or General Black. Either one works; I just prefer *not* 'princess,' 'Your Highness,' or '-jiss.'"

'Hmph, another Vampire,' Djialkan muttered, *'Looks like she was once a Vunsori—a Desert Elf.'*

'You sound judgmental.' I rolled my eyes behind my mask.

"That's right, wind and earth." Aylaena nodded, a cheerful grin on her face. "Do you have all of your things, or should we stop by your rooms first?"

"I have everything," I replied with a shrug.

I fell silent and followed the bouncy Elven—or Vampire?—woman through the ship. By the time we reached what they called the "bridge" of the ship all the windows were filled with portions of Dauthrmir. From what I could tell, with my limited knowledge, it appeared that the bridge was where they controlled the flying deathtrap from. A quick glance toward my twin told me that he must have lost control of his emotions at some point along the way. His eyes were red and puffy. He kept rubbing his nose with the back of his sleeve as if it would keep us from hearing his sniffling.

While I agreed that the surface was startlingly beautiful, I didn't quite understand why he was moved to tears. For me, more than anything, I was excited about the prospect of new prey to hunt—and that certainly wasn't something to cry about.

"Ah, there you are, Arianna-jiss." Eyrian grinned from his large seat when he spotted me. "Let me be the first to welcome you to Vorpmasia."

"Oh…thank you," I replied awkwardly, tugging my hood a little further over my face. For some reason, I suddenly felt much more self-conscious about the elaborate mask I'd chosen. "I hope Mrirtec hasn't been causing too much trouble."

"Hey! I've been behaving!" Darius huffed, indignant, before approaching me, hugging me, and burying his face into my shoulder. *'Ari… Everything is so massive down here. How can the X'shmirans expect me to conquer something on this scale?'*

'The people of X'shmir are ignorant at best, Darius,' I replied with a small sigh. *'Not that we're much better, even with Djialkan and Fraelfnir's help.'*

"You're required to refer to your *brother* as Mrirtec?" Eyrian questioned as he looked between Darius and I with a startled expression. "You said it quite sarcastically…"

The word "Mrirtec" essentially meant "young lord" or "little lord" in Draemiran. Since X'shmiran law was quite particular, it was considered very inappropriate for an Umbral Mage to speak the name of their Astral counterpart. Because of this, both "Darius-zir" and "Darius-y'ric" were out of the question despite being the two highest honorific suffixes for males in the Draemiran language. "Rely'ric" would have been *too* high of a title, however, as that was reserved for deities and rulers despite the suffix version being more lax.

"I detest formalities." I made a sour face and stuck my tongue out at Darius, causing my twin to start giggling. "Djialkan advised me to refer to Darius as 'Mrirtec' instead of the title normally used in X'shmir. Although it *is* in the common tongue, it apparently has a much different meaning Below.

"X'shmiran ways are troublesome, particularly when it comes to being a mage."

"Arianna-jiss, Darius-zir, you should sit down," one of the soldiers spoke, causing me to turn to glance at the Devillian woman, "We'll be landing in a moment."

I hesitated and then turned to make my way over to an empty seat. Glancing toward the row of windows, I crossed my legs and settled back with unease. I had misjudged the scale of the city on our approach. It was so much larger than I originally thought. The city in

X'shmir would probably have fit in *half* of a single Dauthrmiran district.

Eyrian interrupted my pondering by offering me what appeared to be a map. I accepted it with mumbled thanks and then unrolled it, scanning the contents. According to the map, the highest point of the city was indeed the palace and its numerous gardens, stables, and even a barracks and training ground for the Imperial Guard. The next tier down from the palace was called the Sapphire Quarter and was reserved for the rest of the military, as well as the academies for both mages and soldiers, and housing for both.

Following the Sapphire District, in order, were the Nobles, Residential, Merchants' and "Scarlet" Districts. Beneath the Scarlet District, along the surface of the lake, were apparently a mixture of farming and fishing areas worked by the city, along with several piers and boathouses so that flight wasn't required to reach the farmland or fishing spots along the lake's shore.

"Scarlet District?" Darius inquired, befuddled. I gnawed on the inside of my cheek and attempted not to laugh at him when he turned to ask me. "What's that?"

"He...really doesn't know?" Eyrian asked me after a moment, though he seemed to notice my poorly contained laughter; I didn't miss the small smile he tried to hide.

"What *I* would like to know is, why does Dauthrmir have such a large one?" I spoke once I was satisfied that I could speak without laughing. "X'shmir's Red Light District isn't even an eighth of this size."

"Some Adinvyr are ill-suited for other work," Eyrian replied dryly, seeming to ignore Darius' startled yelp. "Even then, the ones that *do* have the capability for other work still need to feed. Unlike X'shmir's prostitution problem, the Dauthrmiran and Draemiran men and women are *willing* employees."

"So, they have a salary, the ability to choose their clients," I muttered, counting off on my fingers. "Perhaps their own lodgings separate from the brothels... They're essentially more 'free' prostitutes?"

"Not *all* of them are prostitutes." Eyrian laughed before circling a little more than half the Scarlet District on the map with his clawed finger. "A lot of them are entertainers, professional escorts, or hosts of some kind. That's why it borders with the smaller entertainment and arts districts.

"Of course, there's a lot of sex trade going on as well. However, many of the men and women that live in the Scarlet District aren't Adinvyr. There's a mix of other Devillian races, some Elves, and even Humans living there. It's clean, it's cheap, and it's well-guarded. A lot of newcomers to the city take up residence in the Scarlet District until they can afford to move 'up.'"

"Literally 'up.'" I glanced out the window and then back to the map.

"So it's a melting pot of cultures?" Darius inquired, causing me to purse my lips at his suspiciously cheerful tone. "Basically, people who either can't or don't want to run their own business in the Merchants' District, don't want to work a 'mundane' job, or don't have the aptitude for mage or combat arts?"

"That was a little more than 'basically,' and you're ignoring the 'newcomers' part, but yes you have the right of it." Eyrian motioned for us to stand. "Still, I wouldn't recommend going down there unless you're both fine with becoming 'food.' You smell unusual for Humans, and you look even more unusual than you smell. I'm pretty sure the patrons and the workers alike would be more than happy to take a piece out of one or both of you."

A crooked smile crossed my face when Darius' face turned a deep shade of scarlet. After a moment, Eyrian's hand obstructed my view as he offered me a hand up from my seat. I hesitated and then decided to let him pull me to my feet. It struck me as strange that he was still treating me as a lady after my display against the Chaos Beast, but it was refreshing at least. Once standing, I folded the map and slipped it into the pocket of my robes.

I fidgeted nervously with my hood as I followed Darius and Eyrian through the hallways of the ship and, eventually, out into Dauthrmir itself. My lips parted and I lifted my nose into the air slightly when the scent of the city enveloped me. I caught myself and glanced around weary, to make sure no one had noticed my behavior.

Everything there hummed with power, but there were several strong, intimidating presences that stood out above the rest. *His* presence, for some reason, was the strongest of them all. Even so, there were many others who were quite powerful in their own right. However, I wasn't sure why *he* was even more powerful than the emperor; perhaps the emperor wasn't here? Or was *he* a higher ranking deity?

"Two more things, Arianna-jiss, Darius-zir." Eyrian grabbed the back of Darius' robes when my twin attempted to dart off. "Darius-zir, *you* shouldn't try to slip away from your sister while here. She can't do the job she's bound to do if you're running away.

"That aside, *both of you* need to stop hiding your power behind your barriers."

"Wait," I protested, turning to look up at the Draekin with unease, "you mean we're meant to release *all* of our power from their constraints while here? All of the time?"

"All of it. All of the time," Eyrian confirmed with a short nod. "If you attempt to hide your capabilities while here our citizens and soldiers alike will think you're trying to hide something *else*. As a whole we're a very warrior-like species. We are wary of anyone who deems it necessary to hide things. The ones that aren't gods or demigods will be unable to tell specifically *what* you are hiding."

"Good, so trust is something mutually earned. Not arrogantly expected from strangers." I nodded my understanding, earning a surprised look from the Draekin. "Very well, I understand.

"Mrirtec, you go first."

Darius turned to pout at me and then sighed heavily, closing his eyes. Several moments of silence passed before his warm power rippled past us and through the city, startling the nearby soldiers and gawking citizens alike. I wrinkled my nose in displeasure when I caught my brother's distinctive floral scent. *'He hid that as well? What on Avrirsa for?'*

"Satisfied?" Darius pouted, looking from me to the startled Eyrian and back.

"I suppose." I shrugged.

Biting back a smirk, I decided to play a fun game with the Devillians.

Without warning I shattered the seals on my power, causing a maelstrom of shadows, ice, fire, and wind to engulf me. Darius yelped and staggered backwards, landing on his rump when the maelstrom dispersed and sent a shockwave outward from me. As startled as my twin was, the expressions on the faces of Eyrian and his soldiers told me they were far more startled than my brother was. Soldiers didn't spook easily, yet they stood there openly gawking at me.

Shrugging again, I clenched and unclenched my gloved hands a few times, working the lingering tingle of magic out of my skin. Satisfied, I placed a fist on my hip and looked down at my pale-faced brother. I couldn't help but smirk now; he even looked a little green.

"Show off," Djialkan snorted from my right shoulder, while Alala chirped from my left. *"Alala, you are not a bird!"*

"Are you just going to sit there, Darius, or are we going to get going?" I asked, offering Darius my free hand. "We've already imposed on enough of General Il'thar's time and that of his soldiers."

"Oh, I'm sorry!" Darius yelped, grasped my hand, and scrambled to his feet before turning to apologize profusely to Eyrian and the soldiers. Eyrian seemed unfazed, but the soldiers didn't seem to know what to think of Darius' rambling apologies.

"Will you be alright to find your way to your lodgings?" Eyrian turned to fully face me and then jabbed a thumb over his shoulder in Darius' direction. "I get the feeling this one doesn't stay focused for very long."

"We'll be alright once he realizes he's hungry," I replied dryly, but with a smile, taking note of my brother already starting to wander down the road. "And that would be my cue to play 'good little escort' it seems. If you'll excuse me…"

Eyrian smiled and then bowed to me before moving out of my way so that I could chase after my brother. I got the feeling that Dauthrmiran laws regarding mages were going to be a pain in my ass, but it seemed better than remaining in X'shmir and dealing with *their* outdated laws. At least here all forms of mages were respected. I could deal with the Devillians being wary of me if I had to.

I picked my way through Dauthrmir's crowded streets and followed my brother, reprimanding him from time-to-time when he darted between people without apologizing. Darius was ecstatic and wove between people with reckless abandon, rushing from one thing to the next without minding where he was going. His manners were already bad enough without excitement added into the mix. He made it impossible for me to enjoy our new surroundings.

As much as I wanted to take everything in, I couldn't take my eyes off Darius until after our exams were over. I was stuck with the duty of babysitting until then—and it looked like I would have to watch him like a hawk. *'Wonderful.'*

At any rate, if I had had any residual doubts about once living in Dauthrmir, they were disappearing. Fast. Everything was so familiar to me that it almost hurt to see or smell. The dark, silver-accented architecture, artfully crafted obsidian and silver street lamps, even the translucent crystal-like roads all seemed familiar. Emotions aside, the city itself was like a work of art. Despite the obsidian, granite, and silver, Dauthrmir had a warm and cozy feel to it. Inviting even.

Yet it didn't feel like "home" there either.

'Just as well…our stay here is temporary after all.' I clenched my jaw, feeling an unwanted lump form in my throat. *'I truly didn't think it was possible that I once lived here, but…'*

I let my thoughts trail off with a sigh and moved to chase after Darius once more. He seemed more eager than usual to slip away from me, and that was dangerous for the both of us. Like him, I wanted to explore our new surroundings and take in the sights, but our mutual safety came first. If something happened to either of us it would be the end for us both. I couldn't let that happen. There were too many things for me to do.

'We can't die. Not yet.'

END OF BOOK ONE
Thank you for reading!

Read on for bonus information about Avrirsa, the author, and social media links!

Also: Please take a moment to leave a review!

Reviews are the lifeblood of any indie author and can make or break the success of a book. It doesn't need to be long, it could be a few words saying what you liked or five things you think could have been done better. Even a sentence or two would mean the world to me and would help me continue to write books in the future.

BOOK ONE GLOSSARY

Adinvyr	A Devillian race with strong ties to sex and sexuality. In order to survive, they must periodically feed on sexual energy which they can take from their prey in various forms.
Akor	A Devillian race characterized by their stone-colored range of skin tones and fiery appearance. The Akor have a close relationship with volcanic areas due to their need to drink and bathe in lava.
Chrot'zi	The Draemiran form of address for an Astral Mage.
fiirzik	A strong alcoholic beverage that is served hot.
Groslturvir	Draemir's winter festival.
jich	A Draemiran curse word that's used in similar fashion to "shit!"
Jrachra	A Devillian race that lives and breathes everything arcane. From a young age they paint aether-infused sigils on their bodies. The number of sigils on a Jrachra indicates power and age. The brilliance of the aether indicates status. The color(s) indicate elemental affinity.
Lyur'zi	The Draemiran form of address for an Umbral Mage.
Mrirtec	"Young Master" or "Little Master" in the Draemiran tongue.
Reiz'tar	A formal way to address women of high status. It is used similarly to "my lady."

	Also used when addressing someone whose name is unknown to you, or if it isn't appropriate to speak someone's given name—such as an Empress.
Rely'ric	A formal way to address men of high status. It is used similarly to "my lord."
	Also used when addressing someone whose name is unknown to you, or if it isn't appropriate to speak someone's given name—such as an Emperor.
Rylthra	A Devillian race with the characteristics of a fox. Although their faces and bodies are similar to that of Humans and Elves, Rylthra have ears and tails like foxes. Their fur and hair color is sometimes mismatched.
	Rylthra are capable of shapeshifting into the full form of a fox. The number of tails is indicative of age and power.
	Those with multiple tails often become priest(esses) or Oracles.
shrizar	A Draemiran term that was popularized during the foundation of the Vorpmasian Empire.
	A "shrizar" refers to the pockets of magic a mage can create and utilize for the storage of items.

Sundreht	The shortest of the Devillian races, Sundreht have ears and tails like a cat. Despite their comparatively small stature, Sundreht are one of the more battle-oriented races.
throstor	A Draemiran word with combined meanings: "die" and "get out of my sight."
varikna	One of the strongest forms of liquor to ever come out of Vorpmasia; even a few sips of this drink is too much for most Humans and Elves.
Varjior	A race of shapeshifters that can take on animal form. Although often confused for Devillian, they are something else entirely.
Vunsori	The proper name for "Desert Elves."
-jiss	A Draemiran honorific used for daughters of royal and imperial families.
-tyir	A gender-neutral Draemiran honorific that is used to formalize addressing someone. Ex. Arianna-tyir, Darius-tyir.
-y'ric	The shortened form of Rely'ric, -y'ric is most often attached to the given name of the person being addressed. Although it is most often used for men of high status, it is not uncommon for people to use –y'ric as a form of address for a man they are courting.
-z'tar	The shortened form of Reiz'tar,

	-z'tar is most often attached to the given name of the person being addressed. Although it is most often used for women of high status, it is not uncommon for people to use -z'tar as a form of address for a woman they are courting.
-zir	A Draemiran honorific used for sons of royal and imperial families.

About the Author

Bonnie L. Price was born in 1990 and has lived in four different states. At the age of twelve, while living in rural Upstate New York, she turned to writing as a way to entertain herself. Without internet or TV, there was little else to do during the long, cold winters.

What started as a way to amuse herself soon became a passion, and she's been writing ever since.

Want to connect with Bonnie?

Fan Group: facebook.com/groups/blp.demonden

Discord: https://discord.gg/gRuGc2r

Author Page: facebook.com/BonnieLPriceOfficial

Series Page: facebook.com/OfAstralandUmbral/

Twitter: https://twitter.com/Bonnie_L_Price

ILLUSTRATION

In love with the cover illustration? Want to see more from the artist? Check out the links below for how to follow her!

LAS-T.DEVIANTART.COM/

LAS-T.ARTSTATION.COM/

FACEBOOK.COM/THANDERLIN.ILLUSTRATION

www.ingramcontent.com/pod-product-compliance
Lightning Source LLC
Chambersburg PA
CBHW020931120726
47905CB00008B/2477